TO DWELL IN SHADOWS

AVALON GRIFFIN

WILD
CLOVER
INK

Published by Wild Clover Ink

TO DWELL IN SHADOWS/Avalon Griffin

Paperback Edition ISBN: 979-8-9866766-3-0

Digital Edition Edition ISBN: 979-8-9866766-2-3

First paperback edition July 2025

Edited by Bethany Seabolt and Samantha | Radiant Editorial

Cover art by Enchanted Ink Publishing

Printed in the United States of America

Dedicated to anyone working on a goal that's taking longer than you initially thought. Keep going.

CHAPTER 1

"We're just going to transport ourselves into the kitchen," Selene said. "Quick and easy."

Sam placed his hands into her outstretched palms. He hoped his human mate couldn't tell how nervous he was. They stood in the middle of their cozy bedroom in the barn loft. A light breeze blew across the top of his head, tickling his sensitive horns. Rainsilver, the horse, chuffed softly from the stall below.

"This is just for practice. If it makes you feel sick or weird, we'll take a break," Selene said. "Go for a walk, jump in the pond, or something like that."

"Or go back to bed?" Sam asked, raising an eyebrow. He looked meaningfully at the large bed in the corner, still disheveled from their passionate coupling last night.

Selene grinned. "You know I'm always up for that. But we need to be serious here. I've never used the traveler's stone with another person before."

"All right." Sam straightened his broad shoulders and took a few deep breaths. Although he was trying to appear unbothered, it felt as though there was a rock in his stomach.

It's going to be fine. This is a completely different situation.

It had been decades since he'd experienced the harrowing sensation of disappearing in one place and reappearing in another. He had been only a boy when it happened, but the memory of the transition still gave him nightmares. First had come the change in the air, the feeling of the ground falling out from under him, and then the pressure that seemed bent on squeezing the life from his body. It was an experience he wasn't eager to repeat.

Selene looked down at their entwined hands and frowned. "I think we need to be closer."

Sam pulled her to him. Selene snuggled against his chest and let out the contented sigh she often made when he held her.

The sound calmed him. It was a reminder that he'd be wrapped in the arms of his beloved mate during this journey through dimensions—not clutched against the chest of a spiteful vampire.

"Ready?" Selene asked.

"Yes."

Selene reached up to touch the gleaming white stone hanging from her neck. She was silent for a moment, then whispered, "Kitchen."

Sam squeezed his eyes shut. As he waited for something to happen, his mind raced with catastrophic outcomes. Was it possible that transporting could be *more* painful now that he was an adult? Perhaps the sensations would be magnified due to his bigger body.

What if Selene wasn't able to transport them both, and they separated? He could end up in their intended destination while she went somewhere dangerous—like the bottom of a lake or the crest of a mountain.

Or what if the traveler's stone had lost its power and was just a useless rock now?

Several seconds passed. Sam remained braced for the jolt but felt no changes or sensations. Selene drew a breath and whispered again, more forcefully this time, "Brunie's kitchen."

Again, nothing happened.

"Well, crap, I don't know why this isn't—" Sam's ears started to buzz just as Selene seemed to be admitting defeat.

It's happening.

Sam's panic rose as his mind took him back to his kidnapping.

Zaybris standing by my bed, looking down on me with disgust. The vampire's dirty fingernails digging into my arm. The odor of rot and dust emanating from his undead body.

The last time he'd smelled that stench was nearly a year ago when Zaybris took Selene from him. That memory was more painful than his kidnapping because it was fraught with so much defeat. Not only was Sam unable to exact his demonic vengeance on Zaybris, but he had failed to protect Selene. And broken his promise to find Queen Thema's missing sister.

Sam tightened his arms around Selene. Then his attention moved from the buzz in his ears to a tug deep in his belly, like the feeling of riding in a carriage when the road dips. Although the sensation wasn't unpleasant, its unexpectedness was jarring.

Pressure began to build as though someone had wound a rope around his skull, squeezing it tighter and tighter. The sound of a yelp unnerved him further. It was a distressed noise that made him fear something had gone wrong.

Then, all at once, the sensations stopped.

Slowly, he realized he was no longer inhaling the scent of the barn's hay and dirt. He smelled lemon and sugar. His eyes opened to see they were in a room with bundles of dried herbs and copper pots hanging from the ceiling. The relief he felt made his entire body sag.

It's over.

They had made it to Brunie and Eldridge's kitchen.

"It worked!" Selene cried. Joy lit her face as she pulled back to look up at him. Sam smiled back, but then they both saw Brunie pressed against the kitchen counter. Her blue wings were shaking with fright.

Selene rushed over to embrace the Harpy. "Oh, Brunie, I'm so sorry! I thought you were in the garden."

"By the wings of Queen Aello, you nearly sent *me* to the Underworld, too!" Brunie said. She pressed a hand to her ample chest, trying to catch her breath. "Practicing for the big day, are we?"

"Yes. I thought it didn't work at first, but here we are." Selene turned to Sam. "How was it for you?"

Sam stretched his neck, looking for any pain or stiffness. "Easier than I expected," he admitted.

"Same here. Even my trip back here from Gaia wasn't that simple."

"Do you think it's because you're in the same dimension?" Brunie asked, her owl-like eyes blinking with curiosity.

"Possibly," Sam said.

"Selene, you might be putting my little horse out of a job!" Eldridge chimed in as he entered the side door. "I'll just have you transport me to and from the village from now on. Quick as a wink."

"No," Sam said sharply. "I don't want to attract attention to Selene and her stone."

Eldridge rolled his eyes good-naturedly. "Twas just a joke, my boy."

"I don't like those jokes," Sam said, his protective instincts simmering. "Think of all who would want the stone for themselves. It can only be taken from her in death."

"Or gifted in charity," Selene added, reminding him of how Zaybris had desperately given her the stone in the Underworld. She tucked it back under her shirt, where it normally rested, hidden from view.

"I should have known better than to jest with a demon about his mate," Eldridge said, chuckling. He wiped garden dirt from his long Goblyn fingers on a dish towel. "When do you expect to leave then?"

"By the end of the week," Sam said. Saying the words aloud made him feel both excited and nervous. "First, we will visit Malkina lands to see if Queen Thema would like to travel with us, then Selene will transport us to the Underworld."

Brunie reached up to pat Sam's cheek. "I'm just bursting with happiness for you. I know how long you've waited for this."

"Thank you," Sam said. "A few boxes of books we ordered for the shop may arrive before we return. Is that all right?"

Sam and Selene had decided that when they returned from the Underworld, they would open Snowmelt's first used bookstore. With Sam's love of books and Selene's love of libraries, they were sure it would be a trade in which they would both find happiness.

"Of course," Brunie said excitedly. She put her arm around Selene, and Selene dropped her head on Brunie's shoulder.

Sam watched them, feeling grateful that Selene thought of Eldridge and Brunie as beloved parental figures, just as he did. He knew Selene's human family had been selfish with her time and energy, often leaving her feeling depleted. From now on, he would ensure she only spent time around those who made her feel cared for.

Looking around the kitchen, Sam considered what an unconventional family they made. It was unusual for Harpies—an all-female race—to mate with a male Goblyn, and Sam had never dreamed that fate would pair him with a human. Yet, each had found a home with their wildly different other half. The loneliness and pain that had plagued him for so many years in Aurelia were now only a memories, as a future with Selene stretched out before him.

Once he reunited with his parents, all that was missing from his life would at last be restored.

CHAPTER 2

Later that night, Selene sat at the mirrored dresser Sam had built, dabbing rose oil on her face while Sam reclined in bed, watching her. Why he was so fascinated by her nightly ablutions, Selene would never know, but the feeling of his eyes on her always gave her little tingles.

"Is there a demon of skin care in the Underworld? I need a moisturizer that's less greasy," Selene said, frowning as she smoothed her cheek in the mirror. She was wearing the same white nightgown with buttons she'd worn the first time they kissed.

"The demons of Vanity might be able to help you. But I'm not certain," Sam replied.

"Demons of Vanity? Would they lower themselves to help a mere human like me?" she asked, turning to him with a smile.

"You are the mate of their prince. I imagine they'll be fighting over who will assist you."

"Does that make me a princess?"

"A princess consort, I believe," he said, then frowned. "I don't remember much about the royal conventions."

"I'm sure it will come back to you, oh great Prince Samael."

Sam gave her half a smile. "I don't plan on performing any princely duties. I'm well past the age when I would have been trained for such responsibilities."

Sadness tugged at Selene as she said, "I hate that you missed out on so much."

"I've accepted it. The time for that has come and gone. I don't think I would like to rule anyway. I don't want to be tied down by duty." Sam shrugged. "I'm mainly looking forward to spending time with my parents. And showing you the wonders of the Underworld."

Selene began brushing her hair. "My last trip to the Underworld wasn't exactly pleasant, but I know this time will be different. I wish there were a way we could send word that we're coming, but I guess it can't be helped. How are you feeling about all this?"

Sam ran a hand through his hair. "I feel many emotions. I dread telling them about all the lives I took in Aurelia, but our reunion will mark the end of a sorrow I've carried a long time. That will bring me great comfort. Are *you* nervous about going?"

Selene slowly untangled a knot in her hair, considering her response. Taking an extended vacation into the realm of the dead was undeniably intimidating. Yet, as Sam's mate, she trusted that no harm would come to her. She was trying to break her old habits of worrying about the unknown and just focus on the fun they could have. There would be an adjustment period, of course, but the rewards—especially for Sam—would make it all worthwhile.

"A bit," she admitted. "But I think that's normal."

"Yes, I agree."

Selene pulled back the covers and slipped into bed. "When I was in the Underworld, your father said something about how I was welcome, but I couldn't stay long unless I wanted to become a demon. What did he mean by that?"

"I'm not entirely sure," Sam said, looking thoughtful. "But we would end our visit long before that happens."

"You don't want me to become a demon?" Selene asked in a teasing tone.

"Absolutely not." He kissed her temple. "I want you to stay just as you are."

Selene stared up at the ceiling, trying to imagine herself with wings and horns. "I wonder what kind of demon I would be?"

"A miserable one. Living between two worlds is difficult enough, and I don't believe a human could be as ruthless as other demons. Not without being born into it. You would always be seen as weak— an easy target for oppression."

Sam's words struck a chord as Selene realized she had already been an easy target for manipulation. For years, she had wrestled with the guilt, perfectionism, and pressure so many parentified eldest daughters experience—until Sam helped her see that her wants and needs mattered too. Breaking those old patterns felt more like strengthening a muscle than flipping a switch, but she was proud of the plans she and Sam had made for their future in Snowmelt.

When discussing their future, Sam had encouraged her to dream big. Having spent little of his wages from Queen Thema, he had more than enough gold saved to indulge her every whim. But what she really wanted was quite humble: a home, a little business to call her own, a vegetable garden, and no family fights to mediate.

When she pictured them both outside a thatched-roof house with red shutters, a thought came to her. "When we return to Aurelia, can we get a pet?"

"Of course." Sam leaned over to slowly kiss her neck. His palm smoothed down her body before disappearing beneath her nightgown.

"Cat or... dog?" Selene asked. Her voice caught as Sam's rough hand glided up her inner thigh.

"You know I'm fond of cats, but we could have both. As many as you'd like." He pressed the heel of his hand against the mound between her legs, which elicited a moan. "Anything you want, it's my pleasure to give you."

She spread her thighs further, signaling she needed more of his touch. Greedily, he accepted her invitation.

"Should we go slow or fast tonight?" Sam breathed against her mouth. It was a game they played sometimes.

"Fast," Selene answered, already rolling her hips. "I want it right now."

Sam motioned for her to straddle him, and Selene did so with gusto. He slid a pillow beneath each of her knees, adding just enough height to keep her comfortable as she moved on top of him. Although their first times together had been wildly passionate, the effort they had spent since then learning how to pleasure each other made their intimacy even more electrifying. Their difference in size sometimes called for creative positioning until they discovered what worked and what didn't.

It didn't take long for Selene to climax, and Sam followed soon after. When they were both satisfied, Selene sank down to press her cheek to his chest, not quite ready to relinquish the bliss of having him inside her. Sam wrapped his arms around her back, and Selene sighed with contentment.

"Love you," she murmured.

"I love you, too," Sam answered, kissing her hair.

Although many unknowns awaited them in the Underworld, Selene drew strength from the knowledge that no matter what unfolded, their bond was unbreakable.

CHAPTER 3

It was a warm, clear morning when Sam and Selene prepared to travel to Queen Thema's castle. After Brunie fed them a colossal breakfast and Eldridge showered them with well wishes, the four of them stood in the front yard.

Sam pulled his long dark hair out from under the straps of his backpack. It was filled with their necessities, while Selene wore a pack filled with cloudberry muffins Brunie had baked for Queen Thema. She was dressed in the canvas human breeches she preferred, with boots, and a cotton shirt. Sam wore his usual black leathers.

"Ready?" Selene asked.

"Yes," Sam replied. Selene wrapped one arm around his waist and pulled out the traveler's stone.

"Safe journeys!" Eldridge called out from the front of the cottage. Brunie rested her elbow on Eldridge's head, waving her hand and shaking her wings. The height difference between the couple had always amused Sam, even though Eldridge was considered tall for a Goblyn. He felt a pang knowing it could be many months before he saw them again.

"Queen Thema's castle grounds," Selene whispered.

Sam closed his eyes and, after a moment, felt his stomach lurch. His ears buzzed, and pressure pounded in his head. Feelings of panic began to rise, but before his anxiety took too strong a hold, the sensations stopped.

The scent of fresh mint enveloped him, and he could hear water flowing nearby.

"We're here," Selene murmured.

Sam sighed with relief. Opening his eyes, he saw they were exactly where Selene had planned—the grounds of Queen Thema's castle. The white stone of the castle walls glinted in the morning sun. Rows of mint growing at their feet swayed in the breeze. The two guards standing on either side of the front gate gaped at them.

Sam kissed Selene. "Well done, my love."

He raised a hand in greeting to the guards.

"Good morning," he said, wondering if they would remember him. When neither guard replied, he added, "We come in peace at Queen Thema's invitation."

"Samael?" the guard on the left gasped. He was more unkempt-looking than the other guard. His black-vested uniform hung crooked on his beefy frame, and several knives at his belt looked in need of polishing. It was Rig, one of Sam's least favorite associates from his time as a royal guard. However, Sam had experienced many changes since the last time he'd seen Rig, so he was inclined to be charitable.

"Hello, Rig," Sam said coolly, then, put his arm around Selene's shoulders. Although Queen Thema had given him a home and a place among her people, Sam had always felt like an outsider among the other guards—especially when they talked about their mates or those they wished to court. It made him relish the words he was about to say next. "You remember Selene, my fated mate?"

"I... uh... yes," Rig stammered. "Greetings, my lady."

"Hello again," Selene replied.

The other guard cleared his throat. "Greetings, Samael. Please enter, and I will take you to the queen." Sam remembered the guard's face but couldn't quite place his name. Before he could ask, the wooden castle gates thundered open, and Arkaya stood in the center of the archway.

"I had a premonition we would welcome visitors today," Arkaya said, smiling. Her tail swayed gently under her dress. "I just didn't expect them to be ones so beloved to our queendom."

"Arkaya!" Selene cried, rushing to embrace Queen Thema's steward.

"Ah, it's wonderful to see you again," Arkaya said while hugging Selene. "Have you been enjoying country life in Snowmelt?"

"Yes, it's been fantastic."

After a moment, Arkaya released Selene and came toward Sam. The ring of keys that dangled from her hip clinked melodically as she patted his arm. "Welcome back, Samael."

"Thank you."

"You look well." Arkaya tucked a lock of gray hair behind her pointed ear. "Come, our queen is in the midst of her singing lessons but will be delighted to see you both."

Selene shot Sam a perplexed look, which he immediately knew translated to *Singing lessons?* He chuckled to himself, loving how the intimacy of their bond went far beyond the bedroom. They also found humor in the same things. Selene slipped her hand into his, and they followed Arkaya into the castle.

They found Queen Thema in the ballroom, standing before a Harpy who looked like her patience had been depleted. The chandeliers were dark, but the room was full of sunshine from the tall windows that lined the walls. The emptiness of the grand space amplified Queen Thema's voice as she ran through a series of scales while they watched from the side entrance. The sound was like the yowling of the castle cats who prowled the Malkina grounds. However, Arkaya seemed enraptured by the queen's efforts. It was only when Thema paused for a sip of water that Arkaya interrupted.

"Glorious. Absolutely glorious!" Arkaya gushed.

Queen Thema turned, saying, "Absolutely hideous is a better description, but I do enjoy the practice—oh! Look who it is! My darling nephew and dearest Selene!"

She rushed across the marble floor to throw her arms around Selene as Arkaya looked on. When they released their embrace, Queen Thema looked over at Sam and winked. She knew he wasn't one for casual hugging.

"What a wonderful surprise," Queen Thema said.

Selene pulled off her backpack. "Brunie sent cloudberry muffins for you."

"Delightful! How thoughtful of her." The queen pulled out a muffin and then handed the pack to Arkaya. "Can you take these to my quarters? I don't wish to share."

"Of course," Arkaya said.

The queen held the muffin to her nose and inhaled its aroma. "I had such a wonderful time at Brunie and Eldridge's cottage. I was so taken by the songs they entertained me with that I am learning to sing." Queen Thema motioned her dismissal to the Harpy tutor. "Now, what brings you back to my realm, dear ones? I hope you didn't walk all this way. I could have sent a carriage for you."

"No need, I brought us over," Selene said, patting the traveler's stone at her neck.

"Ah! An efficient way to travel."

"Queen Thema, we came to ask you something," Selene said.

The queen turned serious. "Anything you need, it's yours."

"It's nothing like that."

Queen Thema shook her head. "I owe you a great debt for my treachery. Although you know I wouldn't have truly allowed Zaybris to make you his blood slave—"

"We've already talked about this," Selene interrupted.

Sam didn't know if he could move past Queen Thema's betrayal as quickly as Selene had, but he understood her inclination to choose peace over bitterness.

Selene gave Thema a soft smile. "We aren't asking you for a favor."

"Then what?"

"We're planning a trip to the Underworld, and we'd like to bring you along."

Queen Thema remained silent for a moment before saying, "The time has come to see Lilith? Truly?" Her golden eyes grew shiny. "I would like that very much."

"She's called Lamia now," Selene corrected.

Arkaya clasped her hands over her heart. "Aurelia's seven sisters can be whole again."

"Yes," Queen Thema said. "Although I don't think she will wish to return if she's as taken with Samael's father as Selene has said she was."

The queen's words made Sam feel warm inside. Selene had told him in detail how his parents looked at each other, how King Asmodeus called Lamia *my treasure*, and how their son's disappearance had not weakened their mating bond. One of Sam's fears was that the pain of his kidnapping would drive a wedge between his parents, so the knowledge that they remained deeply in love was a comfort.

The queen clapped her hands together. "Oh my, so much to do! When are we leaving?"

"We were thinking we could stay at the castle for a few days while you make arrangements. How much time do you need?" Selene asked.

"Just a day or two. I can ask Queen Delphine to rule in my stead. Arkaya, will you contact her?"

"Certainly," Arkaya said.

The queen did an excited twirl on her furred foot. "Let us host a ball in celebration! To welcome you both back and as a farewell jubilee for my journey."

"Wonderful idea, my queen," said Arkaya.

"Samael and Selene, you'll be our guests of honor, and we'll invite all my subjects. It will be one of the biggest and grandest events I've had in years!"

Sam cringed. For him, attending a ball was an experience as torturous as a visit to the Underworld's Sanctum of Agonizing Rectitude. He didn't like the noise, the crowds, or the collective disdain for rules and order. He needed to stop Queen Thema's planning before it went too far.

"No," he said flatly.

Queen Thema's eyebrows shot up. "Excuse me?"

"You don't need to host a ball for us," he said. "I don't want that."

Arkaya gasped. "You're rejecting the hospitality of our queen?"

"I appreciate the hospitality, but I've gone to enough Malkina celebrations. I wish to have a quiet visit before we travel."

Queen Thema made a sound of disgust.

Sam responded with, "You may throw a ball if you like—"

"Oh, may I?" Queen Thema shot back with sarcasm.

"But I will not be attending," he finished.

The Queen crossed her arms and huffed. "Silly me, I thought you enjoyed standing guard at my events."

"It was my job!" Sam said angrily.

"Hey, let's all just take a breath," Selene said, looking between them.

Queen Thema ignored her. "And you didn't enjoy yourself, demon?"

"Was enjoyment required of me?" Sam asked.

"Of course not, but how could anyone not be entertained by the festivities?"

"Too much unseemly behavior ignites my demonic instincts."

"The *unseemly* parts are the most fun!" Queen Thema retorted hotly.

Sam let out a growl of exasperation, causing Selene to hold her palms up in a placating gesture. "Okay guys, that's enough."

He was about to make another quip about Queen Thema's idea of fun, but the worry on Selene's face stopped him. There had been fear in her voice. When she clung to his arm, he realized what he had done. Unwittingly, he had triggered her fear that he couldn't control his emotions.

He knew his exchange with Queen Thema was just banter, but Selene didn't. Too many times, she had witnessed him lose control, and too often, violence had followed. All forms of conflict made his mate uneasy, and now she was assuming the role of mediator and peacekeeper—a responsibility she wished to put behind her.

Sam put his arm around Selene, hoping to signal that there was no cause for worry. He had promised her he would master his demonic instincts instead of relying on her to soothe him—and now was the moment to prove it.

Gentling his tone, Sam said to Queen Thema, "Let us compromise. What if I attended the meal at your ball, then retired to my quarters before dessert?"

"You would choose to skip dessert?" The shock in Queen Thema's voice was clear.

"I would."

"Humph I suppose," Queen Thema replied. "What about your attendance, Selene?"

Selene glanced at Sam, and he gave her a reassuring look.

"I'd love to go and see what the night brings. I may want to stay and dance," she said.

"Fine, fine," Queen Thema said. "Oh, Samael, it was foolish of me to think that true love could turn you into someone merry, but I accept your terms."

The way Selene visibly relaxed made Sam feel relieved. He squeezed her closer, hoping to convey his assurance that she didn't need to worry.

"Arkaya, can you begin the arrangements?" Queen Thema asked.

"Right away," Arkaya said. She looked up at Sam. "Would you like us to prepare a suite, or do you wish to stay in your former quarters? They are just as you left them."

"My quarters will be fine." The thought of being alone with

Selene in his old room made his blood pump faster. "If you don't need us, Selene and I would like to relax after our journey."

"Yes, yes," Queen Thema called over her shoulder as she strode toward the ballroom's exit. "Please, amuse yourselves for I have much to do!"

CHAPTER 4

Selene's heart skipped with anticipation as she followed Sam to his chambers, weaving through hallways reminiscent of English Gothic architecture. Each Aurelian they passed slowed their steps to stare, reminding her of the first time she had found herself in the Malkina castle. But as they continued, she realized the attention wasn't solely on her. Sam drew just as many lingering gazes, despite having once lived among them.

They moved through more winding corridors in the south wing until they reached a nondescript gray door. Assuming it led to Sam's quarters, Selene turned the knob. But when the door opened, she saw it concealed a winding set of stone steps—twisting straight up.

Selene tipped her head back to marvel at the height. "We're going way up there?"

"Yes."

"Were there no other rooms available on the first floor?"

"Yes, but I chose the tower. I liked the view, and there's no one around to bother me."

Selene eyed the stairs with dread. "Okay, let's go. But I'd like to tell you about a human invention called elevators—" she joked.

Suddenly her feet were swept off the ground and she found herself eye-level with Sam.

"Hey! What are you doing?"

"You didn't think I'd make you walk, did you?"

"Well, yes."

"You would have tired quickly."

"True, but I could do it. Eventually. I'm not that much of a weak human."

"I know. But I like carrying you."

"Oh, all right," she said, looping her arms around his neck.

Since she had returned to Aurelia, letting Sam do nice things for her had been harder than expected. He was always looking for ways to take away any pain or inconvenience she might encounter and initially, it had felt like a mind game—similar to when her mother would imply that young Selene wasn't capable enough to do certain things, so Selene would take those tasks on herself. Like shopping for the week's groceries while her mother napped in the car.

It was Brunie who first had brought the issue to Selene's attention. When Sam would do things for her—like run her a bath after she had spent the day gardening or bring her breakfast in bed—Selene had insisted she didn't need him to be so attentive. She was a strong, independent woman, not a delicate flower. But eventually Brunie had pulled her aside and said, "Let him indulge you. He needs it."

Her words had caused a major mind shift for Selene. She was so used to always giving, giving, giving that she'd never considered how she was denying others the pleasure of taking care of her. Selene never quibbled over Sam's ministrations after that.

When it felt like they had been climbing for nearly five minutes, Selene asked, "How is it that you're not even breaking a sweat?"

"I don't mind the exertion. Plus, you weigh practically nothing."

When they finally reached the top, a quick peek back at the path they had traveled made Selene dizzy. Sam set her on the landing before a broad wooden door carved with decorative swirling patterns. She ran her fingers along one of the door's raised lines that curved into something like a fleur-de-lis.

"This is beautiful."

"I carved it," Sam said a bit sheepishly.

"You what?" She moved closer to examine the patterns and textures. "I didn't know you could do this."

"Eldridge taught me. It helped occupy my time here when I wasn't on duty."

"Sam! I knew you were handy with building things, but I didn't know you were an artist, too."

He gave her that shy smile with the dimple that always made her insides flip.

"I love learning new things about you," she said, reaching for his face.

She had meant to brush a soft kiss against his mouth, but when their lips met, he immediately deepened the kiss. Backing her against the door, her arms banded around him.

The rich flavor of his mouth, the feeling of their tongues twining, and the knowledge that they were completely secluded in his towering lair was intoxicating. Even within Eldridge's barn, Selene sometimes worried that the moans and growls coming from their love nest could be heard by anyone outside. But the stone walls surrounding them in the tower were several feet thick, and it was a long way down to the ground.

When Selene rubbed herself against the growing bulge in Sam's pants, he broke their kiss. His eyelids were heavy, irises flickering red.

"Later," he rumbled, taking a step back. "Let me show you inside."

Selene took a second to catch her breath, then passed through the carved door. She was immediately surrounded by bookcases. Each curved wall of the tower held a dark, polished wood bookcase that stretched halfway up the vaulted ceiling. The books were neatly stacked upright on each shelf, but there wasn't an inch of space to spare. The continuous line of bookcases was broken up by pair of glass doors leading out to a balcony. A green velvet couch and leather armchair sat in the center of the room, facing a brick fireplace.

Selene moved closer to the books, skimming over titles like *Quest of Fortune, Nightfall's Desire,* and *Lustful Journeys.* Sam leaned against the doorway, watching her closely.

"I knew you liked to read but I didn't expect this," she said, gesturing around the room. "It's incredible."

"Thank you. I bought most of them from traveling merchants."

Selene pulled a book called *Yearning of the Storm's Kiss* from the shelf. Graphic descriptions of sex leapt off the page as she flipped through it.

"Sam!" she said in mock outrage. "You read smut?"

"What do you mean?"

She grabbed another book at random. This one contained detailed drawings of a furry Lycah couple involved in various obscene acts. The third book she pulled out from a different shelf appeared to be about a group of scaled Drago males and one very satisfied looking Drago female. The book next to that was full of poetry dedicated to the intimate folds nestled within a female Nereid's tail.

"Are all these books about sex?" she asked.

Sam tapped a leather-bound book near his elbow. "This one is about an expedition through uncharted seas. But the others are mostly erotic texts, yes." His eyes were hot on her. "I've been waiting for my mate for a long time."

Her arm trembled slightly with anticipation as she re-shelved the poetry book. "Show me the bedroom."

He led her through another intricately carved door near the fireplace. At the center of the room was an enormous circular bed draped in red brocade. A bathroom was nestled in the corner, while a tapestry rug lay before the dual-sided fireplace. Narrow windows, cut into the walls, allowed soft light to filter in.

"This is the biggest bed I've ever seen," Selene said, trailing her fingers over the bedspread. She could feel the weight of Sam's gaze and knew he was imagining her spread out before him. "Did you build this, too?"

"Yes."

Selene held out her arms and did a little spin. "This is so cozy. I love it."

"I'm glad," Sam said, his voice low. "It's also very private."

He moved toward her with slow, deliberate steps, then pulled her firmly against him. She reached up to kiss him, then hesitated.

"Wait," she whispered.

Sam let out a growl of protest. "What's wrong?"

"I have an idea."

"What?"

She wet her lips, then said, "Bring me your favorite book from the other room. One with something that you used to fantasize about."

"Why?"

"I want to make it a reality."

CHAPTER 5

Selene watched as Sam went to work, flipping through books. He seemed to know exactly which ones he was looking for and where they were. Eventually, he held up a beat-up-looking book bound in purple fabric.

"This one," he said.

He held out the book for her. It was opened to a page depicting a series of penciled drawings of a Malkina couple. In each one, the female lay spread-eagle on a bed, blindfolded, while a male Malkina did wicked things to her body.

"Ohhh," Selene breathed, eating up the image with her eyes.

"Would this be all right?" His words were thick with desire.

"Yes. Do you have a blindfold?"

"I'll find something." The roughness of his tone made moisture pool between her legs. "Take off your clothes, then lie on the bed."

Selene enthusiastically obeyed. As she undressed, she watched Sam dig through a trunk in the corner of the room. Eventually, he pulled out a white tunic and tore a strip of fabric from the hem. He also retrieved something else from the trunk—a shoebox-sized container that he tucked under his arm.

"What's that?" she asked.

"You'll find out." When he came toward her, his eyes glowed red.

"What do you want me to do?"

"Reach back and grab onto the spindles," he said, gesturing to the headboard. Once she had done that, he smoothed her hair away from her face. "Then just *receive.*"

It was strangely erotic to be laid out for him, naked and vulnerable, while he loomed over her. Fully clothed and in complete control. His gaze dragged up and down her body as if making a mental map of everything he would do to her. His features were so intense that Selene involuntarily stiffened, prompting Sam to ask, "Do you trust me, my love?"

"Yes. I just don't want to disappoint you."

"Impossible. My fantasy is only to please you." He moved toward her face, holding out the strip of fabric. "May I put this on you now?"

"Yes."

Sam's heart pounded as he tied the blindfold around Selene's head. He had imagined many scenarios from his explicit books but never dreamed he would be asked to perform one—and within the very chambers where he had first read about them.

His eyes raked over Selene's curves, considering how he should start. So many options. He wanted to make her mindless with pleasure, screaming his name and begging for more. He needed to tantalize every inch of her.

Slow build.

He extended the claw of his index finger and drew it down her arm. "Does that hurt?" he asked.

"No. It makes me shiver."

Perfect.

He repeated the motion on her other arm, and Selene shivered again. Then he gently swept his claw back and forth across her collarbone before moving down her sternum.

Lightly, he traced the sides of each breast. The way her nipples tightened before his eyes made his mouth water, but he didn't stop to indulge himself. He continued to drag his claw downward, drawing lazy circles over her stomach until he skimmed the top of the dark triangle between her legs.

Selene's breaths were coming quicker now. He drew swirls around her hips, then parted her legs so he could caress the sensitive flesh of her thighs. When he moved down to her knees, she giggled.

"Ticklish?" he asked.

"Yes. But don't stop."

When he finally reached the bottom of her feet, he reversed direction to make his way back up her body. But this time, he sheathed his claw. This time, he used his mouth.

He spread her legs wider, kissing and licking her thighs. He wanted to draw her pleasure out for as long as possible but couldn't resist nuzzling his face against her core. When his hot breath skated over her swollen folds, Selene moaned, and he immediately pulled back, delaying her gratification.

"More," she said. He marveled at how her flushed cheeks contrasted beautifully against the white blindfold.

"Patience," he chided. "Try not to come until I tell you to."

"Ugh, you're going to kill me," Selene said, but there was a smile in her voice.

"You're going to feel me everywhere."

She let out a frustrated sigh, which made Sam's desire pound even harder. She was reacting just as he had always dreamed.

When he kissed his way to her stomach, he took extra time to linger over her satiny skin, knowing it was a part of her body she felt self-conscious about. As he squeezed her plush warmth to meet his tongue, her hips began to undulate. He stilled her pelvis with his hands then licked the underside of her breast. Involuntarily, he drove his erection into the mattress.

Must hold out longer.

Leaning up, he closed his lips around one nipple, sucking ruthlessly. The shift from gentle to rough made her cry out and tangle her hands in his hair.

"Hands back on the spindles," he commanded. She obeyed.

He attended to her other breast, but his desire to taste more of her became undeniable. Roughly, he moved down the bed and draped her knees over his shoulders.

When he pressed his mouth to her sex, she cried out, "Sam, please. I can't take much more!"

He delved his tongue into her wet heat, her taste wickedly delicious. In his mind, he had wanted to keep her on edge for hours, but his lust was so strong he knew he needed to make haste. Abruptly, he pulled away from her.

"What is it?"

"Hold on, I want to try something," he whispered. "Just trust me."

Sam slid open the wooden box he had placed on the bed. Nestled within a bed of velvet was a polished column of pink quartz. It was thick and shiny, tapered to be wider at one end.

"This might feel cold," he warned then dragged the crystal across Selene's outer labia.

She startled. "What *is* that?"

"It's a pleasure wand," he said. He moved the crystal over her inner thighs then worked it slowly around her folds. "Do you like it?"

"I... I... yes," she panted.

"A merchant gave it to me many years ago." He teased the wider end around her entrance, making her gasp. "He was under the false assumption that I was buying erotic books for a lover," he explained. "I've always dreamed of using it."

"More, Sam."

Sam began to pump the crystal in and out of her. He quickened his pace until Selene's head thrashed back and forth and she let go of the spindles to claw at the sheets. He didn't correct her. The feeling of having complete control over her passion made him feel wild with lust.

"Sam... Sam, I can't hold out—"

He couldn't hold out either. In a strained voice, he commanded, "Come for me, mate."

Instantly, her body released. He felt her spasms against his hand, and her cries of pleasure made him moan, too. He continued thrusting the pleasure wand until her body stopped shaking.

"Oh my god. Oh my god, Sam, that was incredible." Panting, she touched the blindfold. "Can I take this off?"

"Yes."

Her eyes were heavy-lidded when they met his. He was shaking with pent-up lust. But although he wanted to pounce on her, he held himself back, knowing Selene's body was sometimes too sensitive for more pleasure directly after release.

She sat up, tugging at his pants. "Your turn."

He gasped with relief when she freed his erection from its confines. Before he could question whether she was ready, she bent her head and closed her lips around the head of his cock. He groaned and helplessly bucked his hips.

As she moved her mouth up and down, she grasped his bollocks and tugged them gently, stretching them the way she knew he liked. When her tongue teased the underside of his crown, his hands shook as they pulled at her hair.

"Selene... I'm about to... can't hold out—" He moaned. Her mouth was so hot and wet. She began pumping the base of his cock faster, urging him on. Within seconds, all the tension coiled up in him erupted, lashing him with wave after wave of pleasure. Selene didn't pull away as he came against her tongue, his hips mindlessly thrusting. His roar of bliss filled the chambers.

When it was over, they both collapsed on the bed. They stared up at the ceiling for a moment, until Selene pulled the covers over them.

She curled against him and whispered, "Was that as good as you imagined?"

Sam's breathing was still erratic, but he managed to gasp out, "So much better."

CHAPTER 6

Although Sam would have happily stayed in bed the next day, he knew it would be rude to stay secluded. Plus, Queen Thema had a lot of questions about interdimensional travel.

"What will become of my clothes?" she asked Selene over breakfast in the solarium the next morning.

"What do you mean?"

"As we travel through dimensions, will they disappear? Am I to arrive in the Underworld nude as I do in Gaia? What of my breastplate?" Queen Thema tapped on the metal surrounding her chest.

"You take on your cat form on Gaia," Sam said while buttering a piece of toast. "This is different."

"I don't see any reason why your clothes would disappear," Selene said, suppressing a smile. "I've never appeared anywhere without clothes when I use it."

Queen Thema nodded decisively. "Then I shall wear my cerulean gown with the beaded cuffs. Arkaya! Will you make sure it's steamed and ready?"

Arkaya nodded after setting down a second pitcher of cream at the table.

"Queen Thema, would you like to practice a few times?" Selene asked. "I can transport us someplace within the castle just so you have an idea of how it feels. Sam and I did that a few times in Snowmelt."

Queen Thema looked thoughtful for a moment, then shook her head. "Actually, I would like the entire affair to be a surprise. As old as I am, I rarely have new experiences. I want to arrive in the Underworld full of excitement, warmed by the thrill of adventure!"

"It's not a very pleasant sensation," Sam warned.

"Perhaps to those who are not used to walking between worlds," the queen quipped.

"Sam's right, but if that's what you wish, it's fine."

"Good. I have much to do today in preparation for the ball and also for Queen Delphine's temporary reign. How do you two plan to spend your day?"

Sam replied, "I plan to show Selene around more of the castle and grounds. Unless there's something you need from us."

"I need nothing but for you both to relax and enjoy yourselves in true Malkina fashion."

"Very well," Sam said.

While Sam had been indifferent—or even scornful—toward the famous Malkina opulence during his tenure at the castle, seeing it through Selene's eyes was fascinating. She had only glimpsed a small portion of the castle during her visits, whereas Sam knew every nook and cranny. She marveled at the grand corridors of each wing, gasped when they entered the workshops of the artisans in residence, and even clapped when they ventured into the subterranean crystal gardens. Her perspective made Sam consider that his time at Queen Thema's castle hadn't been as torturous as he had made himself believe. Perhaps it was his loneliness and grief that had colored the experience.

The next day, Queen Thema's farewell ball unfolded just as Sam had expected—with grandiose splendor and far too much drinking and debauchery. He kept his word to attend for dinner but left after Selene whispered that she wanted to be with him. Alone. His pulse had quickened at her words, and a glance at Queen Thema leading a group dance in the middle of the ballroom confirmed that their presence would not be missed.

Wordlessly, they slipped away from the festivities. They made it as far as a nearby broom closet before Sam couldn't wait any longer. He pulled Selene inside, lifted her skirts, and took her against the wall. How Selene's former human lover, Kevin P. Norton, could have spurned her advances, Sam would never understand. There was nothing more rousing to him than being asked by his mate to gratify her desire.

The next morning, Sam woke before sunrise, his body thrumming with anticipation. It was hard to believe that the day he had dreamed of for so long was finally here. He dressed quickly, his movements steady despite the energy coursing through him. Soon, Selene stirred in their bed as well.

By the time they descended from his chambers, the halls were hushed in the early morning stillness. Golden sunlight filtered through the windows, casting warm slants across the stone floor. Waiting outside the doors into her private wing, Queen Thema stood with her hands clasped before her, Arkaya at her side.

"Well, good morning," Selene said. "I didn't expect you to be ready so soon."

"I couldn't sleep all night from excitement," Queen Thema said.

"You only spent a few moments in bed," Arkaya said wryly. "A restful night would have been better advised."

"Perhaps, but I was having too much fun at the ball."

They gazed at each other tenderly for a moment before Thema's tone softened. "It grieves me to leave you, but I will return soon."

"Everything will be taken care of here," Arkaya assured her.

Queen Thema nodded, then pulled Arkaya into a brief but firm embrace, which surprised Sam. It wasn't a secret that the two were lovers. But the queen feared that openly displaying favoritism might undermine Arkaya's authority as steward, so she kept the depth of their relationship discreet.

"Right. Let's proceed, shall we?" Queen Thema said to Selene.

"Okay, no time like the present, I guess." Selene braced her feet and held out her arms. "Everyone, grab on to me. Let's do this."

Sam stood behind Selene, wrapping an arm around her. He could feel the tension in her body as he pressed against her. Queen Thema's usually confident smile wavered as she reached out, gripping Sam's forearm with one hand and Selene's shoulder with the other.

With a determined motion, Selene pulled the traveler's stone from beneath her shirt. She touched her fingers to the glossy white surface, bowed her head, and closed her eyes.

It only took a few seconds before dizziness spun through Sam's head. The air thickened, charged with an acrid smell that clung to his nostrils. Thema's sharp intake of breath told him she felt the shift around them, too.

His stomach lurched as if the ground beneath him had fallen away, and his balance wavered, making it hard to tell up from down. Then came the sound—a harsh, grating buzz, like a swarm of angry bees vibrating against his skull.

Drilling into his head until they spread into his body.

His bones.

Sam's vision tunneled to a pinpoint of light. He tried to focus on it, like a guiding star in a sea of night. But it began to collapse until it winked out completely.

Darkness swallowed him whole.

Sam's breath turned to ragged gasps, his chest tightening with panic. He tried to squeeze Selene closer to him, comforted by the warmth of her body, but the sensation was fleeting. Was she still there? Or was it just hot air slipping from his grasp? The space around him no longer made sense.

It felt as though his body was being twisted into impossible angles. Falling, falling, falling into an abyss of nothing. Somewhere in the void, a raw scream tore through the silence. It was filled with terror, but Sam couldn't tell where it came from.

Was it Selene? Thema?

His throat ached—perhaps it was his own voice he'd heard.

The pressure surrounding Sam's head and body continued to build until he feared his skin might split and his bones shatter.

It was agony. Relentless. Absolute.

Then suddenly—silence.

CHAPTER 7

*S*ulfur.

Scent was the first of Sam's senses to return. It was a familiar scent, one that filled him with nostalgia. The moment he detected the tang of sulfur in the air, he knew their journey had been successful.

Slowly, he cracked open his eyes. Above him stretched a ceiling of carefully laid stone, its rough texture illuminated by a soft glow. His body ached, a dull heaviness settling in his limbs, but none of that mattered.

He was home.

Someone coughed. He looked to his right and saw Selene sprawled on the floor, looking pale. She smiled weakly at him.

He sat up and took her hand. "Are you all right?"

She coughed a few more times and nodded. When she rose to her elbows, Sam followed her gaze, taking in the room around them.

Electric wall sconces glowed on the stone walls, and the marble floor gleamed as though it had been recently cleaned. The room was free of the small furniture Selene had described during at her visit, but the familiar crack running across the mantle of the cold fireplace confirmed it was his childhood bedroom. The door stood slightly ajar, but beyond it lay only darkness.

The room was much smaller than he remembered—probably because *he* had been much smaller the last time he was here. He tried to recall where his room sat in the castle's layout, but his memories were foggy. His parents' suite of rooms must be nearby, yet only silence came from beyond the door.

Queen Thema groaned. She was curled into a ball next to him. "Am I still alive? That was... truly unpleasant."

"Tell me about it," Selene muttered, in that human way Sam had learned meant emphasis. She lightly touched the queen's shoulder. "How do you feel?"

"As though I have just been digested and then regurgitated."

Selene chuckled softly. "That feels accurate."

Thema pulled herself up to a sitting position. "Is this it? Did we succeed?"

"Yes," Sam replied. "We're in the Underworld."

"Marvelous," Queen Thema said in a tone that contradicted her words. She flopped onto her back again with a distinctly cat-like motion.

Selene moved to stand, but her knees buckled. She fell back, wincing and rubbing her temples. "Oh, my head."

Sam pulled Selene into his lap. "Patience," he murmured. "Let's just rest a moment."

Selene relaxed into him. As he stroked her hair, Sam considered their next move. He had pictured reuniting with his parents many times but hadn't considered the awkward space in between their arrival and that moment. So far, no imps had come at the sound of their voices, and the hellhounds had yet to pick up their scent. Was this wing of the castle abandoned now?

Queen Thema cleared her throat, making Sam realize how thirsty she must be. They all needed water, but Selene especially needed food to replenish her strength.

"I'm going to find someone," he said, gently moving Selene off his lap.

The moment he stood, he heard the faint echo of footsteps from outside the room. Pushing the door open, Sam glanced both ways down the dark hall. "Hello?"

The footsteps quickened. An orange light appeared at the end of the hall like a beacon. It grew brighter and brighter until Sam could make out the outline of a winged female holding a flaming torch.

"Who goes there?" the woman called out. She began to run toward him so quickly that Sam took a step back.

"Is it a servant?" Queen Thema asked, rising to her feet.

Before Sam could respond, a demoness filled the doorway. She was tall and imposing, with bronze-colored wings set into her shoulder blades. Black horns were nestled within her long blonde hair, each one curving down and around to frame her ears. A snake tattoo coiled along the length of her right forearm. Sam didn't recognize her, but her red eyes glowed with excitement when they met his.

"Greetings," Sam said tentatively. "I'm Samael—"

"I know who you are," the demoness interrupted breathlessly.

She rushed through the doorway, tossing her torch to the ground where it extinguished the moment it touched the floor. Throwing her arms around Sam's neck, she pressed her mouth to his in a fierce kiss. The surprise of it made Sam freeze. He tried to push her away, but the demoness was incredibly strong. When she finally pulled back, her smile was dreamy.

In a melodious voice, she said, "I'm Vanthee. Your fated mate."

CHAPTER 8

What did she just say?

Selene watched, slack-jawed as Sam struggled to free himself from the grip of the most beautiful woman she had ever seen. The demon... demoness? She-devil? Hell bitch? Whatever she was, she looked like a Barbie doll dressed as a Greek goddess.

Statuesque and blonde, with big hair, big boobs, and big eyes framed by a dark fringe of lashes. She wore a short leather skirt above knee-high boots. A leather harness wrapped around her neck and waist, joined by a central strap that ran down the middle of her chest. Even in the dim light, her breasts were clearly visible through the gauzy top she wore.

"Vanthee... I'm sorry, have we met?" Sam asked.

"No. But your return seals my fate. And yours," Vanthee breathed. "I've dreamed of this day for so long."

Selene had never been the jealous type, but she *urgently* needed to let Vanthee know that Sam was spoken for. She attempted to stand, but the action made her so dizzy, she stumbled back to the floor.

Queen Thema placed a hand on Selene's arm. Artfully, she placed herself between Sam and the demoness. In an authoritative tone she said, "Vanthee, run along and find your queen and king. We have come a long way to see them."

Vanthee looked at Queen Thema as though she had just noticed there were others in the room. She studied her for a moment, as if trying to decipher what sort of creature she was. Queen Thema only stood at eye level with Vanthee's impressive breasts, but her imposing presence made the demoness take a step back.

"And you are?" Vanthee asked, flexing her wings. Despite their delicate webbing, they looked powerful enough to deliver a black eye with a single thwack. Selene thought she saw the tattoo around Vanthee's arm move, too, but she could have imagined it.

Queen Thema's back straightened. "I am Queen Thema, ruler of Malkina in the glorious realm of Aurelia. Also known as Lady of the Flame. The Devouring One. Mother Protector and She of the Change. Most importantly, the favorite sister of your queen. Surely she has mentioned me."

"Not once." Vanthee sniffed, then turned to gaze adoringly at Sam. But the moment Selene entered her line of sight, her eyes narrowed, then widened with disgust.

"Is that human... alive?" Her words dripped with disbelief. She pointed a finger at Selene. "Why is she here?"

Sam's expression turned dark. "This *human* is my fated mate, Selene. And you will treat her with respect." He took Selene's hands to help her stand. She was grateful that his strong arms kept her vertical. "She is the one responsible for bringing me back to the Underworld."

For a split second, Selene saw Vanthee's eyes widen with shock before she let out a haughty laugh. "Demons can't mate with humans. Especially one so... " She trailed off, her lips curling in distaste as she gave Selene a slow, once-over.

Selene's jaw tightened. Since claiming Sam as her mate, she had become far more in touch with her anger. And right now, she could think of nothing more satisfying than slapping that smug look off Vanthee's face.

But since the customs of the Underworld were a mystery to her, diplomacy seemed the wiser choice. Maybe Vanthee was royalty, and it would be an insult to be rude to her. Or she could be a demon of Conflict or Insecurity who fed on negative reactions. Selene had dealt with her fair share of narcissists and bullies and knew not to take their bait.

Pasting on a sunny smile, she said, "Hello, Vanthee, it's nice to meet you. I'm sorry but Sam isn't your fated mate—I've already claimed him."

"You're mistaken," Vanthee retorted sweetly. She tilted her head up at Sam. "My prince, you didn't need to bring these... others along with you. You would have been more than welcome on your own."

Queen Thema placed her hands on her hips. "I beg your pardon, but Selene and I are esteemed *guests*. Come now, girl, we are quite weary. Will you not summon your rulers? Or must I do it myself?" She moved past Vanthee to peer down the hall. "I'm sure Queen Lamia would not want our reunion delayed by your ramblings."

Thema's words seemed to startle Vanthee into action. "All right. I will take you to the king and queen. Their son's return will bring much joy to our kingdom."

Vanthee bent to retrieve the torch she had brought. Instantly, the end blazed with fire. "Follow me."

"Are you able to walk?" Sam whispered into Selene's hair.

As much as she loved their stairway routine at Queen Thema's, Selene had a feeling this was not the time to show weakness. "Sure," she said with false enthusiasm, forcing her legs not to wobble. Sam kept hold of her hand.

They followed Vanthee out of the room and into a dark, narrow hallway. Vanthee led the way, followed by Thema, with Selene, and Sam bring up the rear. The smell of dank earth, sulfur, and smoke made Selene's eyes water. Vanthee's torch was the only source of light Selene could see, but she heard lots of scurrying and scraping sounds from the walls they passed. A hubcap-sized red spider was visible when they turned a corner, and Selene stifled a yelp when something both furry and slimy brushed against her arm.

They passed many closed doors and empty hallways until Sam said, "Why is the east wing abandoned?"

Vanthee paused to face him, her long lashes casting shadows against her cheek. "Because of you, my prince."

"Me?"

"After you disappeared, the queen and king relocated their personal chambers and closed this part of the palace. It was too difficult for them to pass your bedroom, your playroom, and other quarters dedicated to your amusement."

"And why were you here?" Queen Thema asked. "Are you a servant?"

Vanthee seemed offended by the question. "I am the Underworld's Guide. I come to this wing when I wish to be alone and take a break from my duties, if you must know."

"And what do Guides do?" Queen Thema asked.

Vanthee pulled back her shoulders. "I lead souls who have passed on through our realm by lighting their way with my torch. Then I send them through the doors of their destiny with guidance from my key." She held out her tattooed forearm.

"Ah, so you've been trained as an enchantress," Queen Thema said.

"No. But I grew up learning a few things about magick," Vanthee answered vaguely.

Selene estimated Vanthee to be about twenty-five in human years, and wondered how old that was in demon terms.

Queen Thema snorted. "In my realm, one cannot dabble in such arts. Years of dedication and training are required to cast enchantments. And even then, one must be approved by a council of crones before practicing in the community."

"How quaint," Vanthee said, turning away to continue their journey.

"It's not quaint—it's just good sense."

"Do your crones have nothing else to do but meddle?"

"Meddle? How dare you imply—"

The sounds of Vanthee and Queen Thema's argument faded as Selene peered up at Sam. The corners of his mouth were tight, and a deep line had formed between his eyebrows. When he noticed her looking at him, he whispered, "Once we see my parents, we'll find you a place to rest."

"I'm okay. How are you feeling?"

"Better, but... " He hesitated then said, "That encounter was odd."

"Yes. Do you remember her? Why would she say she's your fated mate?"

"I don't know."

"She's quite beautiful," Selene said, unable to stop herself from fishing for reassurance.

"I disagree."

Selene smiled at Sam's matter-of-factness. When she heard a hiss come from Queen Thema's throat, Selene realized her and Vanthee's argument was escalating. It might be a good time to change the subject.

"Vanthee, where are the king and queen right now?" Selene asked.

Vanthee turned her steely gaze from Thema to say, "They usually spend mornings in their private courtyard."

"Is there a way we can go there without passing through the public spaces?" Sam asked. "I would prefer that they are the first to know of my arrival."

Vanthee's face brightened. "Of course. I assumed you would want a reunion free from the prying eyes of courtiers. That is why I'm taking you through concealed passages. Look—here is our first doorway."

Vanthee stopped in front of what appeared, to Selene, to a

random spot in the seemingly endless hallway. Then, she raised her right arm, positioning it in front of a small dimple in the brick.

Selene watched with fascination as the snake tattoo on Vanthee's skin shifted as if it were awakening. The inked head rose up from her flesh into a three-dimensional form. Its tiny tongue flicked out, then struck the stone, sinking in its fangs.

Instantly, the bricks trembled, groaned, and then parted, revealing a hidden doorway.

Vanthee stepped through, her eyes locked on Sam. She lifted her arm, smirking as the snake retracted its head and faded seamlessly back into her skin. "My key."

Sam hesitated, then cleared his throat. "Uh... thank you. That's impressive."

Vanthee's smirk widened. "I have other skills you might find even more impressive." Her voice was a sultry purr.

Selene gritted her teeth. *Oh, come on.*

Vanthee led them through the passage into another hallway, this one colder and more decrepit than the last. She repeated her snake trick several times, unlocking passage after passage, until they finally stopped in front of a towering iron door.

Placing both palms against the metal, Vanthee turned dramatically. "We have arrived. Beyond this door, the king and queen await. It has been an honor to guide you, Prince Samael, and I look forward to growing closer as you settle back into your rightful place."

Sam exhaled. "Thank you for leading us. But I'm only here to visit."

Vanthee's eyebrows shot up. "Is that so? Well, your plans may change when you—"

"Vanthee!" Selene cried. Her patience had finally snapped. "Shut up and let Sam through. He's waited for this moment long enough!"

Anger glinted in Vanthee's red eyes, sending a twitch of fear through Selene. But her words had their intended effect. With a final glare, Vanthee turned back to the door and pressed her tattooed arm against it.

With a low groan, the iron door swung open.

CHAPTER 9

Sam flinched at the rush of light and fresh air. The scents from his mother's prized poison garden patch breezed past him—bitter belladonna, the cloying sweetness of baneberry, the faint almond tang of oleander. It unleashed a flood of memories, making his racing heart pound faster.

This is it. It's about to happen.

There was a murmur of voices, but he couldn't see anything past the thick foliage growing above the hidden door. He took a step forward, but Vanthee pulled on his arm.

"Wait. Let me announce you first," Vanthee said.

Sam paused, then gave a tight nod.

Vanthee turned to Selene and Thema, her tone sharp. "You two, stay here."

She strode ahead, vanishing into the sea of greenery. Pushing through thick, glossy leaves, she called out, "Your Majesties, forgive the intrusion, but I bring news. Joyous news."

The murmuring stopped. Silence fell, then he heard his mother's voice. "Come forward then, Vanthee."

Sam clenched his fists, trying to steady himself, but the sound of his mother's voice caught him off guard. Emotion surged through him. He reached up and pulled aside a curtain of ivy near his face, revealing a glimpse of his father's horns. They were as thick and gnarled as he remembered, but the crown of spikes he wore around his bald head seemed more battered.

As Sam brushed back a hanging cluster of golden laburnum blossoms, he saw his mother's profile. Her auburn hair was braided through her crown, and her gray wings swayed leisurely at her back. They both sat at a small table, sipping from mugs.

The sight of them—real, not imagined—made Sam's legs tremble. He focused on his footing, planting each step deliberately as he followed a few paces behind Vanthee, trying to ground himself in the moment.

When Vanthee reached the table, she dropped into a curtsy. "Fate has bestowed us with a gift."

King Asmodeus looked at her closely, his brows furrowed. "What is it?"

"The most precious gift any of us could dream of," Vanthee replied, still bowed low.

Queen Lamia gave a huff of impatience. "Stand and tell us, Vanthee."

Rising gracefully, Vanthee met their eyes. "I was in the east wing and heard noises coming from Prince Samael's former bedroom."

The pain that clouded his mother's face at the mention of his name was stark. It made him want to burst out to announce himself, but he stayed back.

"More rats?" Lamia asked. "I've told the imps that wing mustn't be neglected."

"No, Your Majesty. Not rats." Vanthee glanced back at Sam before continuing. "Please, prepare yourselves. What I'm about to say may seem... impossible." She took a breath. "Prince Samael has returned."

The words landed like a thunderclap. Confusion consumed both their faces, swiftly giving way to anger. Asmodeus's tone was low and dangerous. "What kind of cruel game is this?"

"Why would you say something like that?" Lamia asked, her eyes wide with hurt.

Sam realized his return must have seemed so improbable that they had taken Vanthee's words as a jest. Before Vanthee could speak again, Sam stepped forward. A dry twig cracked beneath his boot. The sound made them both turn.

"It's not a trick," he called out, his voice shaking. When he pushed the last tangle of vines separating him from his parents, he paused to take in the full sight of them. "It's me, Sam. I've come home."

The king and queen seemed temporarily frozen with shock. They stared at him for a moment until Queen Lamia let out a joyful shriek and dropped to her knees.

King Asmodeus shot to his hoofed feet to rush toward Sam. He enveloped him in a hug so hard it nearly knocked the air from Sam's lungs. He returned the gesture, wrapping his arms around his father's broad back and pressing his palms into the leather cape he wore.

After so many years of being the largest person in every space, it was a strange comfort to be dwarfed in the arms of his powerful father. His scent was just as Sam had remembered—blood and hearth smoke.

The next moment, Sam felt his mother behind him, her small hands clutching at his shoulders. The scent of her pomegranate perfume brought an eruption of emotions. She trembled and sobbed, "My son, my son, my son," against his shoulder. Tears began to flow from Sam's eyes as well.

This was the moment he had waited for—one that had existed only in the sanctuary of his dreams. It was the vision that had carried him through lonely nights. The fantasy that he replayed when nightmares had stolen his sleep. The wish that quieted his demonic urges when they felt too much to bear.

It was real. It was his.

And for the first time, he allowed himself to believe he deserved it.

Sam wasn't sure how long the three of them stayed in that position, arms entwined as if letting go might shatter the reality of the moment. The bond he feared had been stretched too thin by decades of separation now felt strong, making him realize nothing could ever truly sever their connection.

In that moment, nothing else mattered. It was just them, finally together, rebuilding what had once been fractured, piece by piece.

Eventually, Asmodeus stepped back to let out a victorious roar so loud the ground shook.

"Let me look at you." King Asmodeus ran his fingers gently over Sam's face with his clawed hand, then squinted closely at the top of Sam's head. "Have you lost one of your horns?"

"Yes. It's regenerating."

Queen Lamia took Sam's hands, examining the scars that encircled his wrists—a remnant from his captivity in the blood wagons. "And you bear many scars. Were you a soldier in Aurelia? Or a warrior?"

"No," he said softly.

"We have a lot to catch up on," Lamia said.

"I believe he still has your eyes. Do you agree, my treasure?" King Asmodeus asked Queen Lamia.

"Oh yes. He looks exactly the same. Only more grown-up." Queen Lamia searched Sam's face, then hugged him again. "How did you come here?"

"My mate, Selene, brought us here with the traveler's stone."

"Selene. Ah," Lamia said, her smile flickering for a moment. "We didn't know what happened to her when she disappeared. But she must have found her way back to Aurelia."

"Yes, to my great fortune. There's someone else here to see you, too," Sam said. He turned toward the bushes and called, "Come forward."

Queen Thema came running toward them, with Selene close

behind. Without hesitation, Thema bumped Vanthee aside with her hip, her voice breaking with emotion as she cried out, "Sister!"

"Thema?" Queen Lamia gasped, stunned.

She released Sam and launched herself at Thema with such force that the two of them tumbled to the ground, arms wrapped tightly around each other. Their laughter echoed through the garden.

Asmodeus pulled Sam into a one-armed embrace, squeezing his shoulder with pride. "Well done, son."

Sam smiled, then stepped away from his father. He reached for Selene's hand and drew her forward. "My mate, Selene."

King Asmodeus's grin widened. "We have already met. Greetings, Selene." He wagged a finger at her, feigning a scolding tone. "My queen and I weren't pleased about your abrupt departure into the ether, but you have redeemed yourself this day."

"Thank you," Selene said, her cheeks coloring slightly. "I'm sorry about the way I left. I didn't understand how the traveler's stone worked back then."

"And now?"

"Yes. I got us here, at least."

After several moments of laughter and tight embraces between Lamia and Thema, the sisters rose to their feet. Queen Lamia turned to Selene, giving her a slow, assessing look.

"Hello again," she said, her tone cool and unreadable.

Selene offered a bright smile. "Hello. It's good to see you."

Lamia didn't respond. Instead, she shifted her attention to Vanthee. "Excellent work, Vanthee. Your discovery has brought forth the end of a great anguish for our kingdom."

"I know," Vanthee said. The eagerness that shone in the demoness's eyes made Sam as uncomfortable as he was confused. He glanced at Selene. It was she, not Vanthee, who deserved their praise.

Lamia looped her arm through Sam's. She met his eyes with a serious, almost expectant look. "We have much to discuss about your future."

Feeling too buoyant with joy to dampen the moment with heavy conversations, Sam only nodded.

Queen Thema turned to King Asmodeus. "Great king, our journey to your new realm has been arduous. Might we impose on your hospitality for some food and drink?"

"Of course," Asmodeus replied. He stamped one hoof on the ground three times. A band of flying imps with pock-marked wings and arms that hung longer than their legs descended from above. They hovered in the air, awaiting instructions. "Prepare the formal dining room and ready two guest suites—Samael, the lost Prince of Vengeance, has returned!"

CHAPTER 10

King Asmodeus and Queen Lamia led Sam into the formal dining room, their arms draped around him as if they couldn't bear to let him go. Their closeness made Sam feel both comforted and slightly overwhelmed by their protective embrace.

He didn't remember much about the dining room from his childhood, but he was struck by its elegance. Black brocade fabric lined the walls, and metal chandeliers resembling large bats hung from the ceiling. A row of tall windows along one wall looked out onto his mother's second garden—the night-blooming one, where flowers only opened after dark.

The long obsidian table had been set with five place settings clustered at one end. Asmodeus took the seat at the head. When Sam pulled out a chair for Selene beside him, he was stopped by his mother's voice.

"Selene can sit over here," Queen Lamia said, gesturing to the last chair on the opposite side of the table. Her smile was polite, but it didn't quite reach her eyes.

Sam looked at her, blinking. "I'd prefer my mate sit next to me."

"But from there, she'll have a lovely view of the gardens," Lamia replied, her tone smooth and controlled.

"It's fine," Selene whispered. She circled the table and took the seat Lamia had indicated.

Sam sat down, feeling a bit unsettled but not wanting to create conflict.

With a casual wave of his hand, King Asmodeus lit every candle in the room at once, casting a golden glow across the dark furnishings. A trio of imps fluttered in, hovering midair with expectant expressions.

"Tonight," the king announced, "you may have anything your heart desires. Picture your favorite food in your mind, and the imps will guide the demons of Gluttony in preparing it for you."

He gestured to Thema with a smile. "Thema, may I also call you Sister? Please go first."

"You may," Queen Thema said, then scrunched her forehead in concentration. "Raw fish and clotted cream."

One of the imps nodded then looked at Selene. "Can you do human food?" she asked.

"Anything," the king said.

Selene closed her eyes. "I've been craving Southern comfort food, so I'd like hot chicken, macaroni and cheese, fried green tomatoes, and banana pudding."

When she opened her eyes and the imp nodded, it was Sam's turn. There were many dishes he liked in Aurelia, but the foods he had missed most from his childhood were simple—charred bread, fried vulture wings, and cinnamon sweet buns.

When the imps had everyone's orders, they filled each chalice with dark wine and flew away.

Sam toyed with the edge of his napkin. The moment felt too big, and there was so much to say, he didn't know where to start.

Should he ask his parents what they've been doing for the past twenty years? Recount his own story from the moment he was kidnapped? Or catch up on the current news of the realm as though he had never left?

Fortunately, Queen Thema was a skilled conversationalist. "This dining room is absolutely stunning. The chandeliers remind me of the ones you had back home, Lamia. Did you design them?"

"Yes. I wanted something to remind me of my past," Queen Lamia said, referring to the bat—the sacred animal of the Goblyns from when she ruled in Aurelia.

"In my world, humans associate bats with vampires because of you," Selene said. "Isn't that interesting? Did you also have wings like a bat when patrolling Gaia?"

"Those wings were small and weak," Lamia replied with a dismissive wave of her hand. "They called me the Jersey Devil because of it."

She stretched out the elegant gray wings folded behind her back, then snapped them shut with a practiced motion. "Incomparable to the wings I gained when I became a demon."

Asmodeus gazed at her fondly for a moment then turned to Selene. "This must be an exciting time for you. Have you given any thought to what kind of demon you wish to become?"

When she looked confused, the king continued, "What sort of vices are you drawn to? Lust, Greed, Malice, Strife? I estimate the transition will take no more than a season. We should begin planning a celebration for your official transformation." He clapped once, sharp and commanding. "Imps! Come forward!"

Selene turned ashen. "Oh no, I don't plan to become a demon."

"You don't?" Asmodeus asked.

"No."

Lamia made an incredulous sound. "For what reason? Do you not wish to properly join our family?"

"It's not that! I'm thrilled to join your family. It's just that I want to stay... well, myself," Selene said.

"A mortal," Lamia said, the word laced with disdain. "*A human.*"

She began tapping her fingers against the table. "Do you even have any magick?"

"Magick? Uh... no," Selene replied.

King Asmodeus's eyebrows rose. "Truly? No training in enchantments or spellwork? I would have thought you were at least fluent in necromancy to attract a demon."

"Nope, I'm just a regular human," Selene said.

Lamia lifted her chin. "Which is precisely why you should take advantage of this opportunity to transform as I did. To elevate your station."

"Selene doesn't need to elevate herself," Sam said quickly, a knot of dread forming in his stomach. He took a breath, bracing himself. "Mother, you must understand, we're not planning to make the Underworld our permanent home. We're only here to visit."

Queen Lamia recoiled slightly, her eyes wide. "What do you mean?"

"This is only the first of many return visits, I assure you. Selene and I have plans for our life back in Aurelia. But we will visit often."

"Plans?" Queen Lamia asked. "What about your obligations to your kingdom and people? You're their prince!"

"I don't wish to rule," Sam said, quieter this time, but firm.

King Asmodeus leaned forward. "For what reason?"

"It doesn't interest me. Since I wasn't trained for it, I wouldn't feel properly prepared for such duties."

"It is your birthright and destiny!" the king said incredulously. "We can start your instruction tomorrow."

"No. I want to build a life with Selene, and Aurelia is where we are most comfortable. We plan to open a bookshop and live a quiet life." Sam glanced over at Selene, who was staring into her lap. He hated how their plans caused his parents pain, but he wanted no misunderstandings about their intentions.

"That's not going to work for us," Queen Lamia declared. She touched Asmodeus's arm. "Do you want to tell him?"

"Later," the king said tightly.

Queen Lamia pursed her lips and looked up at the ceiling. Then she leaned back in her chair and crossed her legs. "I have an idea." A calculating look fell across her eyes. "Sam, what if Selene leaves you here in the Underworld, returns to Aurelia with her little stone, and then comes back here to visit when you crave a human bedmate?"

The shocked gasp that escaped Selene's lips at his mother's words ignited the tension building in Sam's chest. "Absolutely not. She is my fated mate, and I will not be parted from her."

Lamia's face flushed with anger. "But how can you—"

"Enough!" Queen Thema cut through the tension like a whip. "Sister, you're being catastrophic. Samael has a right to live the way he chooses."

"This is a family matter. We don't need you butting in with your opinion," Lamia shot back.

"I *am* family!" Thema retorted. "Why, this is no different than if you were in Aurelia ruling the Goblyns and Samael lived a great distance away in Vowa lands."

"He must fulfill his duty. His attachment to Selene is holding him back," Asmodeus said.

Queen Thema shook her head. "Nonsense. You both should be filled with gratitude that your son's mate controls a traveler's stone! How else could he visit this realm except in death?"

"Why are you berating me so? I only want to spend more time with my son!" Lamia replied, her voice shaking with emotion.

Sam watched as Selene's eyes nervously flicked between Lamia and Thema. The anger burning in him—the disregard for his feelings and the disrespect toward his mate—was making him feel unbalanced. His claws extended beneath his fingernails, and his horns pulsed with rising emotion.

Queen Thema glanced at him, seeming to notice his turmoil. Pinning him with her gaze, she gave a nearly imperceptible shake of her head.

Then she sighed dramatically and laughed to herself. "Ah, forgive me for raising my voice, dear sister. It's that Malkina moodiness we are so famous for. It's been a difficult journey, so let us speak of more pleasant things. And enjoy each other's company instead of arguing! You can discuss this matter another time, when we aren't all so frazzled."

She looked around the table with a smile, but the steeliness behind her eyes dared anyone to object. "Lamia, I have so much gossip to share. You must hear the story of how Queen Cebna took on a Lycah lover... "

Gradually, the tension in the room dissipated with Thema's jovial story. Soon, the imps appeared with their food, further lightening the mood. Sam tried to catch Selene's eye as they ate, but her gaze remained downcast.

Her discomfort was palpable, making him long to sit closer so he could hold her hand. It pained him to see her like this, especially knowing how much energy it had taken for her to bring them to the Underworld.

Being caught between his parents' expectations and his desire for a peaceful life with Selene was difficult, but he would not tolerate any disrespect toward his mate. He would reiterate his intentions to his parents tomorrow and reassure them that he would always be present in their lives.

CHAPTER II

After the dinner dishes were cleared away, Selene was more than ready to collapse into bed—any bed. She was about five seconds from curling up on the stone floor when Asmodeus finally bid them goodnight, and an imp escorted her and Sam to their suite.

The gothic beauty of their space was breathtaking. Their chambers were comprised of a parlor, bathroom, and bedroom decorated in emerald and black tones. Arched stained-glass windows lined one wall, depicting demons engaged in a courtly dance with skeletons. A fire crackled in the ornate fireplace, and soft light glowed from sconces on the wall. The furnishings were plush but unconventionally shaped. The couch curved in the shape of a C, and several padded stools were scattered around the room—perhaps to accommodate those with cloven hooves.

The stained glass continued into the bedroom. A huge four-poster bed sat in the center, draped in black velvet. An elaborate vanity stood in one corner, and a matching chest of drawers in the other. Selene noticed a set of glass doors near the bathroom that led to a balcony, but she was too tired to explore further.

Sam was still in the hall talking to someone about bringing them toiletries and clothes when Selene slumped onto the bed.

Watching Sam reunite with his parents had been one of the most beautiful moments Selene had ever witnessed. She felt honored to be part of it, and deeply grateful for the winding path that had brought them all to this point. That dinner, on the other hand…

A complete nightmare.

She could understand his parents' desire to keep him close—of course she could. But the pressure they had placed on him to assume leadership mere moments after his arrival felt manipulative. She also hadn't expected them to regard their relationship with such disdain. *A human*, his mother had sneered, as if her son were mated to a diseased rat.

Guilt gnawed at her. It hurt to know they saw her at the center of their disappointment, the living symbol of Sam "failing" to fulfill his destiny. Selene had harbored such high hopes of building a loving relationship with his parents, imagining they would see her as the human daughter they never had—a quirky but welcome outsider, just as she was regarded in Aurelia. But so far, everyone, including Vanthee, seemed to wish she would just disappear.

Selene rubbed the back of her neck. Maybe his parents just needed some time. It was a lot to take in all at once, and they were allowed to have mixed feelings. Was it fair to judge their interaction by human standards—when they were anything but? Once they got to know her, Selene was sure Sam's parents would grow to care for her just as Brunie and Eldridge had.

When Sam finally came into the bedroom, he looked as exhausted as she felt.

"What a day, huh?" Selene said.

"Yes." Sam sat on the bed beside her. "Father wants to take me fishing in the Swamps of Sanctuary tomorrow. It's something we used to do when I was a boy."

"That's sweet. When are you going?"

"At dawn. His schedule is very busy for the remainder of the day."

"I bet." Selene glanced through the balcony doors at the darkness beyond. "How do you tell when it's morning here?"

"The sky changes from black to orange. The Underworld is warmed by fires that burn beneath the ground, not the sun. They ebb and flow like an ocean, creating times of darkness and light. You and Queen Thema might find it difficult to acclimate at first."

"Interdimensional jet lag," Selene said, yawning. She began changing into the nightgown she'd brought.

When they crawled under the covers, Selene nestled against Sam as she always did. He was quiet for a moment then said, "Selene, I'm sorry my mother wasn't very welcoming to you today. The argument at dinner was completely unnecessary."

"It's all right," she murmured. "It was a big day, and everyone had a lot of big feelings."

"Yes. I will speak with them about it."

"Don't worry about it," she said, already half-asleep. "It was an awkward beginning, but they just need to get to know me. I want you to enjoy the time we have here."

"And I want us both to feel comfortable. I'll do whatever it takes to make that happen," Sam replied. "Goodnight, my love."

"Goodnight."

Selene woke up the next day alone. The room was dark, but orange light shone through the stained-glass windows. Rubbing her eyes, she hoped she hadn't slept so long that she'd committed some breach of royal etiquette.

Once, during a Thanksgiving visit to her ex-boyfriend's family, she'd accidentally slept in until 9:30 a.m.—a grave offense to his grandmother, who expected her to rise by six to help with the cooking. The resulting nickname, *Lazybones,* had stuck for the remainder of the visit. Selene could only imagine how Sam's mother might react to an even more egregious faux pas.

Selene slipped out of bed and opened the balcony doors to take her first real look at the Underworld. The orange sky was streaked with purple and pink, like a watercolor painting. A range of ominous black mountains rose in the distance, surrounded by jagged peaks and ridges. A river snaked through the land below, but there were no trees, plants, or vegetation to speak of. This was truly a realm of stone and shadow.

Judging by the clusters of turrets and spires visible below, their suite sat high within the palace. The sound of a door opening drew Selene's attention away from the view. An imp hovered in the parlor, staring at her with an inscrutable expression. The creature was about the size of a two-year-old child. Its ears were long and pointed, and the pinkness of its skin looked more like an infected wound than a spring flower. Its pear-shaped body gave Selene the impression it might be female, though she had no idea whether imps even had genders.

"Awake," the imp croaked, flapping wings that resembled peeling leather.

"Yes, I'm awake. Are you here to help me?"

The imp nodded once.

"I'm Selene. What's your name?"

"Prickles." The imp gestured impatiently to a pile of dresses spread across the couch beside a tray of food.

"Is all that for me?"

Prickles nodded again.

"Thank you," Selene said, sitting on the couch. She glanced at the imp, who hovered in place, peering at her.

Selene frowned. Was this imp something like a lady-in-waiting? Or simply a servant delivering her breakfast? "Prickles, what is your role here?"

"Imp."

"Yes, but what are your duties?"

"To serve."

"Just me? Or do you serve others, too?"

Prickles blinked then said, "Guests."

"I see. Thank you." Selene took a drink from the mug on the tray and immediately coughed. It tasted like the bitterest of coffee mixed with a hefty glug of hot sauce. "What *is* this?"

"Morning drink."

"Okay, wow. That'll certainly wake you up." She sputtered again and asked, "Do you know if there's anything I'm supposed to be doing today? Any appointments I'm expected at?"

The imp cocked her head, looking confused.

Selene tried rephrasing. "Are the king and queen expecting to see me today? To share a meal, or talk, or anything like that?"

"King is fishing. Queen is with sister. No one mention you."

"Got it," Selene said, feeling half relieved and half stung by the rebuff. "Is it all right if I explore the castle on my own then? I mean, is it safe?"

Prickles shrugged. After a few seconds of silent staring, the imp asked, "Dismissed?"

"Of course. You're dismissed. Thank you for helping me, Prickles."

The imp flew off, leaving Selene alone once more. She looked through each of the dresses, all of which resembled something a wicked sorceress might wear. Finally, she settled on a wine-colored velvet number with lace panels across the bodice.

Selene smoothed the velvet and smiled wistfully. The dress reminded her of the costume her sister Cass had worn as a vampire queen for her third-grade Halloween parade. Cass's twin, Evan, had dressed as Dracula and the two of them had been absolutely adorable together.

If only Cass could see me now.

The grief and regret Selene always felt when thinking of her sister were magnified in that moment. It wasn't just the ache of missing Cass—it was the weight of everything she couldn't share. In moments like this, she longed for her sister's presence to laugh with, to vent to, to marvel with at how completely insane her life had become. Cass would've had some snarky, perfectly timed, snarky comment about the Underworld's formal dinners that would've made it all feel a little more manageable.

Evan had taken the news of her departure relatively well when Selene told the family she was moving out of Nashville to live "off the grid" in some obscure eco-village. But Cass could tell Selene's cover story didn't add up. It hurt to imagine her sister lying awake at night, wondering what had really happened.

Selene resolved that once their visit to the Underworld was over, she would return to Gaia and tell Cass everything. No more lies. No more secrets. Her sister deserved the truth—even if she wouldn't believe it.

CHAPTER 12

S am looked up at the sky from the Swamps of Sanctuary and exhaled deeply. His old fishing rod was in his hand and his father sat beside him on the bank. His eyes didn't sting from the harsh rays of sunlight, and his neck didn't ache from looking down at those smaller than him. The smell of wood moss and sulfur enveloped them.

I am home.

After so many years of pining for the Underworld, it still felt unreal to be there. So much of it was darker and grittier than he remembered, but there were still pockets of beauty.

The fishing rod King Asmodeus held jerked. He quickly reeled in the line. A glistening fish with two sets of razor-sharp teeth emerged from the water. The creature snarled and squirmed until the king grabbed it between his massive hands and exclaimed, "Aha! Our lunch!"

"Well done," Sam said.

"Safe travels to the Afterworld, little fish," the king said before removing the hook and dropping it into a bucket. He let out a contented sigh then slapped Sam on the back. "I've missed this, my son."

"So have I."

"I wish your uncle Lucifer was here to join us."

"Where is he?"

"In Gaia. Getting into all types of mischief, I imagine. I'll send word that you're here."

They sat in companionable silence for several moments, listening only to the croaking of spiny frogs clustered nearby. Finally, King Asmodeus tentatively asked, "Did you ever go fishing in Aurelia?"

Sam glanced at his father. They had been at the swamp for hours, and this was the first time their conversation had gone beyond pleasantries. "Sometimes."

"Did Queen Thema teach you as a boy? I know her kind are partial to fish."

"No. I actually didn't meet Queen Thema until later in life—when I was an adult."

King Asmodeus looked surprised. "I didn't realize."

Sam added, "A Goblyn and Harpy acted as parental figures to me, and we fished together occasionally."

The king nodded, dropping his gaze to the ground. Then, gruffly, he said, "Good. That's good that you... had ones like that. I'm glad. Grateful to them." With a flick of his wrist, he cast the line back into the water, the bait making a soft splash as it disappeared beneath the surface.

Several moments passed before Asmodeus cleared his throat, the sound was abrupt in the stillness. "Samael, I... I want you to know that your mother and I spent years searching for you. We never stopped." His voice cracked slightly, though he didn't seem to notice. "You must believe that."

Sam's grip tightened on his own fishing rod. He swallowed, nervous about how deep their conversation was about to go. He watched a line of bubbles break through the water's surface. "I always hoped you did."

His father turned to face him fully, his expression drawn and raw. "You see, we didn't know where you'd gone. One day, we tucked you into bed, and the next morning you were gone. Just gone! Not even a ransom note left." He let out an anguished growl of grief and regret. "Do you have any idea how devastating that was for us?"

Sam opened his mouth to respond, but Asmodeus pushed forward. "Your mother suspected the vampire, Zaybris. I was convinced it was one of my enemies—someone trying to hurt me by taking you. I thought they'd taken you into Gaia or perhaps hidden you away in some obscure dimension like Atlantis." He paused, scratching at one of his gnarled horns, his gaze faraway. "Aurelia never even crossed our minds. It seemed... impossible. A closed dimension, sealed off and tucked away. I deeply regret not considering it."

Sam nodded slowly. "It makes sense you wouldn't think to look there."

"No," Asmodeus said firmly. "We should have tried harder. We should have found you. You must've wondered... why we never came. Why we didn't rescue you." He looked away, jaw clenched. "I'm sorry."

A death-raven launched from a branch overhead, soaring into the trees. The leaves rustled, then stilled, and silence settled between them again. Sam closed his eyes, words knotting in his throat.

Everything his father had said was true.

He had spent countless nights as a child wondering why no one came. Fearing that he wasn't even missed. As a boy, Sam hadn't understood the rules of interdimensional travel. He hadn't known that even beings as powerful as his parents were bound by constraints beyond their control. It had carved deep scars.

"It was... difficult," Sam admitted.

"Of course it was. You were so young and must have been so scared." The king's voice wavered. He roughly wiped his eyes with the back of his hand, then pulled Sam into a bone-jarring hug.

Sam leaned into his father's embrace. It felt strange seeing the king display such intense emotion. He had always seen his father as impenetrable when it came to feelings. Controlled, measured, and even brutal in his rule of the Underworld.

During festivals or grand feasts, he could play the part of boisterous king, but he never lost his temper. Never made a misstep he'd have to walk back. His stoicism was the standard Sam had always compared himself to.

When a fish spoiled the moment by splashing loudly against the water, Sam pulled back. "The past cannot be changed, Father. I'm just glad I can return here without dying."

Asmodeus gave a dry, mirthless chuckle. "Fate had a plan all along, it seems."

"Yes, I suppose so."

Asmodeus regarded him carefully. "Son, I... I need to tell you something. Your return is more fortuitous than you know."

"What do you mean?"

Asmodeus opened his mouth, then hesitated. His jaw flexed as if weighing his next words, but he shook his head. "No. Another time." He bounced his fishing rod a few times then said, "We can speak of royal matters later. Right now, I just want you to know how sorry we are for everything. And how much agony we've been in without you. Your mother cried every night for you."

"I missed you both, too. But eventually, I found comfort and happiness in Aurelia."

Asmodeus let out a ragged sigh. "Will you tell me more of your life there? I want to hear it all—the good and the bad."

"Yes, but... " A cold sweat broke out across Sam's forehead as he considered how much to share. This was the moment he had dreaded—the time to get everything out in the open and reveal his greatest source of shame. For a second, he considered lying but thought better of it. Nothing could diminish the gravity of his actions. Whatever punishment awaited him, he would bear it honorably.

"There is something I need to confess to you. Something that has plagued me for many years."

"What is it?"

"In Aurelia... I know it is forbidden for our kind to kill mortals, but—"

"You killed some mortals," the king finished for him.

Sam paused, surprised that Asmodeus had so easily guessed his turmoil. "I took many lives. Some innocent, some not. In most cases, I felt as though I had no choice. In others, I merely lost control."

Sam winced, half expecting his father to drop his characteristic control and rage at him, but the king's expression remained neutral.

"What were the circumstances?"

Sam started from the very beginning, describing how Zaybris had left him in Aurelia with his vampire brother, who sought to drink only tormented blood. He explained how he had to fight in the blood wagons and how sometimes he lost control and killed his opponents.

He shared how he grew close to Brunie and Eldridge, and the regret he felt over the burns Brunie suffered when he set fire to the blood wagons.

He described how he became a guard for Queen Thema, how he felt when he saw Selene across the crowded ballroom, and their journey to find the traveler's stone.

He told him of the terrible day when he thought he had lost Selene forever—and the joy he felt when she returned.

Through it all, his father listened patiently, though Sam was too ashamed to meet his eye. But when Sam finally reached the end of his story, King Asmodeus didn't even give him a moment to exhale. He simply said, "Son, look at me."

Sam raised his eyes, bracing himself for whatever might come next.

"I absolve you of these deaths."

Sam froze, bewildered. "But I thought—"

Asmodeus raised a hand, cutting him off. "You did what you had to do to survive. And you were in a realm that didn't understand your nature, with rules different from our own."

"Yes, but… "

"I said I absolve you."

"Thank you, I-I'm grateful. Yet I still feel great regret," Sam said, his tone barely above a whisper.

"It will pass," Asmodeus said simply.

Sam picked at a moss-covered rock that jutted from the riverbank. He should be flooded with relief, but instead he felt unsettled. Confused. He had braced himself for more—shock in his father's face, a swift condemnation, followed by the punishment he deserved.

Not the quick pardon of a favored son. It couldn't be that easy.

Asmodeus reeled in his fishing line and rose to his feet. "Come, let us leave the swamps. I have other plans for you today."

"What are they?"

"I want to take you to the Sanctum of Agonizing Rectitude. You can train with the other Vengeance demons to see how they pass judgment on souls and punish them accordingly. Would you like that?"

"Yes. Very much."

"Good. I think you'll find great satisfaction in fully using your powers." Then, in a lighter tone he added, "Perhaps you can also shed some of this contrition you've picked up in Aurelia, eh?

"What do you mean?"

Asmodeus picked up the bucket of fish and said, "Too much mercy can be baneful to our kind. Remember that."

CHAPTER 13

After eating the selection of dark breads and sour-flavored fruits Prickles had brought for breakfast, Selene got dressed and hesitantly stepped out of their chambers to explore.

The hallway was silent and chilled, the air heavy with the scent of old stone. She had no idea where she was in relation to the dining room, but it was obvious their suite was part of the royal wing. Everything around her screamed Underworld opulence—from the thick black carpet underfoot, to the elaborate carvings of skulls lining the walls grinning with gilded teeth.

She followed the trail of skulls, hoping they would lead some-where interesting. The hem of her dress was slightly too long, so she had to be careful where she placed her feet. She wandered past a few empty rooms, occasionally pausing to peer through tall, arched windows. She stopped to run her fingers over the velvety texture of some flocked wallpaper, then paused to admire a painting of a demon perched on a sleeping woman. No one crossed her path, though the soft murmur of voices filtered from behind a few closed doors, reminding her she wasn't entirely alone.

Then she turned a corner and saw Vanthee. She was arguing with another demon nearly twice her size who had goat-like legs.

"You mustn't spurn this opportunity," the demon hissed.

"I'm doing all that I can, Father!"

The demon loomed over Vanthee menacingly, jabbing his finger in her face until her wings wilted. "It's not enough. You're the only hope this family has to—" He paused, sniffed the air, then whipped his head around to look down the hall.

"Oh! Why, it's Lady Selene herself," the demon said in a falsely cheerful voice.

Everything in Selene's body went cold when his eyes met hers. The demon looked like he'd stepped straight out of a horror movie—or worse, a nightmare.

He had horns as large as a water buffalo's set into a triangle-shaped head. His smile was a jagged mess of pointed teeth, and his eyes seemed to twinkle with cruelty. He clicked his long fingernails over his bare, rounded belly, the sound like bones tapping together. On his back, he wore a fur coat made from a creature that must have died from a skin infection.

"Hello," Selene said cautiously.

"Hello. I am Mammon." The demon bowed dramatically, touching his horns to the ground. His cologne—a stomach-curdling mix of rotten fruit and asphalt—wafted toward her. "We're honored to have such an esteemed guest walk among us. You've already met my daughter, Vanthee. We are your humble servants."

"Nice to meet you," Selene replied. Something primal stirred within her, making her feel like a mouse caught between two hungry cats.

Instinctively, her eyes darted around for an exit, but she was trapped in the hallway.

The multiple gold necklaces Mammon wore jangled as he rose from his bow. "And where are you off to on this fine day, Lady Selene? All alone, no less," he crooned.

"I-I'm not really sure. I just thought I'd explore."

Mammon shot a look at Vanthee. "You haven't offered to give our good lady a tour?"

Vanthee went pale. "No, I—"

The sound of a great crack filled the hall as Mammon violently slapped Vanthee across the face. Selene gasped.

"You fall short of your duties as Guide," Mammon said. "Our prince will never favor one so callous to his human."

"No, no, it's fine! I never asked for a tour," Selene said urgently. She was no fan of Vanthee, but she certainly didn't deserve that.

Vanthee stared at the floor, holding her palm against her cheek. "I'm sorry, Father."

Mammon sighed. "I'm disappointed in you, but fortunately, we can fix this slight right now. Vanthee, you will give Lady Selene a full tour of the grounds and take her anywhere she wishes to go. Do you understand?"

"Yes," Vanthee said, still looking at the floor.

"Excellent. I have much to do today so please excuse me," Mammon said. He fluttered two fingers away from his forehead in a salute. "Dark blessings, Lady Selene."

"Uh... same to you," Selene said, watching Mammon clip-clop away.

When he disappeared around a corner, Selene approached Vanthee cautiously. "Are you all right?"

An angry red handprint was visible on Vanthee's cheek. She gave Selene a defiant look. "I'm fine."

"That was *not* okay," Selene said. "At least not where I'm from."

Vanthee rolled her eyes. "Oh, shut up."

Selene bit her lip, feeling completely out of her element. "You don't have to take me on a tour. I can just look around on my own."

"Apparently, I do." Vanthee sniffed. "But it's going to have to just be around the grounds. I don't have time to go outside the gates. Is there anywhere in particular you want to see?"

"I don't know enough to say. How about just a general look at the top spots?"

"Fine. Follow me."

~

Vanthee was a terrible tour guide. When she wasn't striding down the hall so fast Selene could barely keep up, she'd simply wave her arm in the direction of places that seemed important.

"Turret of Whispers," she said, gesturing for Selene to peek out a window. Before Selene could even get a good look, Vanthee was already rushing down a set of stairs that led outside to the main courtyard.

"Crypts of the Forsaken," Vanthee said, pointing at a structure that looked like a decaying mausoleum.

"Chapel of Mourning," she added, breezing past a small building with a hole in the roof. A trio of demons wearing bloodstained robes ignored them as they passed.

"Sanctum of Agonizing Rectitude," Vanthee said, gesturing at an arched doorway that appeared to have survived a fire.

"Wait, wait. Vanthee, slow down!" Selene said when she finally caught up. "What are all these places?"

"The top spots of the Underworld, like you wanted."

"Yes, but what are they for?"

"Lots of different things."

I'm going to strangle her. "I know, but can you tell me a few things about each one? What happens in the Sanctum of Agonizing Rectitude?"

Vanthee smirked. "You don't know? That's where all the Vengeance demons spend their time."

"It is?"

"It's where they go to feel the impact of every wrongdoing a soul has committed in life. Then they take all that suffering and turn it back on them. If they repent, they're allowed to transition to the Afterworld. If not, they go to the Vaults of Eternal Torment."

"Oh."

"It's very telling that Prince Samael hasn't told his so-called fated mate about this."

"We have talked about it. Some."

Selene started to ruminate on how disconcerting it was that Vanthee knew more about something related to Sam than she did, but then a broken cobblestone nearly made her face-plant into a puddle of mud. She caught herself, but not before completely soaking the hem of her dress. The contrast between the well-kept palace and the grounds was odd. Everything beyond the palace walls seemed neglected and run-down.

She followed Vanthee past a cluster of male demons loitering outside what looked like a decaying Southern mansion. As they walked by, the demons began to whistle and hoot. Vanthee made a disgusted noise. "Lust demons."

Selene shot them a nervous glance, which, unfortunately, only encouraged them. One demon, wearing nothing but a leather jock strap, swaggered over and tried to sling an arm around Vanthee's shoulders. Without a word, she raised her arm and delivered a swift backfist to his face. He fell to the ground.

A second Lust demon approached, trying to sniff Selene's hair but found himself with a broken nose after Vanthee slammed his head into a nearby wall. A spray of blood painted the brick red, and the demon dropped with a grunt.

The third came toward them with a sleazy grin, reaching to lift the hem of Vanthee's skirt with the riding crop he carried. She snatched the crop from his hand, snapped it in two, and rammed a jagged piece into each of his thighs. He howled, collapsing in a shrieking heap.

Vanthee turned to the rest of the Lust demons, eyes blazing. "Who's next?"

Silence. Then, as if on cue, the remaining demons backed away, disappearing into the shadows of the mansion and slamming the door behind them.

Vanthee dusted off her skirt with a huff. "That's what I thought."

Selene's jaw was halfway to the ground. "Okay... that was badass."

Vanthee, already a few steps ahead, glanced over her shoulder. "What's that supposed to mean?"

"It's a human term," Selene said, still a little breathless. "It means impressive. Powerful."

Vanthee shrugged. "To your kind, perhaps."

Selene quickened her steps to catch up. "How did you learn all that?"

"What? Defend myself? Everyone should know how to do that," Vanthee snapped. "What else do you want to see?"

Selene scanned the dilapidated buildings around them, looking for something halfway welcoming or appealing. As she did, she kept seeing wispy, human-like figures drifting through the grounds. They seemed agitated and confused, but none of the demons paid them any mind. Were they ghosts? The thought sent a chill down her spine.

While she watched one of the figures vanish into thin air, a demon on all fours suddenly scrambled up a brick wall, startling Selene so much that she yelped. The demon paused to hiss at them through spider-like mandibles, its milky white eye sockets staring with such an eerie, otherworldly presence that Selene couldn't help but shudder.

Vanthee noticed Selene's reaction and laughed. "What's the matter? Are your human sensibilities too delicate for our kind?"

"I'm fine," Selene said, forcing a tight smile. "It's just very different here."

"This isn't a realm meant for living humans."

Selene hugged her arms to herself. "Is there anywhere that's quiet or more pleasant? Like a gallery, museum, or a library?"

"You want to see the library? Fine. But I wouldn't call it pleasant."

CHAPTER 14

Sam gazed up at the towering doors of the Sanctum of Agonizing Rectitude with a mix of nervousness and excitement. The massive stone fortress was bound in thick iron chains, as if straining to contain something monstrous within. At the entrance stood a demon who resembled a statue more than a living being. His body was chiseled like rock, with a heavy brow, a square jaw, and powerful legs. His black hair was cropped short around small, antler-like horns, and his skin was gray-scaled, like that of the Drago race in Aurelia.

"Borias! Meet my son," King Asmodeus said.

Since it looked as though Borias wore a permanent scowl, Sam was surprised when the big demon's face broke into a grin. "So the rumors are true! Our prince is home," he boomed. "It's an honor to meet you."

"Thank you," Sam said.

King Asmodeus looked on proudly. "Borias is a Vengeance demon as well. He's going to show you how he inflicts his gift on those who deserve it."

"I'm looking forward to it," Sam said. Anticipation thrummed faster through him. The opportunity to unleash all the rage and vengeance he had bottled up for so long was here at last. What would it feel like? Intense, certainly, but would he be euphoric after? Peaceful and sated? Or would it awaken something darker, making him ravenous for more?

"I will leave you to it then," King Asmodeus said. He smiled at Sam, gave Borias a quick salute, and turned to walk away.

"Let's begin!" Borias clapped Sam on the back so hard he stumbled slightly. He led Sam through the doors of the Sanctum, where a jangle of screams, pleas, and whimpers hit him all at once. They moved down a long hallway, passing door after door, until they entered a brick-walled room with a single chair in the center.

"This is the judgment room where we'll be working. And it looks like the Magistrate of Souls has brought us a full docket today," Borias said. The big demon scanned a long scroll that was tacked to the wall. "More human murderers, a few thieves—" Borias was interrupted when the soul of a human male was pushed into the room. He was old and hunched, dressed in a worn suit.

"Ah, we can start right away," Borias said to Sam. He gestured to the wooden chair and addressed the human. "Welcome. Have a seat." The human quickly obeyed. His beady eyes darted around, and he gripped the arms of the chair tightly.

"Is this Hell?" he asked. "Are you going to torture me?"

"Maybe. It all depends," Borias said.

"On what?" the man asked.

"On what you've done. You wouldn't be here with us if there wasn't *something* you had to atone for." Borias flashed a smile that made the man start to squirm.

"I haven't done anything, I swear! I was a good person."

"Oh really?" Borias said.

"I volunteered at a soup kitchen every Christmas and always bought Girl Scout cookies. That must count for something, right?"

"Doubtful." Borias slowly walked around the man. His eyes closed for a moment before he said, "Hmm, there's a lot here."

"A lot of what?" the man cried.

Borias ignored him and said, "Samael, why don't you start us off? Tell me what you see."

"Truly?" Sam said, rubbing his palms together excitedly. "I'm not sure how to even begin."

"I've been doing this long enough to see into his soul through sight alone. But you could start with touch. Try his head."

Sam approached the man slowly. Tentatively, he placed his hand over the man's skull.

Fear.

It was the first thing he felt. Not the man's fear but the fear he inspired. This man had done something—no, many things—to make others dread him. They feared the sound of his walk, the resonance of his voice, and the jingle of coins in his pocket.

"What do you see?" Borias asked.

"Many feared him."

"Who were they?"

Faces began to flash behind Sam's eyes. One and then another. And another, and another, and another.

Humans. Females. Mostly children, some older. All had the same fear of this man. They all tried to avoid him or flee when he was near, yet few succeeded.

Shame.

Humiliation.

Guilt.

More sensations were coming to him, faster now.

Sam saw through the eyes of the victims. The man stood before rows of children seated at desks in a large room. His tone was smug with authority. His demands for private instruction, inescapable.

Sorrow.

Pain.

Anger.

At first, Sam felt each emotion separately, but soon they gelled together. Their increasing speed made him gasp. He tore his hand away, trying to stop the flood of images.

But they didn't stop.

The faces returned, more urgently this time. As if each soul demanded to be seen, to be heard. Sam felt the damage this man had done—not just in the moment, but across the lifetimes of his victims.

The agony and relentlessness of the impressions soon made Sam double over. The imprint of this man's lust and need for power was as devastating as it was lasting.

Sam's body began to ache. A violent urge swelled inside him, an impulse to harm himself. If there had been a knife in the room, he might have dragged it across his skin. Shadows gathered around him, but their attempt to soothe only intensified his inner turmoil.

He shook his head violently, trying to dislodge the pain. But it kept coming, wave after wave, until he collapsed to his knees.

"Stay with it, you're doing well," Borias commanded. "Tell me what he's done."

"Abuser. Rapist," Sam gasped out. "He abused children. Many, many children. Girls. For decades."

"Excellent. And you have the feelings of all those victims inside you now?"

"Yes," Sam cried, his body trembling. It was difficult to hear Borias through the sounds of crying and screaming pounding in his head.

"Take all those feelings and send them out through your hands. Deliver them back to him. Make him feel everything!"

Sam struggled to inch closer to the man, still on his knees. Every movement was agony. He could feel not only the pain of the victims, but the echo of it rippling outward—their families, their children, and even generations yet to come.

Finally, Sam got close enough to clutch the man's ankle.

With excruciating effort, he tried to transmute the pain into something else—a shadowy haze, thick enough to smother the man in the very torment he had created. But all he could summon were thin, flickering wisps of vengeance.

He gritted his teeth and moved his hands up to grip the man's leg, envisioning dark jets of shadowy smoke pouring from his own body, seeking entry into the man's flesh. But that wasn't effective either.

"Borias, I can't... It's still within... "

"Concentrate. This is what you were born to do."

"It's too much... "

"Keep trying. His victims deserve it."

Sam squeezed the human's knees, using all his inner strength to project what he was feeling outward. But still, there was no relief. "I can't expel it back. Please. It's agony."

"Take a break. Let me finish," Borias said.

Sam fell back onto the floor.

Through half-lidded eyes, he watched as Borias simply tapped the man's chest. Instantly, the human began to wail. Tears streamed down his face, his body convulsing as he broke into violent sobs. He screamed for forgiveness, shrieking apologies as every ounce of suffering he had inflicted came crashing back on him.

Boris watched him with a satisfied look before turning to Sam.

"The feelings will pass in a moment, Samael," Borias said gently. "Vengeance will soon be fulfilled."

Sam tried to sit up, but Borias touched his shoulder and said, "No. Just rest. Observe the process."

Sam lay on the floor, consumed by helplessness and a crushing sense of ineptitude. What felt like hours passed before the man in the chair finally stilled. He slumped forward, as if he had died all over again, slack and unresponsive when Borias nudged his shoulder.

Borias sighed. "Now, what to do with you, hmm? You're certainly not worthy of the Afterworld, but I hesitate to let you reincarnate so soon." He circled him with a contemplative look. "Are you prone to seasickness? I hope so. Perhaps a few voyages sailing on *Purgatory* will make you more redeemable."

Borias waved his hand. Instantly, the soul disappeared.

Slowly, minute by minute, Sam began to feel lighter. The physical pain he experienced was starting to fade, and the emotional pain dwindled, too.

He began to use the breathing exercises Eldridge had taught him, then focused on the feeling of his cheek pressed against the cold stone floor. The strands of hair clinging to his forehead. The feel of his feet inside his boots. Soon, Sam was able to fully sit up, and after a few more moments, stand.

"That was a rough one," Borias said. "My apologies—I didn't mean to start you so intensely."

"That was nothing like I expected," Sam said hoarsely.

"I'll be honest, your reaction was... unusual. Being in the Sanctum is exhilarating for most Vengeance demons." Borias paused. He rubbed the back of his neck, then said, "Prince Samael, I know it's none of my business... "

"What is it?"

"Do you have a vengeance that's unfulfilled, perhaps? One from your own life?"

Sam considered his words.

Do I?

It was difficult for him to think clearly. Yet after a moment, the image of Zaybris's face flashed through his mind. The shame Sam had felt when the vampire disappeared with Selene from the cave in Aurelia made him swallow hard.

"Yes."

"Is this person still living?

"Sort of. He's actually here... in the Underworld, but... "

Borias's head reeled back. "You have an unvanquished enemy in this realm? Why haven't you addressed it?"

"I just got here," Sam said defensively. "Wouldn't it be best to hone my skills before delivering—"

"No, no, no. You need to do it as soon as possible. Vanthee can lead you to where he's kept."

Sam looked down at his hands, which were still trembling. "I'm not ready."

"You must be," Borias said. "It's blocking you."

Sam's vision was still hazy as he met the demon's eyes. The truth of Borias's words cut through him to the bone. It was a comfort to have a potential reason for why he failed so thoroughly, yet reliving all his own pain, as he had just done with the pain of others, was terrifying.

"I will prepare myself to face him. But not today. I cannot bear any more today."

"Rest up, then. Refresh yourself and we will train again tomorrow."

CHAPTER 15

Selene was relieved to find the Underworld's library in a familiar part of the palace. Nestled at the bottom of a short staircase in the royal wing, it was only a short walk from her and Sam's chambers. The arched doorway, reminiscent of a Gothic church, was well kept and clean. But when Vanthee pulled the door open, Selene was shocked by what was inside.

Instead of a beautifully organized space, the Underworld's library looked as though it had been rampaged by a herd of elephants. Thousands of books were strewn across the floor in a haphazard mess. Broken bookcases leaned against the walls, their splintered shelves spilling volumes onto the ground. Some books had been stripped of their covers, their pages crumpled and tossed into heaps. Others were stacked in precarious towers.

To someone who had always relied on libraries as refuges of order and peace, Selene was appalled.

"What happened here?" She asked.

Vanthee toed away a book covered in mold with her boot. "What do you mean? It's always been like this."

Selene looked up at the vaulted ceiling, full of broken lights and peeling paint. "How does anyone find anything?"

Vanthee shrugged. "How should I know? No one ever comes in here."

Selene picked up the first book from the floor that caught her eye. It was an ancient-looking tome entitled *Malleus Maleficarum*. She immediately recognized it from a high school history unit on European witch trials. It was the infamous treatise known as *Hammer of Witches*.

"This is a human book," Selene said. She wiped dust from the cover and reinserted a loose page of German writing. "My god, it's probably an original copy."

"Probably," Vanthee said, looking unimpressed.

Selene frowned. Although it was a gruesome text, it was hard to see an important piece of human history treated like garbage. She set the book on a nearby table then picked up another. This one was written in a non-human language with beautiful illustrations of seashells. She wiped grime from its soft cover.

"This is such a shame. How could the king and queen let all these books get so—oh!" As Selene spoke, something furry and extremely strong brushed past her hip. She looked up to see that an enormous black dog had burst through the library's door and was now romping among the stacks.

Vanthee scrambled onto a nearby table, her face consumed with fear. "How did she get out?"

Selene blinked, surprised by her fearful reaction. The dog was happily trotting around the library, so full of excitement that she threw her head back and barked. But instead of a "woof" coming out, a blue flame shot into the air. Selene stepped back quickly, knocking over a pile of stacked books. This excited the dog even further, prompting another burst of blue flame from her mouth.

"Get out of here, Zetta! Go back to the kennels," Vanthee shouted. She picked up a nearby book and flung it toward the dog, who interpreted it as an invitation to play. Zetta sprinted for it at full speed. When she came loping back with the book in her mouth, the only recognizable part was the title page—it was the *Malleus Maleficarum.*

Selene winced. "Really? Did you have to throw *that* book in particular?"

"Sorry," Vanthee said, and she seemed genuine.

When the dog picked up another book and began to shake it wildly, Selene called out, "Hey, stop that! Come here. Is your name Zetta? You have to settle down."

At the sound of Selene's voice, Zetta rushed over. In one swift motion, she rose to her hind legs and rested her paws on Selene's shoulders. Then she began to lick Selene's cheek, making her laugh, even though the dog's breath smelled like gasoline. When she ruffled her hands through the dog's shaggy fur, she noticed it was thick in some spots but bald in others.

"What's wrong with her coat? Is she sick?"

"I don't know. She probably has some disease young pups get," Vanthee replied, watching Zetta warily.

Zetta backed down from Selene and zoomed around the library once more.

"She's just a puppy? I wonder if she has mange. Do you have vets here?" When Vanthee looked at her blankly Selene added, "Healers... specifically for animals?"

"No," Vanthee said, as if Selene had asked something incredibly stupid. "Are you hiding meat in your dress or something? Why does she like you so much?"

"She has good taste, I guess," Selene joked. Zetta's powerful tail was wagging so hard it caused a tower of books to collapse. "I take it you're not an animal lover?"

"Hellhounds are vicious. I saw one bite the nose off a demon once just for crossing its path. Another purposely set the last kennel master's home on fire with a single bark."

Selene frowned. "Well, this one is a sweetheart."

Vanthee scowled as Selene scratched Zetta behind the ears, then said, "We need to take her back to the kennels. Ogrin will be furious that she escaped."

Cautiously, Vanthee climbed off the table and led Selene out of the library, which was now even messier than when they'd found it. Zetta didn't need encouragement to follow; she trotted close to Selene's side.

The kennels were in the courtyard, inside a space that looked like a battered greenhouse. Thirteen rusty cages held dogs as black and shaggy as Zetta, only filthier. Some were chained to bolts in the stone floor, others circled their cages anxiously. A few barked at her, and Selene was surprised to see orange flames shoot from their mouths, unlike the blue ones Zetta produced.

"There's the mongrel," a haggard-looking demoness with long greasy hair called out as they approached.

Zetta's jubilant attitude quickly shifted, and she dropped low to the ground, cowering behind Selene.

"She came all the way into the library," Vanthee said.

"Did she?" Ogrin's eyes narrowed. "I'll deal with her later."

"She didn't do anything wrong—she was just curious," Selene said, bending to soothe the dog. The other hellhounds watched her from their cages curiously.

"She needs to learn her place," Ogrin huffed. "Hundreds of years since a Bluebite Howler pup was born, and I have to be the one to train it." She yanked open one of the cages. "Get in there!"

Zetta dropped her body low to the ground and crawled toward the cage. Selene's heart broke for the dog, as well as for the others who looked miserable and frightened.

"What are they trained to do?" Selene asked.

Ogrin eyed her suspiciously. "Who wants to know?"

Selene stuck out her hand to shake. "Hi, I'm Selene."

When Ogrin looked at her outstretched hand like it was stick of dynamite, Vanthee said, "This living human is a guest of the king and queen."

Selene couldn't help but notice Vanthee didn't introduce her as Sam's mate.

"Humph," Ogrin replied, picking at a rust spot on a nearby cage. "Some hounds go to the living world to guard graveyards or burial grounds, and others stay here. They're supposed to herd lost souls who have wandered from their path." She gestured at one of the wispy ghost-like people Selene had seen earlier. Then she pointed caustically at Vanthee. "Since *this one* can't do her job."

"Those are souls?" Selene asked. "Why haven't they moved on?"

Vanthee's eyes flashed with defensiveness, but Selene saw a hint of embarrassment as well. "I do my best to guide them to where they're supposed to go, but sometimes there are too many. Some get missed, and it's nearly impossible to get them back again."

As Selene processed her words, Vanthee marched up to a misty figure. She looked back at Selene and said, "Watch this."

Waving her arms in front of the spirit, she said, "Excuse me—hi. You're in the wrong place."

The figure, who looked like a young man wearing a tuxedo, drifted past Vanthee without even looking at her.

"Sir, you need to go home!" she called after him, beckoning him with her hand.

They watched the spirit continue to hover around the kennels, looking lost and desperately sad. Then he faded into thin air.

"See?" Vanthee's chin trembled slightly when she looked back at Selene. "Now he's gone to haunt someone. Maybe one of your kind can make him move on. Have you had enough of a tour, human? I have other things to do."

It was clear Selene had touched a nerve, so she didn't press further. "Yes, of course. Thank you for showing me around."

"Your chambers are that way," Vanthee said, pointing toward the royal wing. With that, she turned and walked off without another word.

CHAPTER 16

When Sam felt well enough to leave the Sanctum, he found himself heading back to the Swamps of Sanctuary. The stillness of the space grounded him. He perched on a rock, lazily tossing pebbles into the water as he tried to sort through his feelings about his first experience delivering vengeance.

His initial thought was that something inside him was broken. Missing the crucial training he should have received as an adolescent must have damaged some internal mechanism. His second thought followed quickly: maybe even with training, he would have been an ineffective Vengeance demon anyway. Perhaps he was just using his lack of training as an excuse for a fundamental ineptitude.

His third thought was imagining the advice Eldridge would give him. He was fairly certain the Goblyn would tell him he was being too hard on himself. Prone to bouts of melancholy, he often needed Eldridge to pull him out of his dark moods with gentle reminders of how unreasonable he was being.

The Goblyn was probably right, even though his advice was only conjured from Sam's head. It was just his first day in the Underworld, and his first attempt at in the Sanctum. It hadn't gone as he had hoped, but that didn't mean he could never improve.

An imp swooping overhead pulled Sam out of his rumination. It dropped down to hover in front of him and said, "King say you must return to palace. They having celebration banquet for you tonight."

Before Sam could respond, the imp shot back into the sky and flew off.

He rubbed his forehead. Celebration banquet? Why was he constantly plagued by others wanting to hold social events for his benefit? Being the center of attention had never been comfortable for him. What he truly wanted was to take a long nap and then have a quiet dinner alone with Selene.

But as his parents would say: duty calls.

Although it was still light outside when Sam returned to their chambers, Selene was sprawled across their bed, fast asleep. The hem of her dress was filthy, making him wonder how she had spent her first day in the Underworld.

He brushed back a lock of hair from her cheek and said, "Wake up, my darling."

"Mmm," she groaned and rolled over. "What time is it?"

"Evening. My parents are throwing a celebration dinner that we must attend."

"Ugh. Do we have to?"

"I don't want to go either. But the banquet is in our honor. How was your day?"

Selene yawned, then said, "Vanthee showed me around a little. Saw some demons, saw some hellhounds. Went to the library. I must have fallen asleep when I came back to the room." She smoothed back her hair as she sat up. "The Underworld is kind of a mess outside the palace. It seems so, I don't know, run-down. Not neat and well-maintained like Aurelia."

"Yes, I noticed that, too."

"What did you do today?"

"I had a long conversation with my father, and then he left me at the Sanctum of Agonizing Rectitude to practice delivering vengeance for the rest of the day."

"How was that?"

Sam paused, struggling to put the experience into words. "More difficult than I expected."

"How so?"

"It was draining." For a moment he considered telling her what Borias had said about Zaybris but stopped himself. She deserved to never hear that fiend's name again. He gave his mate a forced smile. "I will figure it out, rest assured."

"It's a lot to take in. You're of two worlds now."

"You are, too. Three worlds, if you include Aurelia."

"You're right, I never thought about that." They sat in comfortable silence until Selene sighed. "I'll change so we can go to this dinner."

The celebration was being held in the Underworld's banquet hall, a space Sam didn't remember though he must have visited as a child. Towering columns carved with black goat-headed motifs supported a vaulted ceiling. Rows upon rows of long tables lined with ornate chairs stretched deep into the hall before an elevated platform reserved for royalty.

Green mist seeped from the stone walls, giving the space an eerie grandeur. But Sam barely had time to absorb the scene before an imp led him and Selene into a hidden antechamber at the back of the hall.

A hairless demon with a skeletal smile ushered them in.

"Good evening. I am Ghar, master of ceremonies. It is an honor to meet you both," the demon rasped. "Please be seated. The king would like you to wait here until he arrives."

"What for?" Sam asked.

"That, I don't know," Ghar replied.

Sam and Selene sat on metal chairs between stacks of extra dishes, goblets, and folded linens. While they listened to the muffled clamor of demons filing into the hall, Sam jiggled his leg anxiously.

His parents entered a few moments later, looking serious. Their expressions only deepened Sam's unease.

Queen Thema followed soon after, practically bouncing with excitement. "Our first festive celebration in the Underworld!" she said to no one in particular. She wore a red dress embroidered with gold thread and had a dragon-shaped hairpin tucked into her tower of braids.

"Ghar, please take Selene and Thema to their seats," Lamia said. "We need a moment alone with Sam before the banquet starts."

Selene and Sam exchanged a look before she gave him a reassuring smile, which he returned weakly. She and Thema followed Ghar out into the hall, and then Sam was alone with his parents.

The air seemed to grow heavier once the three of them were alone. Sam waited for his parents to start with some pleasantries— questions about his day or how he was adjusting. But Asmodeus simply began to pace, his heavy hooves making the floorboards vibrate with each step. The room was so cramped that his cape brushed Sam's knees every time he passed. Lamia's expression was grave.

"What is it?" Sam asked, his gaze darting between them.

Asmodeus ran a hand over his head between his horns. "Son, I didn't want to put all this on you so soon, but it's important. Your mother feels we shouldn't wait." He pulled up a chair, the metal creaking as he settled across from Sam.

"What's wrong?"

When the silence stretched, Lamia said, "Tell him, Asmo."

Asmodeus sighed heavily. "All right." When he met Sam's eyes, something vulnerable flickered beneath his powerful, commanding presence. "Son, my time as ruler of the Underworld is coming to an end."

Sam blinked. "What do you mean?"

"My powers, they're starting to fade," Asmodeus said slowly.

"Fade?" Sam repeated.

"My magick is harder to control, and my summoning abilities are becoming less reliable. It started a few weeks before you arrived."

Sam's heart began to thud against his ribs. Asmodeus had always been larger than life, a figure of unyielding strength and authority. The idea of him faltering felt impossible. "Do you need a healer?"

"No," Asmodeus said. "It is not an ailment."

"Perhaps an enchantress then to restore your powers," Sam offered. He glanced at his mother, but she had turned her back to them. "There are some in Aurelia quite skilled in—"

Asmodeus shook his head. "No. It is the natural way. When a celestial event called The Thronefall Flame occurs, the current ruler's faculties fade. So that a new Dark Sovereign may ascend."

"How do you know this?"

"A proclamation etched into the Hall of Demonic Canon commands it."

"What proclamation?"

"One of the oldest, carved in obsidian under a statue of King Baphomet in the Hall," Lamia said. She turned to recite, "When the Thronefall Flame burns across the sky, from its dying light shall rise the Dark Sovereign—one destined to rule dominion over life, death, and all that lies between."

Sam mulled over the words in his head, trying to make sense of them. The dull headache that had started in the Sanctum began to pound. "It sounds like superstition."

"It's not. The last sighting of the Thronefall Flame was about two thousand years ago when I ascended," Asmodeus said.

Sam nodded, struck by the realization that he had never known his father's true age until now. "And how were you chosen as the Dark Sovereign?"

The king adjusted his crown. "I was born on the day foretold in a prophecy inscribed in *The Sovereign's Reckoning*. It was an ancient text my predecessor, Baphomet, destroyed as his reign waned, believing it would keep him in power. But still, I prevailed."

"Do your subjects know you're losing your powers?"

"The mystics do. And those on the Council of Legions—Empusa, Blight, Mammon," Asmodeus replied.

Lamia crossed her arms and leaned against the wall. "Since there's nothing in the Hall of Demonic Canon that clearly names the next Dark Sovereign, some on the council have already begun scheming to influence the outcome. This is why we need to crown your father's successor soon. We have been desperately trying to find someone to take his place... " She pinned Sam with her gaze. "And now you have arrived."

Dread pooled in Sam's stomach. Muffled shouts from the hall mirrored his own growing turmoil. "You don't mean... "

"Fate had a plan all along, it seems," Asmodeus said, echoing the words he'd spoken to Sam in the swamps.

"We could crown you tonight," Lamia said. "But I understand that you need time to integrate back." Her wings began to quiver with agitation. "However, it must be done before the Thronefall Flame appears in three months when the season changes. If no successor is crowned when the veil has thinned for ascension, the realm will become leaderless for a century."

Sam rubbed his hands against his pant legs, trying to ground himself, but his mind was in chaos. He had always assumed his father's reign was eternal. Bearing the responsibilities of prince had worried him enough, but the expectation that he would become king was too much. "No. I don't want that. I'm not suited to rule—"

Asmodeus's face darkened. He stood abruptly, towering over Sam. "You must be."

Before Sam could respond, the door to the antechamber burst open. Ghar stumbled in, panting heavily. "Forgive the interruption," he said, bowing. "But there is trouble in the hall."

Queen Lamia frowned. "What kind of trouble?"

"The demons of Anguish grew bored, so they began reciting

incantations to torment some of the lost souls who wandered into the hall."

"Harmless fun," Asmodeus said dismissively.

Ghar winced. "It... escalated. Vanthee objected, as did Queen Thema, which led to a brawl between the Legion of Ruin and the Legion of Temptation. If you don't intervene, I fear the Aurelian queen will be hurt."

Without further discussion, Lamia, Asmodeus, and Sam rushed out of the room.

CHAPTER 17

Lamia, Asmodeus, and Sam were met with pure chaos when they entered the hall. Goblets were flying through the air, and two of the long banquet tables had been upended. A demon with arms like tree roots was crushing another demon's neck in a headlock, while Queen Thema shouted at a demon plunging forks into another's eyes. Sam watched in horror as a mob of onlookers roared with sadistic delight.

Above the tables, several lost souls floated, engaged in horrific pantomimes. Most were human, a few were Aurelian, and one was from the faerie dimension. One silently screamed, her limbs unnaturally stretched as though invisible chains were tearing her apart. Another frantically clawed at his face and chest with transparent fingers. Some were shaking uncontrollably, writhing in pain, or holding their throats to gasp for air they no longer breathed.

An Anguish demon barreled into Sam, nearly knocking him to the ground. Vanthee was clinging to the demon's back, her arms clenched around its neck as she struggled to shove a lit candle into its mouth. At first, Sam couldn't understand why—until he realized the demon was chanting the incantation that was tormenting the lost souls.

"This is madness! You must disrupt them," Lamia cried to Asmodeus.

The king raised his arms then lowered them quickly, causing the ground to shake. But the tremor wasn't enough to disrupt the demons.

"Again!" Lamia urged.

Asmodeus lifted and lowered his hands again, but nothing happened. He roared in frustration, but the shouting was so loud none of the demons heard.

The king reared back his muscular arm and made a throwing motion. A lightning bolt struck above, but it fizzled out midway through the air.

Asmodeus continued trying to break up the fight by producing gusts of wind, restraint incantations, and blinding flashes of light. But each effort failed.

Sam could see that a trio of demons were beginning to notice their king's futile attempts. Glimmers of scheming anticipation replaced the bloodlust in their eyes as they closed ranks. Doing the only thing he could think of, Sam hurled himself into them, shattering their focus. They crashed to the ground, then immediately turned their aggression on each other, forgetting Asmodeus.

Sam's gaze swept across the cavernous room. Halfway down its length, he saw Selene, and a surge of white-hot panic shot through him. She was crouched behind one of the pillars, safely away from the fighting. But she didn't seem to notice the Lust demons creeping toward her. They soon surrounded her on all sides, leering and licking their lips.

Deep, unbridled rage tore through him at their audacity to even look at her. Normally, he would have tried to suppress those emotions. But remembering that he didn't have to do that in the Underworld made something snap deep inside him.

Protect my mate.

Realizing the chaos in the hall made it impossible to reach Selene in time, Sam summoned the shadows. As he raised his hands, their cold, familiar presence enveloped him. Now there were nine Lust demons closing in on Selene, and Sam cursed that he wasn't skilled enough to send the shadows to strike each one individually. Instead, he ordered them to form a protective shield around her.

But instead of swirling over her as an impenetrable mist, the shadows began to weave together in the air in front of her. Circling, tumbling, and interlacing midair until they formed a solid, unyielding shape.

Within seconds, the shadows had merged into a towering creature—massive and reptilian. Nine serpent-like heads rose from its chest, each one with glowing eyes and gaping maws. Its four legs, like tree trunks, braced against the stone floor. The creature was half mist, half solid. It uttered a low, unearthly hiss that reverberated through the hall.

He stepped back, heart hammering as he stared in horrified awe. It was a hydra—far more nightmarish than any legend he'd ever read. Its heads writhed and snapped, each set of eyes locking onto the demons surrounding Selene with a hunger that seemed almost sentient.

Thick, oily mist coiled around the hydra's sinuous necks. The largest, most vicious-looking head lunged at the Lust demon nearest to Selene. Without warning, it sank its jagged, inky teeth into the demon's mid-section, piercing through his flesh. Yet the wound elicited no blood. A muffled shriek echoed from the demon before the hydra tilted its head back and in one horrifying gulp, swallowed him whole.

The remaining heads whipped through the air, striking down anything nearby that moved. Each attack was swift and brutal, a shadowy blur of snapping jaws and snarls. Sam stood frozen, watching the creature he had conjured tear through the demons with terrifying precision. It wasn't just protecting—it was attacking.

But taking lives was going too far.

I have to stop it.

He tried mentally commanding the hydra, as he often did with the shadows, but it didn't respond. He tried shouting at it, but it didn't seem to hear him. He rushed toward it, but it was difficult to push through the crowds of demons trying to flee.

The hydra didn't falter until Selene raised her hands in a halting gesture. Sam saw her mouth the words, "That's enough," and the creature froze, its heads suspended mid-strike. Then she said, "Go home."

The glow in its many eyes began to dim. Then, as if obeying her will—or perhaps finally sated—it began to unravel. The shadows dissolved into cold mist. One by one, the heads melted into the air, followed by the creature's serpentine body. In moments, it was gone.

In the spot where its belly would have been lay a heap of broken demons.

Sam stared at the aftermath. Once again, he'd lost control of his demonic powers, letting them unfurl on their own accord instead of bending them to his will. And although his father had absolved him of the deaths he caused in Aurelia, surely he wouldn't forgive him of this.

Thank goodness Selene had stopped his creation before it had gone any further.

Sam surveyed the banquet hall, now a ruin of its former grandeur. Splintered chairs and broken tables lay strewn across the floor, mingled with shards of glass and twisted candelabras. The air reeked of blood, sweat, and something acrid.

Sam stared at the wreckage, frustration and confusion merging into numbness. His knees buckled, and he stumbled backward, collapsing into a nearby chair.

He glanced at his parents. His mother had her fingers touched to her lips, looking at him with amazement. His father wore a broad grin, his fanged teeth gleaming. The sight sent a sickening chill through Sam.

Then, in a voice amplified by the acoustics of the hall, King Asmodeus bellowed, "Behold the return of the lost Prince of Vengeance, Samael! Remember this day, for it is but a glimpse of the fury and retribution that will rain upon those who dare to defy his rule!"

CHAPTER 18

Selene's heart ached at the wince Sam gave when the crowd erupted in cheers following Asmodeus's grand introduction.

He stood alone on the raised dais beside the royal banquet table, head bowed, shoulders rigid with the weight of too many memories. She couldn't imagine the pain twisting inside him. He rarely talked about his time fighting in the blood wagons, and Selene never pried. But if there was one thing she knew for certain, it was that he never wanted to kill again.

The strange creature Sam created had made Selene's skin crawl—but now the hollow look in his eyes nearly broke her. Unable to bear seeing her mate so devastated, Selene moved through the hall toward him.

She stopped halfway when Ghar began inspecting the pile of swallowed demons. There were nearly fifty of them—a twisted mass of claws, wings, and scales. When Ghar nudged a demon wedged sideways, its tail twitched. Then one of the demons near the top groaned. Another let out a shriek. The mound began to writhe and squirm.

Selene's eyes widened. *They're not dead.*

Relief cut through the fog of fear the creature had left in its wake. Without hesitation, she shoved her way forward again, toward Sam.

When their eyes met, she shouted, "They're alive!" But he didn't seem to hear her.

As Selene stepped onto the platform beside him, she saw anguish etched into his face.

"I was trying to protect you," he said hoarsely. "I didn't want to kill any of them."

"Oh, honey, you didn't kill anyone. Look." She pointed toward the heap of demons, now beginning to shrink as bodies were pulled free. "They're okay."

One by one, Ghar helped extract the demons from the pile. Some collapsed on the ground; others limped away, groaning. A few clutched broken limbs or staggered with visible wounds. They were gravely injured, yes—but alive.

Sam stared in disbelief. "That creature... I don't know how I created it. I called the shadows, and it just... appeared."

"You have powers you didn't know you had," Selene said gently.

He pulled her closer. "It wouldn't obey me. But it listened to you."

Selene shrugged. "I was just closer to it."

Asmodeus approached them expectantly. "Would you like to address your subjects, son?"

"No," Sam said.

"Come now. You must say something."

"I'd rather not."

"Don't be petulant," Lamia added. "It's as important to build goodwill among your subjects as it is to demonstrate your strength."

When Sam ignored her and turned to sit, Asmodeus grabbed his elbow. "Address them," he barked.

Sam yanked his arm free, but then Asmodeus announced, "And now, a word from our lost prince!"

Selene watched as Sam scanned the banquet hall, taking in the mix of awe and apprehension on the demons' faces. He straightened his shoulders and said, "Greetings. I-I'm grateful to be back in the Underworld." Then, under his breath to Selene, "Should I acknowledge what just happened?"

She hesitated. "Just say something like you're sorry for the interruption."

"Apologies for the interruption. Please be seated, and let's begin the feast."

The unease in the room began to lift when imps swooped in with platters of food. Queen Thema kicked a shattered plate aside and settled near Lamia. Asmodeus reached across the table, patting Sam's shoulder. "Well done, Samael. I've never seen anything like that before."

"It was very impressive," Lamia added with a smile. "And effective."

"I didn't do it on purpose!" Sam protested. "I don't even know how it happened. It's never happened before."

"Even better," Asmodeus said. "You have untapped power within. Now, what caused all this fuss, anyway?"

Queen Thema sniffed disdainfully. "Your subjects thought it would be *amusing* to trick some of the lost souls who roam this realm into believing they were being tortured. Your Guide"—she gestured toward Vanthee, who sat alone with her arms crossed—"attempted to stop their barbaric game. I lent her my support, and a brawl began."

"Seems like a lot of fuss over nothing," Queen Lamia said coolly.

Thema clutched her chest. "Sister, there were *Aurelians* among those being affected. That is unacceptable!" She shook her head, scoffing. "When I host an event, I make certain my subjects are suitably entertained at all points during the celebration. I suggest you do the same."

"Well, this isn't Aurelia, and your unsolicited advice isn't welcome," Queen Lamia snapped. "Those souls are simply echoes, not living beings."

"And that sanctions cruelty? No. The expressions on those poor souls' faces is something I won't soon forget," Thema replied.

Selene silently agreed. Watching those spirits—or ghosts or whatever they were—suffer had been heartbreaking. Why was the land of the dead so callous to the ones already lost? She searched the room for the spectral forms, but they had all vanished.

A pair of imps set down plates of roasted meat before them. Another brought a basket of bread and began filling their goblets with wine. Selene was still buzzing with adrenaline, so she could only pick at her food and listen to the murmur of demon voices humming through the hall.

In between courses, Mammon approached the table and bowed before Sam. "May I be the first from the Legion of Temptation to welcome you home, Prince Samael. I am Mammon, demon of Greed and one of your father's most trusted advisors." Rivulets of grease were running down the sides of his mouth, and bits of shredded meat stuck to his bare chest.

"Thank you," Sam said, obviously trying to hide his revulsion. "I am pleased to meet you."

Mammon held Sam's gaze for an uncomfortably long time, then turned to King Asmodeus. Speaking in low tones, he said, "Your son's emergence signifies a new contender for Dark Sovereign, does it not?"

"It does."

Selene shot Sam a questioning look. He responded by mouthing, *Later.*

"Good, good." Mammon began using his long fingernails to pick his teeth.

He continued to hover, looking between Sam and the king, until Asmodeus said, "Leave us, Mammon. We'll speak of this at a council meeting later."

"Of course." Mammon bowed again and clomped back to his seat.

Taking their cue from Mammon, other well-wishers approached

until it became a continuous stream of demons introducing themselves to Sam. Selene watched the subtle way Sam's posture tightened with each passing minute. He answered politely, even managed a few forced smiles, but she could see he was barely holding it together.

When King Asmodeus finally rose and declared the celebration of Sam's return concluded, Sam didn't waste a second. He reached for Selene's hand and said, "Let's go."

Together, they slipped away from the banquet hall, leaving the noise and crowd behind.

Back in their chambers, the fire in the hearth crackled softly. Selene helped Sam out of his tunic, brushing her fingers over his shoulders. "Do you want to talk about it?" she asked, more invitation than pressure.

He gave a small shake of his head. She nodded, giving him the space he needed. A hot bath would've felt incredible after such a trying day, but she was too tired to do anything but change into her nightgown.

Sam undressed wordlessly and lay back on the bed, eyes fixed on the ceiling. For a long time, there was only the sound of their breathing and the occasional *pop* of fire from the hearth. Finally, he spoke.

"I think the shadows became a hydra because I wanted to protect you from each of those Lust demons. I let my instincts flow, and that's what manifested."

"That makes sense," Selene said carefully.

He was silent for several more minutes. Then he said, "But before the banquet, after you and Thema left... my parents told me something."

"What was it?"

His words came slowly at first, but once he began, the story spilled out in a rush. He told her what his parents had revealed about the Dark Sovereign. Selene listened calmly, even as her thoughts churned. It all sounded like something from a movie. A year ago, she might have dismissed it as fantasy. But now? Anything was possible.

When Sam finished, Selene climbed into bed next to him and said, "No ruler for a whole century? That's terrifying."

"I know," Sam said. He pressed his fingers to his temples. "But why must it be me? Blood alone isn't reason enough. I'm not fit to rule—and I don't want to."

"Did you tell them that?"

"Yes. I said so last night as well. But they believe I will change my mind now that I know the severity of the situation."

"It seems so archaic. Is there really no guidance on who's meant to be the next king?"

"Apparently there was a prophecy in a book called *The Sovereign's Reckoning* that foretold my father's reign, but it was destroyed centuries ago."

Selene turned on her side to face him, propping her head up with one hand. "So if there's no prophecy, how were they planning to find a new ruler before you showed up? What was the backup plan?"

Sam gave a small, humorless shrug. "I don't think they had one. Perhaps a vote by the council? I hate that they've placed all their hope on me like this."

Selene nodded, mulling over the idea that was beginning to take shape in her mind. "Well, here's a thought," she said, lifting a brow, "what if *you* made the plan?"

He turned his head toward her.

"You don't want the throne, right? So be part of the process instead. Use your time here to help find the next Dark Sovereign. You can be Head of Recruitment, as we say in the HR world."

"How would I do that?"

"Interview candidates. Screen them, test them, check their references. What qualities are important for the Dark Sovereign to have?"

"Power and cunning. Decisiveness. Resilience."

"Hmm, that's hard to spot in a sit-down interview," Selene said. Images began to flash through her mind of demons engaged in contests of strength, wit, and cunning, each vying to stand out. "What if you created some kind of trial or games to test the candidates?"

Sam seemed to consider it. "A tournament, perhaps. A gauntlet for those who want to rule. Something to measure their worth."

"Exactly. You could design it, and if someone stands out, you could help them win. No such thing as cheating in the Underworld, right?"

The furrow between Sam's brows began to soften. "This could work."

Selene placed her hand on his chest. "Sam, you've worked so hard to reach a place where you don't owe anyone anything. You don't have to *be* the Dark Sovereign." Her voice softened. "Maybe you're just meant to *find* him."

Sam gave her a small smile. "Once again, you've put my mind at ease. Thank you," he said before turning to kiss her good night.

CHAPTER 19

At dawn, Selene was woken by an imp at their door, summoning Sam for some urgent royal business. He'd barely had time to dress before being whisked away, leaving Selene to her own devices for her second full day in the Underworld.

She lingered in bed long after he left, reflecting on how quiet the space was. It wasn't a peaceful quiet, but hollow. There was a weight to the stillness here—something that made everything feel off-balance. She took her time getting dressed into a fresh wicked sorceress gown and weighed her options for how to spend the day. Wandering the palace alone wasn't exactly appealing, but spending the day confined to their rooms felt worse.

Desperate for a friendly face, Selene knocked on the door of Queen Thema's bedroom across the hall. It opened to reveal a scowling imp who told her that Queen Lamia had taken Thema horseback riding for the day. Feeling a bit stung that she wasn't invited, she thanked the imp and turned away.

Standing alone in the hallway, Selene realized that, so far, Zetta was the only creature from the Underworld who actually liked her. The thought made her smile wistfully.

I guess the kennels are as good a place to go as any.

With that, she set off, her footsteps echoing through the halls.

When she entered the kennel structure, she was greeted by chaos. The air was thick with the stench of raw meat, and Ogrin was in the middle of flinging bloody chunks into cages while screeching at the hellhounds to shut up.

Upon spotting Selene, the demoness narrowed her eyes. "Are *you* the one riling them up so?"

"They must have picked up on my scent," Selene replied. "Sorry about that."

"What do you want?"

"I came to see if I could help out," Selene said, glancing around at the pens. Zetta stood upright on her hind legs, her massive head thrown back in a howl.

"Help?" Ogrin repeated, as though the word offended her.

"Yes. I could take Zetta out for a walk or play with her. I know she has a lot of energy."

Ogrin snorted. "You think you can handle her? Be my guest, Princess."

Selene wasn't sure if she was being addressed by her royal title or receiving an insult, but she didn't comment on it. "Do you use leashes here?"

"Only if you'd like your mortal arm ripped off," Ogrin replied, then laughed in a way that made Selene think of a Halloween witch.

"Okay, got it," Selene said, choosing to be amused by Ogrin's rough manner rather than offended. She reached over the half-door of Zetta's pen to rub her forehead. "Is there anywhere we shouldn't go?"

When the demoness looked at her, Selene noticed the whites of Ogrin's eyes were shot through with black veins. "Just don't leave the palace grounds. Bring her back here before Eventide."

Selene opened the pen door, and Zetta burst out with an

excited yip. She sprinted out of the kennels, which made the demoness cackle. "Better hurry! She'll be halfway to Spirit Veil Valley!"

Selene took off after Zetta, fearing she was about to spend the day running in a gown, but the hellhound was only a few yards away, nibbling at a boulder.

Selene put her hands on her hips and said, "All that fresh meat and you're trying to eat a rock?" Zetta looked at her with a big goofy dog grin, then pressed herself to Selene's hip, earning a scratch under the chin. "Aw, you're a good girl. Shall we go explore? Can you stay close to me?"

Since Zetta was more familiar with the Underworld than Selene, she let her take the lead. First, Zetta zoomed around the courtyard, sniffing everything in sight while Selene trailed behind. Her tail wagged furiously when they came upon a trail of roaches, and a rotten apple on the ground provided several minutes of entertainment. Most demons ignored them, aside from a pair who slowed their pace to stare at Selene, and another who shrieked when Zetta's sneeze shot blue sparks from her mouth.

When Zetta spied a rat heading down a set of rickety stairs, she loped after it. Selene followed. The stairs led them into a crumbling tunnel littered with broken stone. Gingerly, Selene stepped over a pile of rusty nails and tried to remember what Vanthee had called this part of the castle—something like the Catacombs of Doom, no doubt.

It looked like no one had come through in hundreds of years, which made Selene wonder if they were someplace they shouldn't be. But Zetta was happily trotting along, even after losing sight of the rat, so she didn't protest. At least not until the floor felt shaky.

When the wall sconces illuminated how patches of decay had eaten through the floor below, Selene stopped walking. Patting her legs, she called, "Zetta, come here, girl. Let's go back."

The sound of Selene's voice made Zetta do a little spin but didn't stop her. Selene called a few more times, but Zetta ignored her.

"Okay, I'm going up without you!" she called, turning back toward the tunnel entrance to fake her out.

That worked.

Zetta let out a high-pitched whine and came bounding toward her at full speed. Selene tried to sidestep, but the hellhound barreled into her, knocking her clean off her feet.

Then came a *crack*.

The floor gave way beneath her.

Selene plummeted as gravity yanked her downward. A rush of cold air whipped past her ears until she collided with something soft but unstable. It was a mound of loose dirt. Gasping, she pushed her hair from her face and sat up.

Blinking rapidly, she strained her eyes against the sudden darkness. She rubbed the elbow she had landed on, which was already becoming stiff. Above, the jagged hole she had crashed through indicated that she had fallen about ten feet.

She was in a place that looked like the crawl space under her parents' house, but much deeper. There was nothing around her but empty space and stale air. It was a relief to find no immediate threats, but concerning that there was nothing to help her climb back out.

Great.

Selene sat and considered what to do. She called for Zetta a few times but got no response. Not even the faintest scratch of claws. The hellhound was probably long gone by now, off to find her next adventure.

Selene's fingers curled around the traveler's stone hanging from her neck. It pulsed faintly beneath her touch, seeming to recognize her. With a single thought, she could be back in her rooms, curled up under a blanket and away from the musty gloom of this half-buried ruin.

But then what? Zetta would be running wild, terrorizing everyone, and it would be her fault. Definitely not the way to make a good impression on her in-laws. Just as she started rising to her feet, she heard a faint scuffling above—footsteps, cautious and uneven.

Her heart gave a hopeful lurch.

"Hello?" she shouted. "I'm down here! Be careful, the floor is rotted!"

The footsteps paused. For a moment, there was nothing but the creaking of old wood and the groan of shifting beams. Seconds passed, and the footsteps got closer. Then a woman's face appeared over the edge of the drop.

Selene gasped with relief. "Hi, can you give me a hand to get out? The floor collapsed under me and... "

Selene trailed off as she got a better look at the figure peering down at her. It was a woman, but she didn't look like a demon. At least not one she had seen so far. Her features were soft. Pretty.

Familiar.

Golden-blonde hair cut into a messy bob, large eyes, and a sloping nose.

Selene's breath caught in her throat, and her heartbeat became a drum in her ears.

She was staring up at her sister, Cass.

CHAPTER 20

Selene rushed toward the gap in the floor, arms outstretched, even though Cass didn't return the gesture. Her sister wore a billowy white robe belted with a gold braid, but her expression was hard. Selene squinted, trying to make sense of what she was seeing.

"Cass?" Selene called, voice cracking. "Oh my god! What are you doing here?"

Cass's normally expressive eyes were cold. Empty. "Rescuing you from that hole."

"Oh, thank you!" The sound of her sister's voice made tears prick Selene's eyes. "But how did you get here? Did you fall through a portal too?"

When Cass stayed silent for a moment, Selene's mind raced with all the things she wanted to tell her. There was so much to explain. But as Cass stared down at her, Selene realized something about her sister was... off.

"I died," Cass replied. The words were cold. Flat.

Selene froze. It felt as though a sledgehammer had struck her chest. Her gaze traced Cass's features again. So familiar—and yet, too still. Too pale. And then she saw it.

Cass's outline shimmered. She was translucent.

"You... what?"

"I *died*," Cass repeated bitterly. "Why else would I be in the Underworld?" A sickly yellow glow throbbed around Cass's body. It lurched and distorted with each word she spoke.

"No. No, you can't be serious. When?"

Cass tilted her head. "Right after you abandoned us."

The words landed like a slap.

"No..." Selene clutched at her chest, the air squeezing out of her lungs like a vise. Her breaths came faster and faster until she began to hyperventilate. "W-what happened?"

"You were supposed to protect us," Cass cried. "You were supposed to make sure nothing bad ever happened to me!"

"I tried to," Selene gasped. "But please, Cass, how did you die? Were you sick? Did you have an accident?"

"No. I was so upset that you left, I got into some trouble and... " Cass closed her eyes for a moment. Her chest rose and fell as though she were taking several deep breaths. Then she raised her chin and said slowly, deliberately, "I was murdered."

The world tilted and Selene collapsed to her knees. Her hands sank into the dirt as she doubled over, then began to vomit. Again and again until her body was nothing but a trembling shell, her insides raw. Her sobs echoed through the space, thin and broken.

This was it—her worst fear.

And it was all her fault.

Her absence. Her selfish need for escape. Her belief that choosing her own happiness over her family's would somehow make them stronger, that they'd be forced to grow without her. But it must have had the opposite effect.

And now Cass was dead. Not just dead.

Murdered.

"I'm so sorry," Selene whispered. She stretched her fingers toward her sister, desperate to make contact with her.

Cass's eyes glittered with something like triumph. Satisfaction.

"Do you want to know how it happened—"

Her words were cut short by a vicious, snarling bark sounding from a distance. Cass turned, and in an instant, was tackled by Zetta.

"Zetta, no!" Selene shouted.

Zetta clamped her jaws around Cass's translucent throat and bit down. Selene watched in horror as Cass screamed, and her face distorted with agony. Then Selene realized it wasn't agony she was seeing; it was that Cass's face was morphing into a solid form. And a different person.

Cass's blonde hair shriveled like a match tossed on a bale of hay. Her eyes bulged then retreated until they were star-shaped holes sunken within a pasty face. Her white robe split as six spider-like arms burst from her rib cage. Her legs lengthened and her body rose until she was seven feet tall, looming over Selene.

The creature that Cass had become smiled down through a mouth of rotted teeth.

Selene whispered, "Who are you?"

"Greetings, mortal. I am called Drath, demon of Fear." He spoke with a guttural, deliberate cadence that made Selene's skin crawl. Zetta growled and tugged on the tattered black robes the demon now wore. "I was just having a little fun. Eldest daughters radiate with guilt and obligation so sweetly."

Selene opened her mouth to say something, then just stood there, utterly speechless.

Drath crossed his six arms. "My companion and I saw you pass by earlier. He felt all that delicious guilt within you, and I felt the fear. A little deception to feed on those emotions proved... *mmm, irresistible.*"

Selene wiped away the tears still clinging to her lashes. "That was a horrible trick. Why would you do something so cruel to a stranger?"

The sound of Drath's chuckle made Selene so angry she was unable to stop herself from blurting out, "Do you even know who I am?"

"Of course. Prince Samael's mate." Drath leaned down, making Selene realize his face was painted like a nightmarish clown. He extended a leg toward her. The red outlining his mouth split and flaked as he asked, "Would you like help out of that hole?"

"At what price?"

"No charge." Drath wound a hairy leg around Selene's waist and lifted her to stand beside him. "Rest assured, your sister is fine."

"I don't see why I should trust your word on that."

"Suit yourself."

"Don't ever do that to me again."

Drath rubbed two of his arms together. "Ah, but don't leave yourself so open to manipulation and I won't."

Selene wasn't sure how to respond, so she started walking back toward the tunnel's exit. Zetta was at her heels.

Drath trailed beside her, prompting her to say, "Just leave me alone, will you?"

"It's been a decade since I visited your realm. What are your kind most afraid of now?"

"I don't know. The usual stuff."

"Like this?" Drath's body shifted into a giant cobra, startling Selene so much she yelped.

"Yes, that!"

"Or perhaps this?" Drath morphed into a demented-looking dentist wearing a soiled white coat and waving a rusty drill at her.

"Yes. Great trick. You can stop now."

"But what about this?"

Selene's steps abruptly halted as her face and back felt as though they were pressed between two slabs of wood. She tried to turn her head but there was wood on either side as well. She was overtaken with the sensation that she was locked inside a coffin. Claustrophobic panic began to rise, even though she knew it wasn't real. The moment she opened her mouth to scream, the illusion dissolved.

Drath laughed again in a mocking tone. "Still the same as ever, I see. Though I remember a time when things as natural as thunder and lightning invoked human terror. Those were fruitful times."

"Can you just let me go in peace?" Selene craned her neck to look ahead but saw no indication that they were almost out of the tunnel. "You got what you wanted. Now just leave me alone."

"Not when I'm enjoying your company so much. What about this?" Drath's body burst into hundreds of bees. They swarmed at her, and Selene stopped walking and closed her eyes. She let the bees buzz into her ears, tangle in her hair, and land on her face without reacting. She refused to give Drath anymore fuel for his mania.

After a moment, the tone of the bees's buzz changed. When Selene opened her eyes, she saw they had shifted into hornets.

The swarm had doubled and become more aggressive. They were now trying to crawl into her nose and mouth, goading her until she couldn't help but react. They weren't stinging her, but the feeling of a thousand tiny legs crawling on her and two thousand tiny wings beating against her finally became unbearable.

Primal fear made her break into a run while frantically swatting the hornets away. This only seemed to encourage Drath further. The hornets chased after, energized by her fear. They had grown to the size of hummingbirds and were attacking Zetta as well, who howled and trembled.

He's going to continue until there's nothing left of me.

The thought scared her in a different way than all the illusions she had suffered so far. Hunching down, she wrapped her arms around Zetta and clutched the traveler's stone. Using all the energy she had left, Selene imagined being back inside her chambers. Safe and happy.

Drath seemed to sense she was trying to escape and changed tactics. Water began to rush around her feet, icy and smelling like sewage. Then it rose to her hips, her chest, and then her neck, as though the entire tunnel had flooded. She focused harder on the bedroom, visualizing the stained-glass windows and polished floor, imagining herself tucked safe in Sam's arms under the soft bedding.

Zetta was squirming in of her grip to escape the water, but Selene held her tight. She heard Drath's laugh when the water reached her ears, but when it came to engulf her head, they finally transported away.

CHAPTER 21

Selene and Zetta landed in the middle of the bed with a *thump*. Completely dry and insect-free. Zetta, seemingly unfazed by their ordeal, wriggled out of Selene's arms and gave herself a vigorous shake. Selene could only curl into a fetal position. Using the stone was always draining, but this time, it felt like she'd returned to her chambers three-quarters dead.

Zetta zoomed around the room, nose twitching as she sniffed every corner. Selene watched through half-lidded eyes, until the dog leapt back onto the bed and flopped down beside her. Selene draped an arm over the hellhound and buried her face in Zetta's warm black fur. She desperately wished Sam were there, but Zetta's big, teddy bear-like body offered more comfort than she expected. Growing up, Selene had always wanted a dog but was too afraid her mother would neglect it—or worse, abuse it. Who would have guessed she would one day be soothed by a hellhound?

Zetta let out a contented chuff, then turned her massive head to lick the tears from Selene's face. The tenderness of the gesture caused all of her emotions to erupt in a torrent of grief. It was both a release of the utter terror she had felt at believing Cass had been murdered, and despair over how effortlessly Drath had tapped into her deepest fears.

The devastation of her family due to her absence or neglect was a fear she couldn't remember ever being without. It was at the root of everything she hated about herself—the people-pleasing, the poor boundaries, the anxiety, and the lack of identity. These were all traits she thought she was moving past. But perhaps her issues were worse than ever.

Her throat tightened with homesickness. Not just for her family, but for Gaia. For sunlight and grass and trees and places that didn't look like they were made of nightmares. For things like chocolate, reality TV, and smoothies. Her time in Aurelia had made her accustomed to strangeness, but even during the worst of her adventures there she hadn't felt this vulnerable.

Vanthee was right. The Underworld wasn't a place for living humans. For the first time since they had been together, Selene wondered if Sam would be better off without her. This was his home, where he was truly meant to be, and here she was getting effortlessly manipulated because she was so out of her depth.

What if Sam *was* meant to be the Dark Sovereign? Was her attachment impeding him? That was the last thing she wanted. But the thought of leaving him so he could fulfill his destiny made her sob even harder.

Eventually, she must have cried herself to sleep because when a knock sounded at the door, the sky outside the windows had grown darker. Groggy and heavy-limbed, Selene dragged herself upright, silently praying it wasn't one of her in-laws. When she opened the door, Queen Thema stood there, all smiles.

"How are you this fine—" The queen's words faded as she took in Selene's tear-streaked face and puffy eyes. Without waiting for an invitation, she stepped inside and made a beeline for the couch.

"Come," she said, patting the cushion beside her. "Sit. Tell me what's troubling you."

Selene hesitated, then shuffled over to slump into the seat. "It's nothing," she muttered. "Just a bit of homesickness."

Zetta positioned herself between Selene and the queen, her eyes locked on Thema's face. A low growl rumbled from her throat, soft but unmistakably protective.

"Be nice," Selene murmured, resting a hand on Zetta's head. "She's a friend."

As if she understood, Zetta huffed and lowered herself to the floor at Selene's feet, still watching Thema with mild suspicion.

The queen wrinkled her nose delicately. "Dogs. So uncivilized," she said, shuddering. "Now, what brought on this homesickness, my dear?"

Selene didn't really feel up to talking, but she knew Thema wouldn't take no for an answer. Slowly, she recounted what had happened with Drath. Queen Thema listened more attentively than Selene would've expected, offering quiet nods and the occasional "Go on" as encouragement.

When Selene finally finished, Queen Thema was visibly angry on her behalf. "These demons." She scoffed. "They can be absolutely savage at times. I'm sorry you were mistreated by such a brute."

"Thank you."

"Would you like me to speak with Lamia about it? I would want to know if one of my subjects treated a guest so poorly."

"Oh, no. Please don't."

"He should be punished."

"No, I don't want anyone to know. It's kind of embarrassing that I was tricked so easily."

"Let me know if you change your mind," Queen Thema said before her gaze shifted to the traveler's stone hanging around Selene's neck. "However, I have an idea that might help. That stone you carry has another capability—one I believe you've overlooked."

Selene frowned. "What do you mean?"

"Scrying! You can look within it to check on how your family fares anytime you wish."

Selene blinked in surprise, then looked down at the stone. Her fingers brushed over its cool surface. "I forgot it could do that."

Queen Thema nodded, obviously pleased with herself. "Let's try it now."

"But..." Selene hesitated. "If I hold it and think about my sister, won't it transport me to her?"

"Try holding it by the cord. Not the stone itself."

Selene slipped the stone from around her neck and carefully pinched the cord above the gem, avoiding direct contact. Keeping her eyes open, she concentrated on every detail of her sister's face: the freckle on her cheeks, the highlights in her hair, the wry little smirk she made when cracking a joke.

She thought of how Cass's eyes lit up over a greasy slice of pizza, her love for *The Golden Girls*, and the endless stream of funny stories about her disastrous dates. She imagined how much Cass would've liked Sam, how she'd call him a major upgrade from her ex and ask if he could set her up with any single demons.

Slowly, the surface of the stone shimmered. Then, after a moment, a faint image gradually took shape.

Queen Thema leaned closer and gasped. "I see something!"

Relief and gratitude rushed through Selene as her sister's face came into view.

There she was, seated at Maynard's Tavern, the dim but familiar bar where she liked to sip mojitos while sorting through her photography backlog. The details were a little blurred, but there was no mistaking her.

Cass was alive. Safe. Doing something mundane and utterly normal. After a few seconds, the image faded.

"This is incredible," Selene whispered. "Thank you."

The queen smiled, looking satisfied. "I'm glad it brought you peace."

"I want to see my brother now, too," Selene said.

She repeated the process to focus on Evan: his lopsided grin, the scar on his chin from when he crashed his bike, and the shelves full of Bigfoot collectibles in his apartment.

The stone glinted with his profile, then brightened into an image of him sitting on his couch, scrolling through his phone. He looked healthy. A bit bored, but nothing out of the ordinary. Selene breathed a sigh of relief. Then the stone winked out into nothing, as if it had run out of batteries.

"Oh, Thema, I'm so glad you showed me this," Selene said.

"Now," Queen Thema said with a glint in her eye, "let me show you something else. Shielding."

Selene straightened a little. "What's that?"

"It's an old trick," Queen Thema explained, her tone almost conspiratorial. "A way to guard your mind when someone tries to gain access. Arkaya taught me after I encountered an enchantress who tried to bend my will."

She brought her fingers to her temples. "Picture a pyramid," she said. "Strong. Impenetrable. No one can see through it, and nothing inside can be taken out."

Selene nodded and closed her eyes. "Okay."

"Now," Thema continued, "imagine that pyramid protecting your innermost thoughts—your fears, hopes, desires, regrets. Everything that makes you *you*. All of it safe within."

Selene envisioned a great hand, bigger than life, holding a shimmering silver pyramid by its apex. Beneath it, she imagined her brain: pink and fragile, pulsing like a newborn creature, raw and exposed. Every thought, every secret, every memory she held close shimmered faintly within its folds.

Slowly, the great hand lowered the mirrored pyramid until it settled perfectly over her brain, enclosing it entirely. Then the hand twisted the pyramid, locking it into place. Keeping her brain and everything in it safe and protected.

"I see it," Selene breathed.

"Good," Thema said, approvingly.

"Does it really work?"

"Try it," Thema replied, rising gracefully to her feet. "The next time you walk freely in this realm. Don't wait until you're under attack."

"I will. Thank you."

At that moment, the Eventide bells rang out, making Zetta's ears perk up. Selene looked down at the hellhound and said, "I guess it's time to take you back, girl."

Queen Thema stood and yawned. "I should be getting back to my room as well. I've missed my afternoon nap and am feeling the effects."

"Thank you for your help. I feel much better."

"Good. And thank *you* for bringing me along on this journey."

"Have you had fun reconnecting with Lamia?"

"Oh, immensely," Thema said, her smile turning nostalgic. "We squabble, of course, as sisters do, but it's been wonderful to see her again."

Zetta let out a low whine and nudged Selene's hand.

"All right, then. Let's get you to the kennels," Selene said.

She walked Queen Thema to the door, then continued down the corridor with Zetta trotting faithfully at her side. When they reached the kennels, Zetta padded into her pen without protest, tail wagging at the pile of raw meat waiting for her.

Selene lingered at the gate, her hand resting on the cool metal as she weighed her next move. She wasn't hungry, and the nap had left her feeling oddly wired. A hollow ache pressed behind her ribs. She was desperate to see Sam after everything that had happened. But she didn't want to bother him. And truthfully, she didn't even know where he was in the palace.

What she did know was that she wasn't ready to be alone with her thoughts. Not tonight. What she needed was a distraction.

Then she remembered: the library was just a short walk away. If she couldn't escape the mysteries of the Underworld, at least she could escape into a pile of books.

CHAPTER 22

Sam kicked a loose stone along the path to the royal dining room. It had been over two weeks since they arrived in the Underworld, and he'd barely seen Selene. It was making him irritable.

When he wasn't training in the Sanctum, he was being pulled into one royal duty after another. Though no one wanted to speak of the Dark Sovereign when he brought it up, it was clear his parents were preparing him for it. They insisted he observe and take part in every aspect of court life. So far, he'd presided alongside his father at a ceremony honoring the demons of Wrath, signed a decree legalizing nudity in the Chapel of Mourning, and sat through several meals with distant relatives he barely remembered.

Most nights, when he finally crawled into bed around midnight, he and Selene could only exchange a few words before she drifted back to sleep. Once, she'd forced herself to rise at dawn to catch a moment with him, saying something about her sister, but an imp had interrupted them, claiming urgent royal business. For all the supposed privileges of being a prince, Sam was growing bitter that he hadn't managed to carve out even an hour for himself.

And now, his mother wanted to have dinner with him privately.

A demoness bowed as she passed, and Sam gave a curt nod. As much as he had resented being feared by the Aurelians, being revered by demons was worse. Every word, gesture, and expression seemed to invite commentary and exaggerated praise—especially from Vanthee, who never seemed far from his side.

When Sam pulled open the doors to the royal dining room, he was surprised to see the space dark. A large blanket had been spread in the corner of the room, and Queen Lamia was lighting candles around it.

"What is this?" Sam asked.

"There you are," Queen Lamia said, turning to him with a smile. "I thought we could share a picnic on the dining room floor as we used to. Do you remember?"

When Sam was a boy, he usually took meals in the kitchen since he was too small to fit in the large dining room chairs. One night, after begging to dine with his parents, his mother had taken pity on him and moved their meal to the floor, picnic-style. This had delighted young Sam so much that it became a tradition for him and his mother on evenings when Asmodeus was engaged elsewhere.

Lamia settled herself on top of the blanket then patted the space beside her. Sam sat down. He realized he was now more than a head taller than his mother, even while sitting. On her face he could see worry lines carved between her brows and signs of age on her hands. Though she was a demi-goddess, it seemed she was not immune to the effects of time.

Lamia gazed out the windows into the night-blooming garden while Sam adjusted the clasp of his boot. This was the first time they had been truly alone since his return, and each seemed unsure of what to say.

"How was your day? Were you training in the Sanctum?" Lamia said.

"Yes," Sam replied. His ability to deliver vengeance was improving, but he evaded the question every time Borias asked when he was going to face Zaybris.

"The imps should be here soon with our meal," Lamia said after a moment.

"Excellent."

"The last time we did this you only drank juice. Do you drink wine now?"

"Yes. Though I prefer ale or mead."

"So grown up," Lamia said. "What was your favorite food in Aurelia?"

"I ate all manner of dishes, but the pies they prepared at Queen Thema's were my favorite. I also spent time with a Harpy who was an excellent cook. Everything from her kitchen was delicious."

"A Harpy? Was she your lover?"

Sam blinked at the boldness of her question. And the absurdity. "No, Brunie was… " He stopped himself from saying *mother figure,* for fear of upsetting Lamia, "Much older than me and mated to a Goblyn."

"A Goblyn and a Harpy? How unusual."

"Yes, but they are well matched," Sam said. "I imagine your marriage to Father was also unusual. A demon king with an Aurelian queen must have been unprecedented."

A trio of imps appeared above them. They swooped down to place trays of food before them.

Lamia poured them both a glass of wine. "We kept our relationship hidden, so no one ever questioned us. I was the one most surprised by our pairing."

Sam took a sip of wine. It tasted of smoke and spice, much headier than the wines of Aurelia. "When did you become a demon?"

"Not long after Asmodeus brought me to this realm. The mystics locked me in the Turret of Whispers for thirteen days. There, I could ruminate on the virtues and vices of demonhood in complete darkness and silence. I took no water or sustenance for those days, until my flesh became weak and my mind grew addled. It was a difficult process, especially since you were in my womb and I feared the ritual would cause you harm. But on the thirteenth day, my Goblyn body expired. Yet, I rose up, reborn. From Lilith to Lamia—mate to Asmodeus and Queen of the Night and the Underworld. Asmodeus claimed me as his mate and we held a coronation ceremony the next night."

"Did you feel different?"

"Oh yes. More powerful and stronger. It was a glorious change. I felt more capable of ruling my new realm."

"Do you ever miss Aurelia?"

For the briefest of moments, he saw sadness color his mother's face. "Sometimes. I grieve that the Goblyns and vampires do not have a queen of their own. But Thema tells me they are faring well."

They ate in silence for a few moments. Learning more about his family lore filled an ache inside Sam that he had endured for too long.

Eventually, Lamia asked, "How did you meet your human?"

Sam explained how had Selene come to Aurelia through a trap set by Queen Thema, and her plans to use Selene as bait to steal the traveler's stone from Zaybris. Lamia listened without interruption, her features neutral at first. But when he shared how he started the claiming ritual in the cave, her expression shifted. She began to look suspicious. Skeptical.

Once Sam finished his story with how Selene had returned to him in Aurelia, Lamia didn't speak for a moment. Then she bluntly asked, "Was Selene the first to share your bed?"

Sam's face heated. "Yes."

"Ah, I see." Lamia flipped her long braid over her shoulder. "I think you should try bedding a few other demonesses while you are here. Vanthee is quite taken with you."

Sam drew back, horrified. "Absolutely not."

"How can you know Selene is your fated mate if she's the only one you've ever known?"

"Because I just know."

"How?"

"I felt the bond come into place."

Lamia gave him a pitying look. "I fear you may have confused feelings of lust for the mate bond. Demons can't be fated to mate with humans."

"No. I have had... feelings of lust before meeting Selene, but what we have is different." He shifted his sitting position on the floor. Sharing such personal details made him feel deeply uneasy. "Even before we claimed each other, Selene was able to wield control of the shadows. You saw what she did with the hydra. Doesn't that prove she's my mate?"

"It was probably you controlling them instinctively." Lamia paused to chew an olive, then gestured at him with her fork. "Wouldn't you like someone to match your strength and power? An equal?"

"Selene *is* an equal to me."

"My darling son, she's not. Even if I had stayed a Goblyn, I would have still been a worthy mate to Asmodeus. We are both royalty and possess magick. But a human and a demon? She brings nothing of benefit to our family. Or your kingdom."

His spine stiffened. "I disagree. She has the ability to calm and soothe me. It is a gift I cherish deeply."

"Dear one, you're being silly. Even if you want to keep Selene as a lover, you would still be free to take another wife. Or several wives. Ones more advantageous to your status."

Sam stared down at the fresh greens on his plate, their taste turning sour in his mouth. A familiar sensation rose up in him—one he had thought he left behind in Aurelia.

It was the feeling of being not quite enough. Of being an outcast. Of disappointing everyone around him by not being who or what they wanted him to be.

He had known his parents would find his relationship with Selene unconventional, but he believed that would be overlooked since the will of fate had brought them together. Their pairing was preordained in his mind and not up for debate.

How had their pleasant evening turned so tense? He forced back the angry feelings that were beginning to form by taking three long, slow breaths. "Mother, I ask that you respect my choices. When the season ends, Selene and I are leaving. I don't wish to discuss it further."

Lamia's wings snapped. "A few months is hardly long enough to make up for the time our kingdom has been without their prince. This is where you belong. This is where you were meant to *rule*."

Sam shook his head. "I'm not the Dark Sovereign."

"Ha! You believe fate matched you with Selene, yet you reject the idea that fate wants you to be the Dark Sovereign?"

"The Dark Sovereign should be one who wants to lead. One who craves power and seeks to make the Underworld stronger. I wouldn't be suitable for it. The idea of having subjects or advisors or courtiers repels me. I want to answer only to myself."

Lamia's mouth thinned, obviously displeased with his answer.

Sam continued, "It pains me to disappoint you, and I hate that Father is losing his powers. But... "

He hesitated, then straightened his posture. "I have an idea. Actually, it was Selene's. Let me serve my royal duty by helping you find the Dark Sovereign."

Lamia took a sip of wine. "And how would you do that?"

"What if we hosted a tournament or series of trials to find the Dark Sovereign? Then the demon most suited to rule may prove himself worthy."

Lamia's eyes narrowed. "What sort of trials do you propose?"

"I'm not sure yet, but we can design them," Sam replied. "What skills or traits do you think are most crucial for ruling?"

Lamia's response was swift and decisive. "Unholy strength, the endurance to withstand suffering, mastery of negotiation, and, of course, a talent for deceit."

"Then we'll create tests to determine which demon excels in those areas."

Lamia looked thoughtful for a moment. "Hmm. We could start with a wide pool of contenders then narrow them as they move through each challenge."

"Yes, that would work. Anyone still standing by the end would be eligible for Father to crown them Dark Sovereign."

"Mmm," Lamia replied evasively. She wiped the corners of her mouth with a napkin. "But we mustn't let any of our subjects know your father's weakened state."

"I agree." Sam swirled his wine in the glass. "Perhaps we could frame the trials as an amusement or a competition to become the king's favored champion."

"Intriguing," Lamia murmured, her gaze sharpening. Then she tilted her head, a smile playing at the corners of her lips. "Very well. I'll agree to these trials. On one condition."

"Yes?" Sam asked warily.

Lamia's eyes glittered with triumph. "*You* must compete in them as well."

Sam let out a heavy sigh.

Endless clashes with his parents, or a set of games he could shape... and deliberately lose? The choice was clear.

He looked her in the eye and said, "If that's what it takes, I agree."

CHAPTER 23

Sam awoke the next morning with dread in the pit of his stomach over what he needed to do. Last night, he and Queen Lamia had spent the rest of their meal compiling ideas for the Dark Sovereign Trials. While Sam pushed for games that required skill and intelligence, Queen Lamia wanted challenges that relied on luck and physical strength. They came up with a list of twenty-five possibilities, which his father and the Council of Legions would narrow to three.

The trials would be vigorous, but that didn't frighten Sam. What did was the need to conceal his true motive—finding the competitor most worthy of ruling. For that, he'd need his powers at full strength.

And that meant facing Zaybris.

He didn't wake Selene. If he did, he'd be tempted to linger in bed, wrapped in her softness. Instead, he slipped from their room and summoned an imp to see if Vanthee was available.

A few minutes later, Vanthee met him outside the Sanctum. Her cheeks were flushed as though she'd been running. Her expression was serious before it shifted into dreamy adoration.

"I am here for you, my prince," she murmured.

"Do you know where the vampire Zaybris is kept?"

"Of course. He's in the Vaults of Eternal Torment.

"Can you take me to him?"

Her eyes sparkled with excitement. "It would be an honor."

Vanthee led him past the Sanctum and into the Chapel of Mourning. There, behind the dais, she revealed a hidden passage with her tattoo. It was an entrance that opened onto a narrow spiral staircase. She offered her hand, which Sam ignored, and they began their descent.

Sam had assumed Zaybris would be held in the Crypts of the Forsaken, but the deeper they went, the more he realized the Vaults of Eternal Torment made far more sense. It was a place reserved for the worst, most irredeemable souls—those devoid of remorse, whose crimes demanded further punishment before justice could truly be served. It was also where the Vengeance demons cast souls they deemed unworthy of reincarnation, even if they sought it in the Afterworld.

They walked in silence for several moments, until Vanthee spoke. "May I speak freely?"

Sam cringed. "If you must."

"If Zaybris had stolen my child, I would have found a way to destroy him by any means necessary."

"But then his punishment wouldn't be eternal."

"Perhaps. But my rage would be boundless. I would be a protective, devoted mother. If given the chance." She glanced over her shoulder. "Do you want children?"

Sam's jaw tightened. "That's not your business."

"I ask only because it's unheard of for a mortal to bear a demon's seed. The idea that you may never become a father is a sad one."

Irritation made his already heightened emotions simmer. He and Selene had talked about children, but neither had a burning desire to have them at the moment. "Grieve not. Selene and I can plan our future without your input."

"But surely you must want your bloodline to live on. You owe that to your kingdom."

"Don't tell me what I owe," he snapped. His hand tightened on the staircase railing. "Please, I need to prepare myself. I don't care to chat."

Vanthee went quiet.

They continued to descend what felt like thousands of steps—far deeper into the Underworld than Sam had ever ventured. The air grew heavier with each step, thick with the stench of misery and decay. In the flickering torchlight, a vast labyrinth came into view below them, its corridors twisted at unnatural angles. The very architecture felt wrong, as though the place had been designed to unsettle. Most paths led to abrupt dead ends or plunged into darkness, likely crafted to crush any hope of escape. Moans and distant screams echoed from unseen cells.

When at last they reached the bottom, Vanthee tried to take Sam's hand again.

"The way to Zaybris is treacherous. Let me lead you."

"You can lead without touching me," he said. Vanthee pursed her lips, but she didn't push further.

He continued following her past cells filled with the depraved and corrupt. Most ignored them, though a few pleaded for freedom, or simply for attention. At last, Vanthee's pace slowed. She stopped before one of the most decrepit cells they'd seen. Sam peered inside. It was dark, but he could make out a figure lying on a metal cot at the back, staring up at the ceiling.

Zaybris.

A jolt of anticipation surged through him. His fingers trembled at his sides from the overwhelming pressure of everything he had carried for so long now about to pour out.

"Here he is," Vanthee said. "May I stay to watch you inflict your wrath?"

"I'd like to be alone." The words came out breathless. This was it, the moment he had envisioned in countless daydreams and nightmares. It was meant to be just him and Zaybris. He didn't want an audience.

Vanthee's face fell. "I will leave you then. But call for me when you're finished, to help you out."

"I will. Thank you."

Vanthee walked away with slow, languid steps, obviously delaying her departure. When she finally disappeared around a corner, Sam extended a claw and tapped against the bars of the cell. The sound made Zaybris sit up, though it seemed to take great effort for him to stand.

Sam was shocked by his appearance. When he had last seen the vampire in Aurelia, he'd looked just as Sam had remembered him—healthy, despite his paleness, tall, blond, with a bearing of pure arrogance.

The creature before him now was skeletal. Only a few strands of hair clung to his scalp where the bonewhite of his skull wasn't peeking through. His nose had completely rotted off, leaving two empty slits at the center of his face. The clothes he wore were tattered and filthy, most likely the same one he had worn when he transported Selene to this realm.

Zaybris shuffled closer to the bars, then gazed up at Sam with sunken, rheumy eyes.

"It's you," Zaybris said, his tone was surprised, like he was being visited by an old friend.

"Yes."

"You've come home."

"I have."

Zaybris tried to peer behind him. "Is your mother here? Has she mentioned me?"

"No."

Zaybris curled his fingers, the remaining nails cracked and blackened, around the bars, leaning in. "She is busy with her royal duties, no doubt. Is she not the most glorious queen?"

"Indeed."

"I know she'll be here to visit me any day now. Have you brought me some blood? It's been many weeks since I received my last drop."

"No." A bead of sweat slid down Sam's temple, despite the chill in the air. He could tell that Zaybris was not in his right mind, but that didn't change what he intended to do. "Vampire, can you guess why I am here?"

Zaybris blinked, then scratched at what was left of his ear. "Is this a game?"

"It is not a game." Sam leaned closer to the iron bars. "I am a demon of Vengeance. Had you not ripped me from my home, my role here would be to make the dead feel the pain they caused others in life."

Zaybris swallowed. "I see."

"And now it's your turn."

Zaybris began to hobble backward. "But that was so long ago. Surely, you're not still dwelling on such things."

"Oh, I've dwelled on it for decades."

"Y-you had a perfectly adequate life in Aurelia. Enough food to eat, shelter, and few enemies." His voice rose with desperation. "And wasn't it there that you found your beloved human? I did you a favor, taking you from this godforsaken place!"

"A favor?" Sam's hand shot through the bars and closed around Zaybris's throat. The vampire's flesh squelched wetly beneath his grip, fragile and decayed. Sam had to remind himself not to squeeze too hard, not yet.

Just as he had practiced in the Sanctum, he gathered all the pain inside of him into a pulsating ball of energy. He didn't need to dig deep to access it—it was always there, just beneath the surface. But as it surged out of him and into Zaybris, something strange happened.

His suffering poured out as flashes of searing color.

Black for fear. The fear I felt when I woke up to see Zaybris looming over my bed. For the terror that consumed me when he grabbed me, then plunged me into the abyss of darkness. Black for the horror of being aban-

doned in an unknown realm, not knowing where I was or how to get home. Black for every moment of blinding panic I ever felt in Aurelia, even after I had escaped the blood wagons.

Blue for loneliness. Icy, bleak, bitter loneliness. The loneliness of being the only one of my kind. The loneliness I felt when Aurelians would look at me and quake with fear. For all the times I watched everyone around me dance and fall in love at Queen Thema's balls. Blue for the nights I spent alone in my chambers, comforting myself with texts describing acts of love I was certain I'd never experience. Blue for the pain of being ripped away from my mother's affection and denied my father's guidance.

Red for anger. Blistering, throbbing, vivid anger. Red for the volatile emotions I still struggle to control. For the trauma and sheer injustice of what was done to me as an innocent boy. Red for how my demonic instincts are a burden in Aurelia — a defect I was expected to overcome in exchange for grudging acceptance.

White for hopelessness. The absence of color, light, or meaning. White for the day I accepted that I would never reclaim what was taken from me. For all the nights I shivered in the wagon next to Eldridge, unable to imagine a life that wasn't filled with misery. White for the many years I lived without joy, comfort, and peace because of one vampire's selfishness.

Sam's body trembled, every muscle quivering under the strain of channeling so much heartache. Yet his grip on the vampire's throat never wavered.

At first, Zaybris had screamed. Long, guttural wails of agony that rang through the dark halls. The other souls began to wail too, echoing the suffering of both Zaybris and Sam. But as the tide of Sam's memories and emotions crashed over him, the vampire's screams faltered. They fractured into gasps, choked sobs, and eventually, silence.

Finally, Zaybris just stared, lips parted, eyes wide with something closer to understanding than fear. When Sam felt the last reserves of his power flicker and fade, he released his grip. Zaybris crumpled to the stone floor, thudding against the cold ground.

Sam looked down at him, chest still heaving. He braced himself for the rush of satisfaction he had dreamed of—the thrill of justice fulfilled, the victory of vengeance complete.

But it never came.

There was no triumph. No relief.

Just emptiness.

All Sam could feel now was a cold, aching void.

He rested his forehead against the bars, struggling to reconcile the emotions he'd anticipated with the stark weight of reality. He stayed there for a long time. Then, when he couldn't bear to be in the vaults a moment longer, he called out, "Vanthee?"

Within seconds, she appeared from around the corner, rushing toward him. Her expression was awed. "Oh, Samael, that was absolutely magnificent. I've never seen such—"

"Were you watching?"

"I couldn't help myself. I wanted to see you in your full power!"

"I said I wanted to be alone."

"I know, but... what's done is done, and I don't regret a second of it." Boldly, she placed a hand on his chest and stepped closer. "Let me take you to my chambers to unwind. I have wine, or perhaps you'd like me to bathe you?"

Sam ripped her hand away. He was tired of being polite, especially to someone who didn't respect his wishes during such a private moment. "Stop! Selene is my mate and the only one I want to be with!"

The enticement in Vanthee's gaze shifted to fury. "She can't love you as I would!"

Sam backed away irritably. He felt too drained to argue with her, especially when he knew a long stair-climb back up awaited them. "Just take me back to my chambers. I need to see Selene."

"Of course," she said in a clipped tone. "But at this hour, she's probably working in the library."

"What do you mean, working?" Sam snapped. "Did someone dare to assign the princess consort *chores*?"

"No, it was her choice. When I took her on a tour of the palace, she was shocked by the library's poor conditions, so she took on its revitalization as a project. She visits the hounds most mornings and works in the library throughout the afternoon."

Sam gave a terse nod. Realizing he had no idea how Selene had been spending her time for the past two weeks made his gut churn with shame. What kind of a mate was he for not making an effort to connect with Selene every day?

"Take me to her."

CHAPTER 24

"Eww, what *is* that?" Selene said to herself, peering at a book covered in pulsating green goo. It was wedged behind a bookcase so rickety it looked like it would disintegrate if she breathed too hard.

Since she had started cleaning up the Underworld's library, she'd faced a constant game of picking her battles. Some sections just needed the dust swept away, while others had surfaces that required vigorous scrubbing. The gooey book fell into the *no way am I touching that* category, so Selene avoided that corner, and continued stacking books by category and condition.

Zetta napped on a pile of crumpled pages nearby, snoring out puffs of smoke with every exhalation. Since had Selene decided she needed a project to keep from going stir crazy, Zetta rarely left her side. They had settled into a daily rhythm. Each morning, Selene helped Ogrin feed the hellhounds, despite the demoness's constant grumbling. Then Zetta kept Selene company in the library. Even with the occasional icky moment, working amid the dust and decaying tomes of the library was an introvert's dream: quiet, peaceful, and without distractions. Zetta also seemed to enjoy the break from her cage and the noise of the other dogs.

Selene picked at the flecks of disintegrated book bindings clinging to her dress. She was wearing the most utilitarian thing Prickles could find—a blue Victorian-inspired, high-necked frock with tight sleeves that didn't get caught on everything. She had asked for pants or something resembling a simple T-shirt, but so far Prickles hadn't delivered.

After setting down yet another battered book on war strategy, a hardback titled, *Lonely Nights and Magic Delights* caught her eye. She flipped through it, hoping it was the type of erotica Sam liked. It turned out to be a crumbling manual on sleight-of-hand tricks. She tossed it aside and tried not to let her thoughts drift to how much she missed Sam. Or wonder why it had been so hard for him to make time for her.

In Aurelia, when she and Sam had talked about coming to the Underworld, Selene had naively pictured them exploring the realm together. Sam would act as her tour guide, and they would both get reacquainted with his parents over family outings, shared meals, and whatever else demons liked to do for fun.

So far, the only meal she hadn't eaten alone in her room occurred on the night of their arrival. Prickles brought her trays of food like clockwork, but the imp didn't like to stay and chat. Playing with Zetta and the dogs helped ease her loneliness, but she couldn't help feeling a little abandoned. Selene had barely even seen Queen Thema since learning how to scry and shield.

"Selene? Are you in here?"

The question startled her. It came from a voice that sounded like Sam's, but she held back from answering. Was this another trick? Had Drath or another demon sensed she was thinking about Sam and come to torment her?

She covertly peered around a bookcase. Sam—or someone who looked like him—stood near the library's entrance, surveying the space with a scowl. There were dark circles under his eyes and his shoulders were slumped, but when he caught sight of her, his face brightened.

As he came toward her, Selene held up a hand. "Wait. How do I know you're really Sam?" Quickly, she imagined the pyramid slamming down over her mind and thoughts.

His forehead creased. "What do you mean?"

"I need to know you're real."

Sam stared at her for a moment, then said, "I'm real."

"Prove it."

"How?"

Selene looked him up and down, considering. "Tell me the name of the Harpy I sang a song to in Iriswood."

"Pydiana," he replied without hesitation.

Selene exhaled with her entire body and rushed toward him. "Oh, thank god." But right before she reached him, she stopped, remembering how filthy she was. "I'm dying to kiss you, but I'm covered in dust. What are you doing here?"

Wordlessly, Sam pulled her into his arms, dust and all, and crushed his lips to hers. She threaded her fingers through his thick hair, sinking her nails into his scalp. His hands cradled her face so he could take her mouth hard, undulating his tongue against hers. His scent, the wetness of their mouths, and the nearness of his body made her blood spark with fire.

From the corner of her eye, Selene saw Zetta wake up long enough to let out a soft whine as she yawned, then fall back asleep.

After several blissful minutes of kissing, Sam pulled back. "Why did you think it wasn't me?"

"I had a bad experience recently. I'll tell you later." She laid her cheek against his chest. His clothes smelled funny, like wet stone and rusted iron, but she didn't care. His heart thumped beneath her ear. "I'm just so glad to see you."

"What bad experience?"

"It's nothing. How have you been?"

Sam grasped her shoulders, forcing her to meet his eyes. "What bad experience? Tell me what happened."

She bit her lip. "I'm afraid of how you're going to react."

"Were you harmed?"

"No. Well, not physically." When Sam growled, Selene cupped his jaw and said, "I'm fine, I swear. I'll tell you, but you must promise not to storm off and do vengeance."

Sam sigh wearily. "I don't think I could if I even wanted to right now. But yes, I promise."

Slowly, Selene explained how she'd been spending her days and what happened with Drath in the tunnels. Recounting the story made her more emotional than she expected, especially remembering how happy she had felt seeing Cass at first. With every word, Sam grew more tense. When she finished, she watched his irises flash from black to red then again.

Quietly, he said, "I will deal with Drath. Rest assured. He will know pain and fear like he's never experienced before. But that can come later." He pulled her close again. "I've missed you. I hated being away from you so much."

"I missed you, too."

"I tried to come back to you early every night, but there was always an interruption. I'm sorry." He looked around the library again. "I hate that you've been spending your time in a place like this."

"Oh no, I like it. It's so satisfying to bring order to chaos. I've made a lot of progress." She gestured to two bookcases of neatly stacked books in the corner. "That section is for books on plagues, the other is for confessionals, and I'm starting one on war strategies."

Sam nodded and Selene noticed a slight tremble in his hand as he raked it through his hair. "You seem a little off. What's going on?"

The look he gave her was stark. Raw, unfiltered emotion. "I just faced Zaybris."

"You *what*?" Selene cried.

"I faced him where he's being imprisoned and I... I gave him vengeance."

Selene gaped at him. "And? How do you feel?"

He didn't reply, just pulled her into another kiss—harder this time and laced with urgency. "I don't want to talk. I just need to feel you."

Between kisses she said, "You're sure? It's a lot to process."

"I'm sure." He covered her breast with his hand and whispered, "We should go to our rooms."

"We could, but no one ever comes down here," she whispered back. "We could... "

Without a word, Sam lifted Selene against him, pulling both her legs around his hips. He set her on the nearby table, then swept away the piles of books with his arm.

The ferocity of the gesture made her giggle. "You just ruined three days of work," she cried. Sam looked panicked, but Selene pulled open his pants and said, "Worth it."

When she curled her fingers around his length, he hissed out a breath. He leaned further into her touch while pulling her skirts to her waist. He slid his warm palm up the delicate skin of her thigh, while his other hand thumbing her nipple through the fabric. He began feeling around for a zipper or set of buttons to undo, but the dress was corseted. Tricky to remove.

"I have to feel more of you," he growled against her ear. "Do you want to keep this gown?"

"Yes, don't tear it. It's the best one... for working," Selene panted. The feel of his fingers stroking over her panties made it difficult to form complete sentences.

He looked frustrated, but then said, "Lie back. I want to try something."

She did as she was told, anticipation already soaking her panties. Sam loomed over her for a moment with his hands bunched in her skirts. Then he closed his eyes and went very still. Just as she was about to ask what he was doing, a dark shape darted out from a corner and slipped under her dress. She yelped in surprise as something cool and tingly swirled over the bare skin of her stomach. Sam's look of concentration deepened until she felt the sensation glide up over her rib cage—then her breasts—dancing and skimming around the sensitive skin, twisting and pulling at her nipples until she gasped.

It was strangely wonderful, and deliciously wicked.

"Sam... what are you... how?"

"The shadows," he said. "A Lust demon gave me the idea. Do you like it?"

"I-I... love it."

He chuckled softly. "Lift your hips." She complied, and in an instant, her damp underwear went fluttering to the floor.

While the shadows continue to sweetly torture her on his command, Sam dropped to his knees. Roughly, he draped one leg over his shoulder and pushed her other leg aside so she was completely open to him. Although she could tell he was coiled tight with desire, he didn't pounce right away. The intensity of his gaze made her squirm as he stared at the most intimate part of her and murmured, "So beautiful."

Then he set upon her wildly. Licking and sucking as though he were a starved beast. His claws extended, digging into her thighs in a way that was sure to leave marks. She moaned and pressed herself closer to his mouth.

The unhinged way he devoured her made her briefly think of how her ex-boyfriend Kevin never went down on her. He claimed it "hurt his jaw" or he "didn't know how," despite all the times she had tried explaining that she didn't want a masterful technique—passion and enthusiasm went a long way.

How lucky I am that Sam has both.

With the shadows driving her wild beneath her dress, Selene reached down to stroke Sam's horns. She had quickly learned he loved this, especially when she did it to give him feedback. Telling him "a little to the left"—and pulling him in that direction with his horns— only seemed to amp him up further.

When he slipped his fingers inside her, she couldn't help but buck her hips. With his lips sucking her clit and his strong fingers pumping in and out of her wet sheath, she felt herself unraveling. Knowing he would stay on his knees for hours if she let him, she said, "Stop, baby. No more. Come inside me. Now, Sam."

He shot to his feet. In one swift motion, he plunged into her, pulling her hips to him so he could sink in deeper. She locked her legs around his waist and arched her back, meeting his thrusts.

This caused the shadows to writhe and pulse around them both. Selene watched Sam motion to them with his eyes. Then she felt the mist undulate down between her legs, brushing against her clit as Sam pounded into her. His expression was anguished. Desperate.

So good.

She couldn't hold out a second longer. Driving her head back, she let out a moan as waves of pleasure crashed over her again and again while she called his name. Seconds later, he went over the edge too. Groaning and gasping, then plunging into her as hard as he could.

"Selene," he cried, then collapsed over her, his head resting on her chest. They were both panting and sweaty. Sated.

Together again.

"Ahem," said a voice from behind them. "Um... pardon the interruption."

To Selene's horror, she turned to see Vanthee standing in the library's doorway.

CHAPTER 25

Selene's face flushed with humiliation as Sam pulled down her dress to cover her bare legs. He hastily fastened his pants.

"What do you want?" Sam barked.

"I was sent by Queen Lamia to bring you upstairs for dinner," Vanthee said. Her tone was formal, but her eyes shone with jealousy.

"Tell her I'm busy," he said.

"Apologies, but I can't do that. They are meeting with the Council of Legions and one of the generals wants you to join."

Sam's glower showed equal parts resentment and frustration. Selene slipped off the table, whispering, "It's all right. Just go."

"I'll come if Selene is allowed to dine with us," Sam said.

Selene shook her head. "Oh no, I'm not dressed for—"

"That's fine," Vanthee interjected. Then she smirked at Selene. "But she'll need to wear panties."

When Sam bared his teeth, Vanthee tossed her hair and backed out of the room. "I'll give you a moment to regain your composure."

When the library doors shut behind her, Selene covered her face with her hands. "Oh god, that was mortifying."

Sam began placing the books he had knocked over back on the table. "Don't let her antagonize you."

"Sam, I can't go to dinner with your family now. I'm all sweaty and covered in dust."

"Nonsense. You look perfect."

Cringing, she bent to retrieve her underwear from the floor. "But I don't know the protocol for meeting dignitaries. I can just finish up here and meet you back in our rooms later."

"No," Sam said firmly, stepping in front of her. "You're the princess consort now, and I want you by my side for events like this. I'm not letting anyone keep us apart that long again."

Selene scrunched up her face in a final, silent protest, then sighed.

"Fine."

~

Selene was surprised when Vanthee led them in the opposite direction of the royal dining room and into a small state room in the north wing. Sitting at the table were Asmodeus, Lamia, Mammon, and two demons Selene didn't recognize. One was a female with frizzy gray hair and an eye patch. She was shaped like a cannonball and making gestures with a gnarled cane. The other was a reedy male, dressed in something like a Civil War uniform that was neatly pressed with gleaming gold buttons.

Vanthee cleared her throat. "Forgive the interruption. I have brought the prince. And... her." She elbowed Selene.

Lamia rose with the grace of a trained hostess. "Excellent work, Vanthee. You're dismissed." She pulled out a nearby chair. "We already have a seat prepared for Sam. We'll have the imps fetch one for Selene. Please, meet our guests."

She gestured first to the thin demon. "This is Blight, general of the Legion of Punishment. Mammon, from the Legion of Temptation. And Empusa, from the Legion of Ruin."

"Good queen, just introduce me as general of the superior legion —it's faster," Empusa said with a deep, throaty chuckle. Her small wings, riddled with faded scars, swayed leisurely.

"You all know my son, Samael, and this is his human, Selene," Lamia added smoothly. "How lovely that you brought her to dine with us tonight, Sam."

Everyone nodded at them. If Selene had thought Lamia's politeness meant she had suddenly decided to like her, the "his human" remark squelched that. An imp scurried over to place a chair awkwardly at one corner of the table. Moments later, a glass of wine and plate of food were set in front of her.

Empusa rested her palms on the top of her cane. "Prince Samael, thank you for coming. Since you'll soon be crowned the Dark Sovereign—"

"I'm not—" Sam began, but Empusa spoke right over him.

"I wanted to share my concerns with you as well as the king and queen. I've already warned Mammon and Blight, but they seem to think I'm joking."

"No one's been named the Dark Sovereign yet," Sam said. "But go on—what concerns you?"

Empusa inhaled deeply, seemingly for dramatic effect, and closed her eyes. Then she opened them and declared, "A plague is afoot."

"Nonsense," Mammon mumbled through a mouthful of food. "One demon struck ill doesn't constitute a plague."

"Agreed," Blight said, squaring his narrow shoulders. "The Legion of Ruin has always been prone to exaggeration and embellishment."

Empusa lifted her fist. "Is that so? Well, perhaps if you—"

"Silence!" Asmodeus said sharply, startling Selene so badly she dropped her fork. "Mammon, Blight, do not speak again until I ask you to. Empusa, continue."

Empusa inclined her head. "A laborer came to me claiming he saw a patch of rot creeping near one of the lakes of fire. A fungus of sorts, but dark, crystalline, and jagged. I was ready to thrash him for wasting my time, until he showed me his hand."

She lifted her own hand in demonstration. "The two fingers that touched the fungus had turned black with rot. Brittle as charred wood. And the decay was climbing. Spreading up his arm so rapidly, I fear it will consume his whole body soon. Just from the briefest contact."

"That is concerning," Sam said.

Empusa smirked at Mammon and Blight. "See? The wise recognize danger."

"How long as it been there?" Sam asked.

"I'm not sure," Empusa replied. "This occurred a few days ago."

Sam looked to Asmodeus. "Has anything like this ever happened before?"

"Never." Asmodeus stroked his chin. "Perhaps we should close off the area around the lakes for now. Forbid anyone to enter the territory until it's safe. Or at least until we know what it is." He glanced at Lamia. "Your thoughts, my treasure?"

"I agree."

Asmodeus rose from his seat, gesturing for Sam to follow. "Empusa, I am grateful to you for bringing this to our attention. We are going to look at it right now."

"At a safe distance, if you please," Lamia said with a pointed look.

"Your Majesty, should you really venture down there? In your weakened state?" Mammon asked in a falsely concerned tone.

Asmodeus's nostrils flared. "Excuse me?"

Mammon looked around for the other generals to back him up but they avoided eye contact. "I only meant... "

"I know what you meant," Asmodeus said. He leaned down, putting his face right in front of Mammon's. "You were trying to undermine me."

"I wasn't!" Mammon protested.

"You'd better not be," he said in a voice that sent a chill down

Selene's spine. "I'll deal with you later. My queen, will you finish hosting our guests?"

"Of course," Lamia said.

Sam gave Selene's shoulder an affectionate squeeze as he passed behind her. Although a flesh-eating fungus sounded serious, watching him leave the room made her stomach sink.

Once they were gone, Empusa leaned back in her chair, a satisfied smile curling her lips. Queen Lamia sipped her wine as Selene pushed around the food on her plate. For several moments, only the sound of Mammon gnawing on a bone filled the room.

Then Empusa fixed her one eye on Selene and said, "Human woman! Tell me of yourself. What interesting vices of ruin do you possess?"

Selene laughed nervously. "Vices? I'm not sure what you mean."

"Are you prone to gossip, jealousy, or hatred?"

"I try not to be."

"Do you slander others or indulge in excessive laziness?"

"No, not purposefully."

"Oh." Empusa puffed out a breath. "How dull."

"What's the most ruthless way you've sought revenge against your enemies?" Blight asked.

"Well, I... " Selene started to say she'd never had enemies, but stopped herself. Her instinct had always been to be sweet and agreeable, molding herself into whoever others wanted her to be to keep the peace and win their approval. But here, in this place... it was a whole new ballgame.

And besides, saying she had no enemies wasn't even true.

C'mon, Selene. This is your chance to impress your mother-in-law.

"I killed a vampire once. Staked her right in the heart," she said, trying to sound casual. "Does that count as a vice of ruin?"

CHAPTER 26

The moment they realized they were dining beside a vampire-killer, both Empusa and Blight's eyes lit up.

"Oh ho, that definitely counts as a vice of ruin!" Empusa cried excitedly. "Give us all a bit of sustenance. Spare no detail."

Slowly, and as gruesomely as she could, Selene described the encounter with Margery. How she and Sam were tricked. How Sam was injured. How Margery tried to bite her. And how Selene's rage summoned shadows to her aid.

Blight gasped. "But how could a human have the gift of shadow manipulation?"

"From her mate, you simpleton." Empusa scoffed. "Didn't you see her tame that hydra at the banquet?"

"But I didn't know Prince Samael was my mate at the time," Selene added. She could feel Lamia's eyes on her, so she continued, "He had fond memories of learning the shadows from Queen Lamia, and I was grateful even a sliver of that power transferred to me. It saved my life."

"Or perhaps Sam sent them to protect you," Lamia said sweetly.

Selene gritted her teeth. "He was unconscious, but that's a lovely thought."

"What did it feel like sinking the stake in?" Blight asked, rubbing his bony palms together. "Did you do it quick and neat? Or slow and languorous?"

"How much blood was there?" Empusa asked, vying for Selene's attention. "Did the vampire expel the life fluid of all those she had consumed?"

The moment she had killed Margery had replayed in Selene's dreams many times. "There was no blood. What I remember most is how her face changed. When the stake went in, Margery's expression was surprised. Then confused. Then at peace. I wasn't sure what had happened at first. But when she stopped moving, I knew. She was truly dead."

"Ah, your first murder," Empusa cooed.

"And what of the corpse?" Blight asked.

"Her body turned to dust when the sun rose. All that was left were her clothes."

Empusa practically panted over that detail. "Fascinating. Do vampires still remain in Aurelia?

"Yes, they do," Lamia snapped, unexpectedly. "And my sisters handle them just fine. Queen Thema is resting—otherwise, I'd summon her to tell you herself."

She turned her gaze on Selene. "I never intended for their immortality to end at the tip of a stake. Surely, there was another way to defeat her that night."

Selene looked down, feeling completely intimidated. "I wish there had been."

"Bah. Violence can solve any problem," Empusa said firmly. "You did well, human."

"I disagree," Lamia said coolly. She took a sip of wine, then set the goblet down with precision. "It's important for a demon's mate to have skills in diplomacy, as well as strategy and wisdom. Confidence, strength, and charisma. But so far, I haven't seen evidence that you have any of those."

Selene blinked at the boldness of her words, then swallowed at their impact. She had endured years of insults from her mother, but rarely had they landed with such precision. "I'm sorry you feel that way," she said quietly.

"As am I," Lamia replied. "If I must indulge my son's infatuation with you, then I believe he would benefit from a second wife—one better suited to his nature."

The words hit Selene like a punch to the gut. "But I'm his fated mate."

"He can still take another bride."

"Vanthee would be an excellent choice, my queen," Mammon said, spitting out bits of food with every syllable.

"You look pale Selene. Do you believe your love is not strong enough to welcome a second wife?" Lamia asked.

"It's not something we ever talked about."

Empusa glanced between Selene and Lamia like she was watching a thrilling tennis match. "I know—let's play a game," she said, practically bouncing in her seat. "Human, tell us why you should be the prince's *only* bride."

"Well, I..." Selene's mouth went dry. Her mind blanked.

Why *was* she the better choice?

On paper, they didn't add up: demon and human, light and shadow, calm and chaos. But somehow, they *worked*. She brought him peace. He gave her fire.

But sitting there now, under the weight of their judgmental eyes, she was struggling to articulate that. And why someone as ordinary as her could possibly be a better partner to Sam than the beautiful, powerful, and thoroughly *demonic* Vanthee.

Lamia's stare remained fixed and unflinching. Selene fumbled for something—*anything*—to say. But then her gaze shifted, just past Selene's shoulder.

Asmodeus and Sam returned to the room, their expressions grim.

"Well?" Blight asked.

"Empusa was right," Asmodeus said. "A creeping rot is spreading through the land. We didn't touch it, but the look of it is abominable. It's clinging to the edges of two lakes now."

"We must stop it!" Mammon said, spraying crumbs.

"For once, I agree with him." Empusa muttered.

"Let's send a few imps to touch it. Then we can monitor their reactions and track the process of the disease," Lamia said.

"No," Sam protested. "Mother, that is cruel."

Lamia rolled her eyes. "Oh, Sam. You're far too merciful at times."

"Listen, everyone. The rot is a concern, but fear not." Asmodeus crossed his arms, grinning. "I know when it will disappear."

"When?" cried Blight.

Asmodeus cast a proud glance at Sam. "Once we crown the Dark Sovereign."

CHAPTER 27

After her humiliating meal with the Council of Legions, Selene had kept a low profile at royal events. She hadn't even been present when King Asmodeus announced the upcoming competitions to select a royal champion—and for that, she was grateful. He'd made the declaration during a public sparring match between demons of Brutality, and the bloodthirsty cheers alone would have haunted her for days.

The first trial was named Infernal Combat, and while Sam seemed to think it would be a piece of cake, the thought of watching him compete—getting beaten, tortured, or subjected to who knows what kind of indignities—was agonizing.

Sam had been making a conscious effort to spend more time with her, and walking her to the kennels each day had become part of their new routine. That morning, they'd talked about the first trial, and he'd told her she didn't have to watch it. She could stay curled up with a book in their chambers. Or, if she preferred, Prickles could deliver regular updates so she'd know what was happening without having to witness it firsthand. But Selene wouldn't hear of it. Even if she ended up watching the whole thing through her fingers, she was going to be there for Sam.

When they got to the kennels, they found that Ogrin had taken all the dogs out for a training run. Selene felt a pang of disappointment, but after kissing Sam goodbye for the day, she decided to make the most of her time in the library and get more work done.

A few minutes of walking brought her to the library's arched doors. But as she jogged down the short staircase leading to the entrance, she nearly collided with a spirit. Its wispy paleness stood out starkly in the dark alcove where it hovered.

Selene stepped back, a chill of fear washing over her at being so close to an actual ghost. It seemed oblivious to her presence, and she hurried to enter the library, leaving the spirit to its own business. But when the ghost suddenly began slamming itself against the wall, Selene couldn't look away.

She watched as it floated back, then hurled itself forward with breathtaking force to collide with the stone wall. Then the spirit did it again. And again. Over and over, relentless and mechanical, as if trapped in a loop.

The figure appeared to be a woman, dressed in a 1920s-style drop-waist dress. Her mouth was stretched wide in a silent scream, her agony almost palpable. Selene watched, transfixed, as the ghost repeated the ritual. She wondered what had prompted such desperation.

Each collision became more forceful. More tortured. The impact didn't make a sound, but it made Selene flinch each time.

Finally, she couldn't bear it. She held up her palms and said, "Stop it, stop it! Please!"

Instantly, the spirit paused, just before she made contact with the wall. Slowly, she turned her face toward Selene and blinked. It was dark in the alcove, but the confusion on her faint features was clear. When they locked eyes, a voice rang out in Selene's mind.

I can hear you.

The words sounded faraway, like an old gramophone recording, but the diction was clear. The disorienting sensation made Selene take an unsteady step back. Just as she was about to question if she had actually heard anything, the voice came again:

Can you hear me?

Hello? Miss?

Once again, the words echoed in Selene's mind, bypassing her ears entirely.

She nodded earnestly, rubbing her arms to chase away the goosebumps prickling her skin. Concentrating on the strange presence before her, she deliberately formed the thought: *Yes, can you hear me?* Then she mentally pushed the words outward, projecting them with just the force of her mind.

But the spirit didn't react. She continued to look at Selene with an achingly hopeful expression. Selene tried again, practically shouting the words in her thoughts: *Can you hear me?*

Still nothing.

Selene took a tentative step closer to try a different approach.

"Can you hear me?" she asked aloud, her words slicing through the silence between them.

Both watched as a thin tendril of shadow curled out from Selene's mouth, then darted toward the spirit. It spiraled around the ghost's head, then her face brightened.

Selene saw the spirit's lips move, and another shadow zipped from her mouth to toward Selene.

The words—*Yes! I hear you!*—echoed clearly in her mind.

She gasped, realizing the shadows were carrying their words back and forth.

"Do you need help?" Selene asked.

The spirit nodded, clutching her hands against her thin chest.

I can't escape.

"How long have you been here?"

I don't know.

"What's your name?"

Ruth.

"I'm Selene."

I'm most grateful you can hear me.

"Do you know when you passed?"

Ruth looked puzzled, so Selene repeated herself. When Ruth still didn't answer, Selene asked, "What year were you born?

1901.

Selene tried to keep her expression neutral, even though it was painful to consider how long Ruth had been trapped here.

Where am I? I need to go home.

Dread twisted Selene's stomach as she realized the truth of Ruth's situation. She wet her lips, searching for the gentlest way to say what needed to be said. But there was really no way to soften it.

Carefully, she said, "Ruth... do you know that you've died?"

Ruth's misty form jerked with surprise.

Died?

"Yes. This place you're in? It's the Underworld."

Ruth floated in silence for several moments. The way her features morphed from confusion into anguish was heartbreaking to see.

"I think you're supposed to be somewhere else," Selene said gently.

Ruth began to hover back and forth, as though pacing in midair.

Sometimes I'm here, and sometimes I'm in a place that looks like my house... but it's different. I remember getting sick but then—

Ruth covered her face with transparent hands. Her form quivered as silent sobs wracked her body.

I thought I was having a nightmare.

"I'm so sorry," Selene said, swallowing hard. "You must have gotten lost along the way."

I died. I am dead.

Ruth sobbed then dropped her hands from her tear-streaked face to peer at Selene.

But you're not?

"No," Selene said tentatively. How to explain the complexities of being a demon's mate? "I'm alive, but I'm... different."

Ruth began to cry again.

I want to go home.

"I understand. I don't know how it works here, but I can find someone to help you cross over," Selene said, glancing around helplessly, as if the answer might reveal itself.

That upset Ruth even more. She shook her head fiercely, her eyes wide.

No, no! I want to go back to the home I grew up in. Not... whatever comes next.

She turned away, as if ashamed. Wisps of hair that had slipped free from the chignon at the nape of her neck floated around her bowed head.

I'm not ready.

"Why not?"

Silence filled the hallway for so long, Selene wondered if her ability to hear Ruth had faltered. She held her breath, waiting. Then at last came the fragile, trembling words:

I'm frightened.

Selene sighed, wishing she could hug her. Even in death, she realized, it was easier to cling to familiar pain than to face the uncertainty of the unknown. It was a feeling Selene knew all too well.

Words of encouragement danced on the tip of her tongue. She was about to tell Ruth she was stronger than she knew, that she deserved more than existing in this half-life of sorrow. She wanted to urge Ruth to have courage and promise that what lay beyond wasn't as terrifying as she feared.

But she held back.

Because Selene remembered what it was like to be stuck. When she was in Ruth's place, no amount of wisdom or well-meaning advice would have pulled her out of her own toxic patterns. The life of obligation and self-sacrifice that she had built was suffocating, but also safe. By constantly meeting the needs of others, she had maintained a false sense of control over them. And by not setting her own goals, she had shielded herself from the sting of failure.

Letting go of all that hadn't come from someone else's words. It had been a choice she had to make alone.

"All right, Ruth. You don't have to go now," Selene said.

Ruth's ghostly form wavered at the edges, as if she trembled with relief.

"But when you're ready, come find me."

CHAPTER 28

At the end of a long day of delivering vengeance in the Sanctum, Sam huddled with Selene and other demons on the Bloodstone Plateau, an outdoor stadium and the largest gathering space in the kingdom. Terraces had been carved into the stone for seating, and below them, dancers from the Legion of Temptation entertained the crowd with a sultry dance routine. A howling wind whipped through the stadium, tossing Sam's hair around his horns.

Apparently, today marked the anniversary of the eclipse Asmodeus claimed credit for—one that ended an empire on Gaia. He had commanded his subjects to assemble in celebration, but Sam knew his father's true motives stretched beyond revelry.

Everything was in place for the first trial to begin.

He felt ready. Borias had been right—his abilities in the Sanctum had improved since his visit to Zaybris several days ago. Images of each soul's past deeds came to him more clearly, and he was becoming better at letting the pain of others pass through him without taking root. He hoped the mental clarity he'd gained would help him to find the Dark Sovereign.

Imps flew about, roughly chasing away roving lost souls, causing Selene's brow to crease with disapproval. When she'd told him of her ability to speak with the spirits, it had concerned Sam. The souls sent to the Sanctum had a specific reason for staying in the Underworld. But those who were merely lost? They weren't bound by clear rules or judgment. To Sam, their presence suggested chaos and imbalance, a crack in the Underworld's order. And that unpredictability, combined with Selene's unique gift, could make her even more vulnerable than she already was.

Selene interrupted his thoughts by gesturing to a demon sitting nearby, who was loudly snacking on strips of dried meat. "Zetta would love those."

"We'll have to find her some," Sam replied. Though the hellhound was indifferent to him, he was grateful that Zetta had taken such a strong liking to his mate. Especially since most demons were terrified of the hellhounds. He couldn't stay by Selene's side throughout the day, but knowing Zetta was near eased his fear that she might be tormented again. As she had been by Drath.

Just the thought of the demon of Fear made Sam's muscles tense with rage. Yesterday, he'd overheard Mammon bragging that he'd placed a substantial bet on Drath winning all the trials. Sam hoped he'd have the chance to face him today. He was determined to channel every ounce of anger and fury he had built up and eliminate Drath without hesitation. The demon would pay in blood and suffering for disrespecting his mate.

When the Legion of Temptation dancers finished, Asmodeus rose to address his subjects. Sam could tell his father was in good spirits, though his fading ability to project his voice was apparent from the funnel he used to amplify it.

"Good evening, and welcome. On this day when darkness dominated over light, so shall our kind rise!" Asmodeus raised his arms, inviting cheers. To his left, Queen Lamia gave a noble wave. When the crowd quieted, he continued. "I have gathered you all here tonight in celebration, but also for a special purpose. The time has come to separate the strong from the weak."

Selene gave Sam a worried look. "Oh no. This isn't—"

"It is," he said quietly.

"Why didn't you tell me?"

He threaded his fingers through hers. "I didn't want you to worry."

King Asmodeus stamped his hooves excitedly before continuing. "As you know, I am searching for someone very special, and tonight marks the beginning of a series of challenges. Trials of skill, cunning, and brutality—all carried out to find the demon most worthy of serving this realm..." He paused dramatically. "As my champion!"

The stadium erupted in a chaotic roar. Sam wondered what favors they assumed the king's champion would receive. Riches, certainly, but the promise of power was more alluring. The demons of Greed were visibly salivating, and several demons of Pride had already began to preen.

Asmodeus raised his palm to the darkening sky in a beckoning motion. "Now, I summon all who hunger for my favor to step forward. For tonight, at this moment, the Infernal Combat Trial begins!"

"They're really doing this now?" Selene squeaked. "Do you have to?"

"I'll be fine," Sam said, cupping her face to kiss her. "You forget I once spent every day battling for survival. This will be easy for me."

He motioned to Queen Thema, who sat near Lamia, a few seats away. "Will you sit with her?"

"Of course," Queen Thema said, sliding across the rock to link arms with Selene. "Don't be nervous, dear girl. How glorious to watch your beloved dominate all the other demons! Let us cheer him on—hurrah!"

Sam joined the other demons descending the terraces to gather in the center of the arena. His strategy for this trial was to surreptitiously observe any demons who stood out to him— while fighting for his own self-preservation, of course. He knew the price might be a few bruises, maybe even some broken bones, but securing his future with Selene in Snowmelt was worth every bit of pain.

Ghar, who had traded his usual master of ceremonies duties to administer the trials, stood waiting on one side of the stadium. He drew a line in the gravel with a long, sharpened bone.

"May all who wish to compete stand behind this line."

The demons complied, and Sam sized up the contenders. He estimated hundreds had gathered, mainly hailing from the Legion of Ruin and Legion of Punishment. He studied their faces, searching for some inkling of Dark Sovereign potential, but he saw only expressions of arrogance, bloodlust, or avarice. Some were already jostling for position, elbowing one another or exchanging threats.

When all the competitors had assembled, Ghar addressed them with solemn authority.

"To compete in the next trials, you must heed these rules." He produced a large hourglass from thin air. "Combat will last as long as it takes for the sand to run from the top of the hourglass to the bottom. Once the last grain falls, any demons who remain standing are declared victors. Any weapons on your person are permitted, excluding fire."

Ghar signaled his readiness to the king. Asmodeus looked down at the contenders with satisfaction. When he caught Sam's eye, he winked.

Rearing back on his hoofed feet, Asmodeus shouted, "Begin!"

CHAPTER 29

Demons began to pile on Sam the moment Asmodeus's command left his lips, surging toward him in a wave of claws, teeth, and aggression. They came from all sides, each one vying to be the first to draw blood. But this was no surprise. Sam had known from the start that he'd be an obvious target. To the others, he was a pampered prince. An outsider with an unfair advantage and the one most likely to win the king's favor.

He didn't flinch. Instead, he drew himself inward, gathering his energy like a snake coiling before the strike. He let the demons believe they were overwhelming him, that he was caving beneath their assault. In truth, he was conserving strength, building power, waiting for the perfect moment.

His movements became smaller, tighter, more deliberate. For a heartbeat, doubt flickered in his mind. What if Selene, watching from the stands, thought he'd already fallen? He pushed the thought aside

Survive the onslaught. Then strike when they least expected it.

A small, spry demon yanked clumps of Sam's hair with gleeful malice, while another raked his claws down his bare arms, leaving trails of blood. A demon with a bull-like head was butting him in the stomach while simultaneously kicking at one trying to bind his feet. Each wanted the glory of taking down the lost Prince of Vengeance. But none of them knew what he was capable of.

In Aurelia, he had to temper his strength and restrain his inclinations for violence. But here, there was no reason to hold back.

He let them brutalize him for one second longer, then exploded out of his defensive crouch in a wild burst of aggression. First, he grabbed the demon near his feet by the throat and flung him across the stadium, where his body crashed into a cluster of rocks with a sickening *thud*.

Then, he seized the bull-headed demon by the horns. With a flick of his wrists, Sam bent the demon's horns toward each other at a 90-degree angle. The demon collapsed, letting out a long, guttural low of pain.

The one clutching fistfuls of his hair began chanting a curse, his voice rising in manic glee. Green pustules erupted across Sam's skin, oozing with dark magick. But Sam wasn't fazed. He reached up and with a single, punch, shattered the demon's jaw. The demon's teeth scattered across ground like broken glass, breaking the curse instantly.

Suddenly, an enormously tall demon grabbed Sam around the middle and hoisted him off the ground. As he hung in the air, Sam quickly scanned the stadium, now a whirlwind of chaos. Bodies of fallen demons lay scattered, while most continued to clash in fierce combat. A moment later, the demon slammed Sam into the ground, sending a cloud of dust billowing into the air.

But the demon didn't realize Sam had long since learned how to soften such impacts. He went limp as his body hit the ground, letting the force disperse through his body.

He sprang back to his feet and in the next instant, the towering demon found himself airborne as Sam wrenched *him* off his feet, then drove him into the ground. The demon lay there, staring up at the sky in disbelief.

Sam wiped the sweat from his forehead and braced for the next assault. He noticed demons beginning to avoid him now, perhaps realizing he wasn't such an easy target. Crimson bursts of light and waves of heat, typical of defensive magick, soared past him. He scanned the stadium, searching for contenders who rose above the rest, until his gaze landed on Drath. The demon's tattered robes flapped as his spidery arms jabbed at those around him.

Sam smiled.

Vengeance.

He charged toward the demon, plowing through lesser adversaries without slowing. With a burst of ferocity, he slammed into Drath, tackling him to the ground. In one swift motion, Sam wrenched all of the demon's limbs together and pinned him beneath his weight.

"You dared to torment my mate?" Sam seethed.

Drath struggled uselessly. "What of it?" he spat.

Sam tightened his grip, pulling the demon's limbs until he gasped in pain. "Why would you disrespect her in such a way?"

Drath's eyes gleamed like glowing pinpricks deep within his face. They locked with Sam's, and he said, "She... she was alluring. Irresistible."

Red flashed across Sam's vision. He drove his knee into Drath's stomach. "That was the wrong thing to say."

"Was it?" Drath coughed, grinning. "How telling. What do you have to fear from others being tempted by her charms?"

"She is under my protection."

Drath's painted lips curved into a smile. "Do you fear she would leave you for another? Perhaps... one more *human?*"

Sam's fury surged.. Losing Selene that first time, when Zaybris took her, had left him terrified of it happening again. The months they'd spent apart were filled with tortured days and sleepless nights. Feeling as though he had failed her. Wanting to simultaneously destroy everything in his path and crawl into a hole to die.

It was like tiny thorns were piercing his mind as he relived those memories. Sharp, biting, and precise.

He realized he was being baited.

"Get out of my head," Sam snarled.

Drath's voice turned silky. "Perhaps I could take Selene as my human bride. She must grow weary of your long absences... serving the kingdom—"

Sam punched Drath in the face, breaking his nose. Black, sticky blood instantly coated his hand. The demon's chuckle came out as a wheeze. "I may not have your physical strength, but I could easily drive you to madness."

"I'm afraid not."

"Then kill me," Drath hissed. "You could do it. Deliver a lethal blow I could not survive. You've done it so many times, haven't you? To ones more innocent than I... "

Unbidden, the faces of the Aurelians Sam had killed flooded his mind. First in a blur, then one by one, vivid and slow. Each face burned with fear, twisted in pain. Their eyes haunted him, staring through time, accusing and unrelenting. Again and again, they came —until Sam gasped, his breath stolen by the weight of his guilt.

"Stop... " Sam protested weakly.

"Never," Drath hissed.

Sam knew he was feeding Drath with his torment, but it was difficult to break free of his influence. His hold on the demon's limbs faltered, just enough for Drath to slip one spidery arm free.

With a sickening ease, Drath reached up and tapped Sam's forehead. Instantly, the guilt and anguish surged—tripling in weight.

Sam rolled off him, hitting the ground hard. Drath followed, his limbs slithering over Sam's body to intensify his cruel power, tapping him in a rhythm that seemed almost gleeful. Sam tried to buck him off but failed.

Then the demon leaned in close, breath hot and rancid, to whisper, "I told you I could evoke madness."

Sam tried to turn his face away when, suddenly, someone

appeared behind Drath. Before he could blink, a hatchet sank into the demon's skull with a *thunk*.

Drath's head snapped back as the attacker wrenched the handle with brutal force. The demon let out a shriek. Instantly, the images invading Sam's mind vanished.

Gripping the embedded hatchet, the mysterious figure drove Drath facedown to the ground, where he stayed, writhing in pain.

Sam looked up at his savior. It wasn't a hulking beast, as he'd expected, but a slight, agile demon. Wrapped in head-to-toe leather armor, with a steel helmet crowning his head. A hinged visor bearing an image of a flame concealed his face, making it impossible to tell friend from foe.

Sam tensed, ready to defend himself against a new threat.

But then the figure lifted the visor and Sam's breath caught.

It was Vanthee.

Strands of blonde hair clung to her sweat- and dirt-smeared face. She grinned, then raised a finger to her lips in a silent *shhh*. Extending a hand, she helped him to his feet.

"I have many skills," she said.

"What are you—" Sam began, but blaring horns drowned out his words. Winged demons swooped overhead, blasting trumpets that left trails of fiery sparks across the sky.

Ghar stood beside the king and queen, raising the drained hourglass high. Sam stared, surprised the trial was already over. It felt as though it had barely begun.

King Asmodeus surveyed the stadium. "Cheers to an invigorating first trial! All of you fought bravely, but only those who remain upright will move to the next round. Look around, my contenders—these will be your opponents when we gather again."

Sam turned, expecting to see Vanthee but she had vanished. Scanning the bloodstained ground, he counted around thirty demons of various shapes and sizes still standing. To his dismay, Drath had managed to pull himself up to his knees, swaying in pain with the hatchet still embedded in his head.

Sam narrowed his eyes, taking mental note of the other survivors. He didn't know who they were, not yet, but he would. Names, allegiances, power levels, ambitions—he intended to uncover it all.

In the crowd, he spotted Selene clinging to Queen Thema. They both waved. Selene's smile, so beautiful and full of relief, made some of the anguish Drath had left behind begin to fade.

How lucky he was to have something so precious to fight for.

CHAPTER 30

Selene sat on the Bloodstone Plateau for nearly an hour after the trial had ended, feeling deeply unsettled. Queen Thema had invited her to join a private post-trial celebration that Lamia had planned, but Selene declined, knowing she wouldn't be welcome. Besides, the last thing she felt like doing was celebrating.

Although Sam seemed to have come out of the trial with no lasting damage, watching him get pummeled had been sheer torture. She had felt so alone, so out of place, wincing and gasping while everyone else cheered wildly with each punch thrown.

She brushed dirt from her dress, stirred up by the dust rising from the stadium floor. Clusters of demons still remained, some reenacting fights they had seen, others drinking heavily and singing songs of victory.

"Excuse me. You must be Lady Selene, the princess consort," a deep voice said.

She looked up to see a huge demon with gray-scaled skin, short black hair, and the physique of a professional wrestler looming over her.

"Yes, that's me."

"My name is Borias. I'm a Vengeance demon who works in the Sanctum with Prince Samael. I just wanted to introduce myself."

"Oh, hello Borias. It's nice to meet you." She was always guarded when meeting new demons, but Sam had spoken highly of Borias, and his dark eyes seemed kind. He was actually a bit handsome, in a rough-edged, brawler kind of way. "Did you enjoy the trial?"

Borias raised one eyebrow, but the rest of his face remained neutral. "I prefer celebrations that include cake."

Selene couldn't help but laugh. "So do I."

"Did you enjoy it?"

"To be honest, I hated it. I'm far too human for games like this, I guess."

Borias smiled, flashing straight white teeth. "If I may also be honest, I didn't enjoy it either. There's a time and place for violence, but it shouldn't be a qualifier to become the king's champion."

"I think you're in the minority here," Selene said, gesturing to a pair of demons who were simultaneously choking each other.

Borias rolled his eyes. "Being a demon isn't just about cruelty. When I was in Gaia, there were many demons who left the Underworld because they'd grown tired of those who reveled in pain."

"You lived in Gaia? When?"

"About three hundred of your years ago."

Selene's mouth fell open. "You were around in the 1700s? Where?"

Borias sat beside her and shrugged. "Here and there. I mostly spent time in Europe. A few years in Russia."

"Did you enjoy your time there?"

"Somewhat. I liked the sunsets."

"I miss those. I'm probably developing a serious vitamin D deficiency here," Selene joked. "I never knew demons walked among humans until recently. I actually met a demon in Nashville, where I'm from, once. He said he came to Gaia through a séance."

"Yes, some demons will take that route when they need a quick escape. What was his name?"

"Halphas. Or Hal, is what he goes by. Do you know him?"

Borias's dark eyebrows shot up. "Yes. He was the cavalry officer for the Legion of Temptation's mounted troops, but he deserted. Did he seem all right?"

"Yes. He was very kind to me."

"Good. Some demons take to human life well. Others don't. Do you plan to become a demon yourself?"

"No. We're just visiting." Selene gave him a sideways look. "But maybe if I did become one, I wouldn't be so squeamish about watching people get beat up."

"Doubtful. I don't know exactly how it would work, but I imagine traits you have suppressed as being undesirable would rise to the surface. It wouldn't necessarily make you bloodthirsty or sadistic. You might sprout wings, though."

"Now, that sounds cool." Her smiled faltered as darker thoughts drifted by.

"What is it?" Borias asked. "Something grieves you."

She bit the corner of her lip. "It's just that... sometimes I feel like I'm holding Sam back. Like maybe I should become a demon so he can stay here longer."

"But do you *want* to become a demon? Really want it?"

"No."

Borias gave her an assessing look. "I know your type. I see it in the Sanctum all the time. Not as one to be punished, but as one whom others manipulate. The ancient word for it is whim-shifter."

Selene drew back, slightly offended. "What does that mean?"

"You try to be what others need. Reshape and shift yourself to please others, or act as you think they want you to."

Selene's face flushed. "That's exactly what I do," she said softly. It felt as though Borias had just stripped her naked and paraded her around the stadium with his words. "We call it a people-pleaser in my world."

"Don't look so horrified. It's not always a bad thing. It's just that in my experience, whim-shifters never get what they truly want. They put forth a lot of effort for little reward."

Selene gave a small snort. "Tell me about it. So, what's the remedy?"

"Start pleasing yourself. If you don't want to be a demon, don't become one. I've never heard Prince Samael say he wished you weren't human. He seems to love you as you are."

"He does. He absolutely does. But his parents… " she trailed off.

"See? There you go again. Forgive me for being so bold, Lady Selene, but you're trying to shift yourself to please someone else."

"Good grief," she said lightly. "Since when are Vengeance demons so perceptive?"

"I'm very wise," Borias said with a wink. Then he added, "I've also seen inside the souls of many humans."

She rubbed her fingers between the fabric of her dress. "I hate being this way."

"I didn't mean to make you feel bad. Your ability to understand others is a strength. In some realms it's a form of magick, used for gaining secrets, negotiation, and winning favor. You just have to make sure it doesn't consume you."

"That's good advice. Thank you."

"My pleasure." He stood and stretched his arms overhead. "I don't know about you, but all this noise and commotion has me ready to turn in."

"Yes, that sounds good to me, too. Have a nice night, Borias."

Borias bid her goodnight, and Selene watched him walk out of the stadium and back toward the palace.

Eventually, she left the stadium as well, thinking about how Borias was the second demon to hold up a mirror to her face and force her to confront the truths she'd been avoiding.

If only it were that easy.

CHAPTER 31

Since winning the Infernal Combat Trial, Sam had tried to keep a discreet presence in the palace to observe the other contenders, but his parents made that difficult. Earlier in the week, his father had him sit in for him during open court, the time when his parents heard petitions, settled disputes, and addressed grievances from their subjects. It was mind-numbingly tedious, yet Sam forced himself to nod along to each plea and attempt at flattery. If his parents thought the experience would make him more amenable to becoming the Dark Sovereign, it had the opposite effect. He hoped the next trial would provide a better opportunity to see a potential candidate shine.

Sam was sweeping the floor of one of the older judgment rooms, when he heard the click of the door latch shut. Quickly, he spun around to see who it was. Vanthee stood, leaning against the closed door, gazing at him with heavy-lidded eyes. She'd applied red gloss to her lips and wore a skin-tight gown made of transparent lace.

"May I help you?" Sam asked.

"Hello," she whispered.

The sultriness of her gaze made him tighten his grip on the

broom handle. Every encounter with Vanthee felt like a chore, and he wasn't in the mood for her games. The scent of her generously applied cherry-and-clove perfume filled the room, making him rub his nose.

"Have you come to assist me?" he asked. A recent surge in condemned souls had forced him to use a rarely visited chamber that was badly in need of cleaning. "You can start by scrubbing the floor with that sponge and bucket over there."

"I didn't come to clean," she purred.

"Suit yourself."

Vanthee watched him sweep for a moment, then crossed the room and slipped behind him. Her arms slid around his biceps, and she rested her head against his back. "I came because I want to be with you."

Sam pulled away at once.

"I've tried to catch you alone for so long," she murmured, then tried to embrace him again.

"Don't touch me," he snapped.

"No one needs to know. I won't say a word."

"Nothing is going to happen between us. Go find a Lust demon to meet your needs."

"I saved you in the trial. Doesn't that prove my worth to you? Don't I deserve a reward?"

"You have my gratitude," Sam said flatly. "There's your reward."

Vanthee's dreamy expression shifted to something darker. "Stop pretending to be so noble. You're not in Aurelia anymore. There's no need to cling to their foolish ideas of fidelity."

She trailed her fingers down his chest, but Sam blocked her with the broom handle.

"Haven't you ever wondered," she whispered, "what it's like to be with a demoness?"

"No. You need to leave."

She inched closer, until her breasts brushed his Sam's knuckles where he gripped the broom. "I used to dream about you. The shining lost Prince of Vengeance. So handsome and brave. I always knew our destinies were intertwined."

Sam's unease grew. He was used to confrontations where force, or the threat of it, spoke louder than words. But this was different. A female who ignored his wishes and pushed past his warnings presented a different kind of challenge. Since violence wasn't an option, he tried a different tactic.

"Yes, our destinies are intertwined," Sam said evenly. Vanthee's eyes lit up—until he kicked the cleaning bucket toward her with a clatter. "We were meant to clean this room together."

The anticipation on her face shifted into irritation. Then hardened into resolve.

"Fine," she said, smoothing her dress. "I'm not afraid of hard work. Allow me to demonstrate just how agile and flexible I can be."

"If you can lift that stain on the floor in the corner, I will be impressed," he joked.

His jest made Vanthee's cheeks flame. Careful of her tight dress, she lowered herself to the floor. She dunked the sponge into the soapy water and began scrubbing.

Though they worked in silence, the room was thick with tension. Sam could easily walk out of the Sanctum to escape her, but he knew Borias would chastise him for leaving a room only half-cleaned. If Vanthee was angling for some private time with him, he needed to make it clear that this was all she was going to get.

"Do you like seeing me on my knees, great prince?" she said, leering up at him.

Sam didn't respond. Instead, he focused on knocking down a stubborn cobweb clinging to the corner of the ceiling. The scent of cleaning solution was beginning to drown out her perfume and for that, he was grateful.

"Be sure to really scrub hard when you get to the skirting board," he instructed.

Vanthee glared at him then said, "Yes, sir."

After several minutes, she sat back on her heels and wiped the sweat from her brow.

"Growing weary, are you?" Sam asked. "Perhaps it's time you went home."

"I'm not as strong as you, that's true," she replied, her voice edged with challenge. "But I'm tough. Tell me, great prince, do you ever worry about breaking your little human when you're pushing inside her?"

A red haze swept across Sam's vision. Her crude question ignited a raw urge to lash out—to snarl, to rage, to terrify her so thoroughly she'd never dare approach him again. But he held himself back. He knew exactly what Vanthee was doing: prodding, provoking, trying to prove that he belonged with a demoness, not some fragile human.

Usually, when he was unsure of how to act, he asked himself what Eldridge would do. But this time, his thoughts strayed to Brunie. He remembered how impossible she was to rattle, how effortlessly she defused barbed remarks with raw honesty. What seemed like innocence had a way of shaming her challengers, leaving her the quiet victor.

"No," he said lightly. "Selene is able to accommodate me."

Vanthee's mouth opened in surprise at his composed reply. She tucked a strand of hair behind one horn then asked, "But surely you must crave someone to match your power."

"Not at all. We've figured out what works and what doesn't."

Vanthee pressed her lips together. Her attempt to shock and provoke him was unraveling, yet she wasn't relenting. "Most demons prefer a lover they don't have to treat like she's made of glass."

Sam stopped sweeping and leveled a look at her. "For the last time, Selene is my mate. I don't want anyone else. Whatever you're trying here, it's pointless. Surely you have plenty of suitors more worthy of your time."

"That's where you're wrong," Vanthee snapped. "I don't have a lot of suitors. My father won't allow it."

A flicker of pain crossed her face, and for a moment, Sam almost pitied her.

"Interesting," he said. "Mammon never struck me as the protective type."

"He's not. I'm just an asset to him." She scrubbed harder at the floor. "I was betrothed to Drath to settle one of Father's debts but thankfully, Drath called it off."

Sam's eyebrows lifted. "Because you tried to split his head open?"

"Something like that," Vanthee muttered.

Slowly, the pieces fell into place, and Sam began to understand the logic behind her obsession with him. To Mammon, aligning with Sam held more promise than a pact with any other demon, and Vanthee was the perfect pawn to make it happen. Mentioning her father seemed to unlock something in Vanthee. The seductive facade slipped away, replaced by something rawer, more real. Sam watched her attack the floor with renewed aggression.

"Are there any demons you would choose to marry, if it were truly your choice?" Sam asked.

Vanthee let out a dry laugh. "There's no such thing as choice for me."

"Why?"

"It's just the way it is. I'm not a royal offspring like you."

Sam ignored the jab. "What did your mother think of your betrothal to Drath?"

"I don't know. I never met her."

"Truly?"

"She's dead. After I was born, 'someone' threw her into one of the lakes of fire. I'm fairly certain it was my father."

Sam inhaled sharply. "Why is he allowed to walk free? He should be in the Vaults of Eternal Torment."

Vanthee shrugged. "He claimed it was an accident, that she tripped. Or at least, that's what I was told. I was just a baby."

"That's unacceptable. Was there even an investigation?"

She scoffed. "Do you think we're in Gaia or something? No one cared."

There weren't many ways for a demon to truly die, but being consumed by the flames of a lake of fire was one of them. Sam knew what it felt like to be separated from his parents, but never knowing one at all? And worse, knowing one had likely killed the other? That was a different kind of devastation.

"I'm sorry," he said.

"It happened just after you were taken," Vanthee replied, somewhat apologetically. "I'm sure the king and queen had more pressing concerns."

"Still, an act like that should've been punished."

"Perhaps it would have been once. Elders have told me that after you vanished, the king and queen began to neglect their duties. The realm started to decay. Laws went unenforced, the land was left untended, and more souls were lost. A lot of them, actually."

This caught Sam off guard. He'd noticed parts of the Underworld were in disrepair, but he hadn't realized the neglect stretched across the entire realm.

"Is that why there are so many lost souls roving about?"

"It's not my fault!" Vanthee protested. "There were Guides before me, nine of them. But one by one, they grew tired of Underworld politics and left for Gaia. I was only an apprentice when I was forced to take over and guide all the souls alone. I begged for help from my father—from the king and queen—but no one listened. They've desecrated what this realm was meant to be. It was created to judge the dead and guide them to their next journey—not serve as a playground where demons indulge their every whim."

Before Sam could respond, Vanthee rose to her feet. "I've had enough of this," she muttered, tossing the sponge back into the bucket. "If you ever get tired of your human, come see me. Otherwise, clean this room yourself."

CHAPTER 32

I want to go home.

The words echoed through Selene's mind, sudden and loud. She whipped around so fast that several books tumbled from her arms, hitting the library floor with a *thud*. It barely mattered, given the dozens already scattered across the room.

There was Ruth, hovering over a chair behind a desk, poised like someone ready to strike a bargain. Her face held a blend of fear and yearning, but she seemed more determined than the last time Selene had seen her.

Selene set down the remaining books she held and wiped her dusty hands on her dress.

"Are you sure?" It had been three weeks since she first made contact with Ruth, and she wasn't sure if that was considered a long or short time to decide to stop being a ghost.

Yes, miss. I'm ready.

"All right," Selene said firmly. "Then I'm going to help you. First, I have to figure out who we can talk to."

Ruth nodded as Selene ran through the short list of demons she'd met. The sound of Zetta gnawing on a hunk of brimstone nearby made her briefly consider Ogrin—but she dismissed the idea. Ogrin had little patience and even less sympathy for lost souls. Empusa was probably too busy, Blight and Mammon were too creepy, and as for Queen Lamia... Selene would rather become a ghost herself than ask her for help.

A knot of dread tightened in Selene's throat as realization dawned. Vanthee was the only one who could probably help her.

"Right," Selene said to herself. Then, in a coaxing tone so as not to shatter Ruth's resolve, she asked, "Ruth, can you follow me, or do you want to stay here while I see what needs to be done?"

The spirit's eyes flickered toward the dim corridor outside the library, then back to Selene.

I'll follow you, miss.

"Great. Let's go." Turning to Zetta Selene said, "You stay here."

After some minor whining from Zetta, Selene left the library and headed toward the places she'd seen Vanthee lingering. Ruth floated along behind her. Selene stopped to ask a few passing demons if they'd seen Vanthee, hoping for a lead. One demon shrugged, barely glancing at her; another simply shook his head before slinking away.

Eventually, Selene spotted a familiar figure approaching—a demoness with wild gray hair and an eye patch. When she caught sight of Selene, she boomed jovially, "Vampire killer!"

Selene smiled, grateful for a friendly, if eccentric, face. "Hello, Empusa. Have you seen Vanthee? I'm looking for her."

"She's recharging in the Serpent Burrows, I'd wager."

"Could you take me there? I need her help."

"Yes, but... " Empusa's gaze focused behind Selene. "Did you know there's a spirit following you?"

"Yes."

Empusa gave her a skeptical look, then shrugged. "Follow me, then."

As they walked, Empusa pummeled Selene with more questions about when she killed Margery like, "When the vampire turned to dust in the morning, did you breathe it in? What did it smell of?"

Selene disappointed her by confirming she had not, in fact, inhaled vampire dust. Still, she continued trying to placate Empusa's curiosity for fear the demoness might lose interest and abandon them to find the Serpent Burrows on their own. Eventually, the solid terrain beneath their feet became soft and uneven.

"There she is," Empusa said, pointing in front of them.

Up ahead, Selene saw mounds of dirt pocked with openings that looked like gaping mouths. Vanthee sat cross-legged in the center of the largest mound with her eyes closed, looking like a glamorous yoga teacher deep in meditation. Sparse patches of grass and twisted, thorny plants surrounded her. The air was dry and still, making the whole place feel desolate.

Selene eyed the holes in the ground uneasily as they came closer. Then she clapped a hand over her mouth when she saw the nest of snakes squirming in Vanthee's lap. Their scales gleamed in shades of green, brown, and red, their bodies pulsing and slithering over one another like a living tapestry.

"Vanthee!" Empusa's voice rumbled through the air. "This human wants to see you."

Vanthee''s eyes flew open, and her copper-colored wings gave a single sharp twitch. Her eyes fell on Selene, then narrowed. "What do you want? I'm preparing for the Hailing of Souls."

"I'm sorry, but I need your help," Selene began. She hesitated— torn between the urge to flee from the nest of snakes and the pressure to find the right words. After steadying herself, she gestured behind her.

"This is Ruth. She's been here for a very long time." The ghost placed a cold, translucent hand on Selene's shoulder. A chill radiated through her, startling but not unpleasant. "She's told me she's ready to go home."

Vanthee's face drained of color. "She what?"

"She wants to go home," Selene repeated. "To whatever happens next."

"You can hear her?" Vanthee asked. The snakes in her lap grew restless. Some wound up her arms to drape themselves around her shoulders, while others slipped back into the dark burrows beneath her feet. "How do you know this soul's name?"

"And that she's ready to go?" Empusa added. She leaned on her cane as though she feared falling.

"She told me," Selene said. "We can communicate through the shadows."

Vanthee's expression shifted, just slightly. Selene saw her disdain give way to something deeper, heavier. Like grief.

But just as quickly, Vanthee masked it with a smirk. "Prove it," she said. The snakes hissed as if echoing her demand.

"Come on. She's not a trick pony," Selene said. When Vanthee failed to drop her challenging glare, Selene sighed. "Ruth, would you please hold up three fingers so they know you can hear me?"

Instantly, Ruth's translucent form responded, raising a ghostly hand and spreading three fingers.

Empusa pressed her hand to her chest. "Damnation and ruin, she's telling the truth! How is this possible?"

"Is it just her, or can you speak to all the lost souls?" Vanthee asked, her expression curious now.

"I don't know, she's the only one I've ever tried," Selene said. When the two demonesses continued to stare at her, she added urgently, "Can you help her?"

Vanthee got to her feet with fluid grace. "Yes, of course. It's nearly time for me to go anyway." Selene noticed that some of the snakes coiled around Vanthee's arm melted into her tattoo, disappearing. "This spirit belongs in the Afterworld. Ask her to follow me."

Selene turned and gently said, "Ruth, this is Vanthee. She's going to guide you home. Go with her—it's time."

Ruth's form quivered, shifting from a gray wisp to a black, pulsing mass. She began to twist and flicker, spiraling in turmoil.

No! Not without you, miss!

Selene felt a pang in her chest at the spirit's agitation. She must be so frightened. "All right, Ruth, it's okay," she murmured. Turning to Vanthee, she said, "She wants me to come with her."

Vanthee let out a sigh, dramatic and exasperated. "Fine. But listen, you absolutely cannot get too close to the gateways. Understand?"

Selene nodded.

Vanthee withdrew a long piece of wood looped through her belt, and with a flick of her wrist, it ignited, casting a warm glow on her face. Selene realized it was her torch. "Let's go."

Selene turned to Empusa, who was still staring at her with awe. "Thank you for your help, Empusa."

"It was my pleasure, vampire killer," Empusa said, raising her cane in a mock salute. "Farewell, and dark blessings!"

CHAPTER 33

Selene estimated they had walked at least a mile past streams and barren fields toward a looming range of black mountains before Vanthee finally came to a halt. Far behind them, the palace stood like a dark specter, its jagged spires slicing into the red sky.

In front of them, the land dropped off sharply, revealing a vast, desolate basin nestled between the mountains. At its center, three enormous rock domes jutted up from the earth, perfectly arranged in a triangle. Each dome emitted a different glow. The largest radiated a piercing, otherworldly white light; the second shimmered with a serene blue haze, and the third pulsed ominously with a deep red.

"Follow me," Vanthee said irritably and began her descent down a treacherous staircase carved into the cliffside. The stone steps were narrow from age, worn smooth by time.

"What is this place?" Selene asked, trailing behind her carefully. She wore a long velvet gown with bell sleeves, and though she was deliberate with her footing, she nearly slipped off more than once. Ruth sweetly reached out to steady her elbow, but her hand passed right through.

"Spirit Veil Valley."

"What are those domes?"

"Those are the thresholds," Vanthee replied as though Selene had just asked something painfully obvious. "The white one leads from the living realm into the Underworld, the blue goes to the Afterworld, and the red leads to the Sanctum of Agonizing Rectitude."

By the time they reached the bottom, Selene was breathing hard, her skin damp with sweat. Then Vanthee startled her by pressing a hand to her sternum and pushing her back against the mountainside.

Vanthee's red eyes locked onto hers. "It's nearly time for the souls to arrive. You have to stay right here. Got it? No matter what you see or hear, do not move from this spot."

Selene nodded. Her pulse quickened in anticipation.

"We don't have much time." Vanthee added, then she pointed to the dome glowing with the blue light. "Tell Ruth that's where I'll take her."

Selene looked at the dome then up at the spirit hovering behind her. "Ruth, it's time for you to go. You need to follow Vanthee to the blue light over there. Then you'll be home."

Honest to goodness?

"Yes. You can do it," Selene urged gently..

Ruth pressed her hands together and bowed.

Thank you, miss.

Vanthee made a beckoning gesture, and Ruth floated behind her.

With each step toward the Afterworld threshold, Selene watched the fear etched into Ruth's ghostly form melt into relief. Her shoulders relaxed and her haunted eyes softened with a quiet acceptance.

When they reached the entrance, Ruth paused. She turned back toward Selene and lifted a hand in salute. The grateful look on her face brought a lump to Selene's throat.

Vanthee then raised her tattooed arm and swept it in an arc over Ruth's chest. With a sudden whoosh of unseen power, Ruth was pulled forward. The blue dome's light embraced her instantly, wrapping around her until her figure dissolved into the brilliance. Selene squinted through the glow, watching its hue shift from deep sapphire to sky-blue.

And then Ruth was gone.

At peace.

Selene sighed gratefully. The sense of accomplishment that swelled in her chest was unlike anything she had ever known. To witness something so beautiful—and to have played a small role in making it happen—felt like a profound privilege. Tears welled in her eyes, the moment forever etching itself into her memory until Vanthee's voice cut through.

"All right, flesh-bag, I'll be back soon. Don't do anything stupid!"

Selene laughed through her tears at Vanthee's bluntness. She lifted a hand in a small wave, watching as the demoness disappeared into the large white dome, her torch flickered until it was swallowed by darkness.

Wiping away her happy tears, Selene glanced around the valley and shivered. There was a strange energy to this place. The air was still, but beneath her feet pulsed a low hum, almost too deep to hear, but impossible to ignore. Overhead, the sky churned with bruised purple and gray, hinting at a storm that would never come.

It felt like a place not meant for mortal understanding.

She stared at the dome Ruth had vanished into, still struggling to grasp the enormity of what she was seeing. It was almost too much to comprehend, being privy to the place where souls went after death. The soft, shimmering light emanating from the blue dome filled her with a sense of calm and made her feel hopeful. Serene.

She looked over at the white dome, waiting for an emotion to stir, but nothing came. Only curiosity about where it led.

But when she turned her focus to the red-lit dome? That hit different.

Staring into the dome that led to the Sanctum consumed her with a thick, creeping dread. Suddenly, every regret she'd ever had came rushing back. Every shameful deed, cruel thought, and mistake she wished she could undo resurfaced. They tumbled through her, growing louder, heavier—like a snowball gathering mass as it rolled downhill—until all she could feel was shame.

Thankfully, the sound of voices and approaching footsteps from the white dome pulled her gaze away. Moments later, Vanthee emerged, trailed by an enormous crowd of spirits drifting silently in her wake.

They moved in unified procession, their translucent forms flickering. Vanthee led them to the center of the triangle formed by the domes, where she held her torch high, casting a warm light that cut through the eerie twilight around them.

One by one, each spirit approached her, as if instinctively understanding that their final journey would soon be determined. Vanthee placed a hand over each spirit's heart, then nudged them toward either the gate with the blue light or the gate with the red light. Her movements were steady and practiced, as though she'd performed this ritual countless times.

As the spirits crossed their designated thresholds, each gate reacted differently: the blue light of the Afterworld embraced its travelers, growing brighter as they dissolved within it, while the red light leading to the Sanctum flickered and flared, swallowing its chosen ones in an angry flash.

It all happened quickly. Selene estimated that Vanthee directed thousands of souls through in just a few minutes. And they weren't all human. She saw many Aurelians, three giants, several dwarves, and a handful of faeries. Most went to the Afterworld, but the ones bound for the Sanctum received an extra hard shove from Vanthee.

A few souls drifted away from the herd, looking lost and unmoored. They drifted around the valley, further and further from Vanthee, until like moths to a flame, they glided toward the palace.

Selene watched the whole process with awe. Knowing she was the only human to witness such a sight left her deeply humbled. Every person she had ever lost had come through the Underworld.

Both sets of grandparents. A co-worker with cancer. A friend who died in a car wreck.

All of them had been guided by Vanthee.

After the seemingly endless line of souls crossed over, Selene assumed the ritual was finished. But then she saw a final figure stumble out of the gateway—a human boy, perhaps no older than six. He wore a hospital gown that swayed around his ghostly frame. Unlike the other spirits, whose faces held a serene acceptance, this child's face was streaked with tears.

Selene watched as Vanthee approached him slowly, moving with an unexpected gentleness. She knelt down to his level and extended her torch toward him. With a subtle wave of her hand, the flame shifted, transforming from fiery orange to a soft flicker of pink, blue, and green. The colors danced like a quiet rainbow in the dim light, and the boy's tearful expression softened. His mouth curved into a tentative smile.

Vanthee then extended her forearm, and a snake's head rose from the tattoo on her skin. It observed the boy curiously, tilting its head like a puppy. When the boy reached toward it, Selene held her breath, half-expecting the snake to strike, but instead, it arched with pleasure as the boy stroked its scaly skin. He began to giggle.

Once the snake finally retreated beneath her skin and the boy's tears had dried, Vanthee pointed toward the gateway to the After-world. The boy nodded. Together, they walked toward the shim-mering threshold. As he stepped closer, his expression shifted—from fear to pure, radiant joy—and the sight made tears stream down Selene's cheeks.

Vanthee blew him a kiss. He beamed, then stepped forward into the embrace of the blue light.

And he was gone.

After watching a few moments to ensure the boy had fully disap-peared, Vanthee returned to the white gateway, presumably to check for any other stragglers. Finding none, she blew on her torch to extinguish it, looped it back into her belt, then turned toward Selene and frowned. "What are you crying about?"

"What you do... it's beautiful," Selene said, wiping her eyes.

Vanthee seemed disarmed by her words. "I take my job very seriously."

"I can tell. And you do this every day?"

"People die every day."

"Yes, you're right," Selene said, still sniffling. "How do you know which gateway to send them to?"

Vanthee held out her tattoo. "The snakes tell me. They determine who deserves punishment and who can pass."

"What deserves punishment?"

"Why don't you ask your Vengeance demon mate?" Vanthee shot back. When Selene didn't react, she continued. "Punishable acts are murder, cruelty, rape, assault, theft, fraud... anything that violates someone else's trust or safety."

Vanthee began climbing the stairs out of the valley, and Selene followed. "The snakes just tell me who deserves punishment. The demons in the Sanctum decide how much to deliver."

"I can see why some of the souls got past you," Selene said quietly. "It's so easy for them to drift away."

"Thanks for the reminder," Vanthee snapped.

"Maybe I could help—"

"Maybe you could shut up," Vanthee cut in quickly.

Selene stepped carefully over a broken stair. "I didn't mean for it to sound like criticism. No one could herd that many souls. You're doing the best anyone could. Probably better."

"Yeah, right."

"No, I mean it. Truly, I'm blown away by what you do. You probably have the most important job here."

Vanthee stopped walking abruptly. "Stop. Just stop what you're doing."

Selene blinked in surprise. "What am I doing?"

"You're trying to get on my good side with all your flattery and *empathy.* I don't need it."

"I really wasn't."

"Sure seemed like it."

"Don't worry, I know you can't stand me," Selene replied with a chuckle.

"It's not that I can't stand you." Vanthee kicked a loose pebble off the step. "It's that… "

When she didn't continue, Selene gently probed, "What?"

Vanthee's eyes snapped to hers, hot with accusation. "You took something from me."

"Me? I've never taken anything from you."

"Yes, you did!" Vanthee stared at her for a beat, then her words came in a torrent of anger. "You don't know how many nights I used to dream about the lost prince returning to the Underworld. After my father promised me to Drath, I could only think of one way to escape. There was only one path that would free me from the betrothal—if I was the lost prince's fated mate."

She rubbed her palm over her snake tattoo in a soothing gesture. "And then you took that from me." Her voice cracked with emotion.

"I… " Selene's words faltered. "I didn't know."

"When you came with him from Aurelia, I tried to convince myself my dream wasn't dead. At first, I thought—there's no way you could be his fated mate. But when I found out you can wield the shadows, that hope crumbled. Still, I told myself I might have a chance. Maybe as his second wife or mistress. Maybe I could win him over, or at least prove I was a worthy match. I even tried to seduce him—"

"Wait, you did what?" Selene gasped.

"I tried to seduce him but it was a complete disaster, okay?"

A small flicker of satisfaction warmed Selene knowing that Sam's love for her had withstood even a demoness's attempt at seduction. But she didn't dare let it show.

Vanthee was quiet for a moment, then sniffed bitterly. "He really loves you. And he wants nothing to do with me."

"Do you truly have to marry Drath?"

"I don't know. Probably. He called it off after I tried to murder him, but lately he's been asking about me. I don't know what sort of deal he and my father have now."

A single tear tracked down her cheek. Then she turned and continued up the stairs.

Selene shuddered. There were few things she could imagine worse than being Drath's wife. They resumed their slow ascent, the silence broken only by Vanthee's quiet hiccups as she tried to stifle her tears.

When they reached the top, Selene felt as though she should say something, but didn't know what. Finally, she settled on, "Vanthee, I'm sorry that Sam couldn't give you what you wanted. Is there anything he or I could do to help you?"

"Still trying to get on my good side," Vanthee said bitterly, wiping at her eyes with the back of her hand.

"No—"

"Here's what you can do. Just let me be miserable in peace."

CHAPTER 34

Sam was with Borias outside the Sanctum, discussing a soul who had damaged one of the judgment doors in an escape attempt, when the sound of heavy footsteps interrupted them. He turned to see Drath approach. A bandage was wound around his head, and he wore an unsettling grin.

Sam looked away, hoping Drath was merely passing by, but then he stumbled toward them. Borias's thick arm shot out, stopping Drath from colliding with Sam.

"Watch where you're walking," Borias growled.

"A thousand apologies," Drath drawled, pointing at the ground. "I nearly tripped on this loose cobblestone."

Sam glared at him but didn't respond.

"Pay attention next time," Borias said.

"I will," Drath replied, then took a step closer to Sam. "However, someone should do something about the decay that has beset this realm, don't you think?"

Drath looked expectantly between Sam and Borias. When neither responded, he crossed his multiple arms and added, "It wasn't always like this, was it Borias?"

"No," Borias said coolly. "But I am not so fragile that it bothers me."

Drath huffed out a rusty laugh. "It's not luxury and comfort I seek, but discipline. If a ruler cannot maintain appropriate standards —if he lets things as simple as a broken road slide—there should be consequences."

He turned his painted face to Sam, giving him a meaningful look that instantly put him on alert. "What is your meaning?" Sam asked.

Drath used the heel of his foot to realign the loose cobblestone. "I mean that I would like to see the Underworld commanded by someone with true power and ambition." He locked eyes with Sam and licked his lips. "Someone more ruthless than your father."

Borias seized Drath's cloak and yanked him forward, their faces inches apart. "How dare you insult my king! Especially in front of Prince Samael."

"I was only stating facts," Drath spat. "When the next trial takes place, I intend to rise above the rest. To secure my place. If our great and powerful king wants a champion, then let it be me."

Drath squirmed out of Borias's grip and then turned his sunken eyes back to Sam. "It will be me."

The unspoken meaning of his words made Sam's blood run cold. *He knows the true purpose of the trials.*

"Why are you bothering us?" Borias asked. "Go rant and rave somewhere else."

Drath's mouth stretched into a grimace. "When I am *champion*, this realm will brim with horror as it's never known. All the dead will be punished, perhaps for eternity. Our lakes of fire shall churn with writhing flesh, our abyssal pits will echo with endless screams, and the eternal flames will consume all they caress."

"Whoa, I think you need to calm down," Borias said.

Drath let out a hissing sound. "How can I remain composed when so much is at stake?"

"They're only games," Borias replied.

"Games that I am meant to win!" Drath said. "For I will—"

"Your head wound is starting to bleed again," Sam interrupted, gesturing at the red stain seeping through Drath's bandage.

The unexpectedness of Sam's observation made Drath falter. Cautiously, he raised one limb to the back of his head.

"Oof, looks painful," Borias added.

"It must be time to change the dressing," Drath said, backing away. He seemed unnerved by this accidental display of vulnerability.

"Unless you'd like us to make the whole bandage red," Borias said, flashing a crooked grin.

"He's right. You'd better go take care of that," Sam said. With a rough push on Drath's back, he sent the demon moving in the opposite direction. "I'll see you at the next trial."

Drath seemed confused for a moment, then pressed a limb to his oozing gash and began to shuffle away. "Yes. Yes, you will."

Borias waited until Drath was out of sight before saying, "His arrogance is loathsome. I agree that some things that could be improved here, but the last thing we need is more horror."

"What did he mean when he said it wasn't always like this?"

Borias leaned against a nearby column and shrugged. "I'm nearly five hundred years old and this is the worst condition I've ever seen the Underworld in."

"What do you believe is the reason?"

Borias glanced at Sam hesitantly. "Uh... that's a tough question."

"You may speak freely." When Borias continued to look uneasy Sam added, "Please, I'd like to hear your thoughts."

Borias scrubbed a hand over his wide jaw. "Your father has reigned a long, long time. Sometimes I wonder... well, perhaps it's a foolish idea... but maybe if someone new, someone fresh, could take some of the burden of leadership off him, things could improve."

The relevance of his words settled like lead in Sam's gut. He didn't respond for a moment, then said, "What would you like to see changed?"

"So much," Borias said. "The very bones of our realm need

tending to—the roads, bridges, caves, and towers. Everything is falling apart."

Sam nodded, which encouraged Borias to continue. "In a way I agree with Drath that there's a lack of discipline. I don't like the way other demons are free to act out their most depraved urges. There used to be more order."

Just then, a lone spirit drifted past them. It was an old man, barefoot and dressed in a bathrobe, clutching his heart.

Borias pointed up at him. "And that," he said. "We never used to see innocent souls trapped here. It's not right. They should be at rest."

Sam took in the spirit's lost expression and grief stirred in him. He realized he had been willfully blind to the Underworld's growing disorder. He had convinced himself it had always been this way, blaming his fading memories for any sense of change. But hearing Drath and Borias echo his observations was sobering.

For the first time since his parents had told him of the Dark Sovereign, Sam began to consider what would happen if he accepted the role. He had always resisted the idea of rulership. Having absolute power over others held no pull for him, and he abhorred pageantry. Yet he had spent little time considering the good he could bring about as king. The positive changes he could command. The many wrongs he could right.

Borias let out a weary sigh. "It's not my place to question how Asmodeus rules, but sometimes I wish... "

"What?" Sam urged.

"I want a king who understands he's meant to *serve* the realm. Not simply exist within it," Borias said. He turned away before Sam could respond, muttering, "I need to fix that door," as he walked off, leaving Sam alone with the weight of his thoughts.

When Sam finished delivering vengeance for the day, he took a long walk around the weedy grounds outside the palace. It was quiet there, and any imps his parents might send to summon him would have a harder time tracking him down. A handful of scavenger vultures pecking at the remains of a rat peered at him but didn't approach.

He watched a silk weaver spider skitter across the ground and let his mind wander. How would he change the Underworld if he were in charge? First, he would reestablish proper law and order. Perhaps a robust royal guard to patrol the realm and ensure demons stayed within their limits of behavior.

Then he would repair the infrastructure. Address the poor roads, eliminate the creeping rot, and repair or replace the many crumbling buildings.

He would make sure the imps and other beasts were treated humanely. Selene's beloved hellhounds would receive new, clean kennels and a spacious area for them to train. In fact, he would build Selene an entirely new library so she no longer had to toil in the decrepit one. As the Underworld's beloved queen, she could have anything she wished—

He abruptly stopped in his tracks.

If he were to stay as the Dark Sovereign, Selene would have to become a demon. She would have to abandon her humanity and mold herself into something else entirely. Permanently change herself in response to a decision he made about both of their lives.

The idea made him feel nauseous.

He snapped off a thorny branch from a nearby shrub as he put more distance between himself and the palace. The transformation process his mother described had been harrowing. The changes Selene's body could face included sprouting horns, growing fangs, and losing the soft curves Sam loved—replaced by sharp, unforgiving angles. Even if Selene was agreeable to becoming a demon, what if she hated the person she became?

During his time in Aurelia with Zaybris's former colleague,

Waldron, the vampire had confided in Sam how much he despised his new form. Turned against his will, Waldron found it utterly torturous to adapt to hungers and urges that violated his deepest morals. Though he longed for an end to his suffering, that release was denied to him. For Waldron could not leave the world in the same form in which he had entered it.

The truth was that Selene would never be happy here. This realm wasn't meant for someone like her; it was too steeped in darkness and death.

Yet her uncanny ability to speak with the dead gave him pause. It made him wonder if that gift was proof she belonged here more than she knew. As his mate, perhaps she possessed hidden protections that could soften the passage from mortality to demonhood. If the power of their bond could shield her from the worst of the change, she might have a gentler descent into the dark.

It was a notion not easily dismissed.

CHAPTER 35

The week after sending Ruth home, Selene found herself squeezed between Queen Thema and Empusa on a bench fashioned from scaffolding along the River of Hatred. Only an hour earlier, she and Sam had been rudely awakened by an imp who informed them that the next trial would take place at the river...

Immediately.

A few days ago, Queen Thema had announced that she was ready to return to Aurelia, and apparently King Asmodeus decided that his sister-in-law deserved a proper send-off. So, in true royal fashion, that meant spectacle. Why not knock out one of the trials at the same time?

Selene glanced around uneasily at the swarm of demons clinging to the scaffolding. The entire structure looked as though it had been slapped together hours ago—rickety, swaying, and packed with creatures eager for chaos. Some demons sat shoulder to shoulder on narrow planks; others dangled by their tails or clawed feet.

Although a channel of the River of Hatred ran past the palace, they were gathered in a part of the Underworld where Selene had never ventured into before. Having grown up near the Cumberland

River—a body of water about a mile wide that wound through Nash-ville—she had expected the trial would take place near something similar. But this was no ordinary river. The widest part of the River of Hatred was so vast she could only see the far shore if she strained her eyes. The waters were also heavily polluted with discarded metal, torn netting, and other debris.

Empusa, seated to Selene's right, poked a finger beneath her eye patch to scratch an itch. Selene had come to realize that all demons had their own peculiar scents, but Empusa's was perhaps the strangest yet—an odd mix of patchouli, rusted metal, and the faintest trace of bourbon. When she let out a thunderous burp, Queen Thema, sitting on Selene's left, pinched her nose in disgust.

"Oh, do pardon me, Aurelian queen," Empusa chirped in a high-pitched voice, thick with mockery.

Queen Thema gave her a withering look. "I will certainly not miss the lack of *manners* in this realm."

"Empusa," Selene asked, tucking back the strands of hair that kept blowing in her eyes, "do you know what the king wants the competitors to do for this trial?"

"Traverse the river, I imagine."

"You mean like swim?"

Empusa chuckled darkly. "Only if they want to become a part of it. The waters are poisonous. If anyone falls in… " Empusa snapped her fingers. "Gone! Dissolved into nothing."

"They die?"

"Yes. But also no. Their body perishes, but their spirit becomes part of the river. If you look closely at the currents, you can see the faces of those it has claimed.

Selene's throat tightened. She watched the competitors pacing along the riverbank, noting how carefully they avoided even getting their feet wet. Sam stood apart from the rest, arms crossed, his gaze locked on the river.

"How are they supposed to cross it, then?"

Empusa gave her an exaggerated wink. "That's the challenge! See that demon with the lesions on his skin? That's who I'm cheering for."

Selene spotted a short demon below them with tiny holes scattered across his body like coral. "Oh?"

"My nephew. He's a demon of Mishap. He doesn't have much chance at outshining your mate, of course, but competition builds character!"

"Uh... yes."

"No one is strong enough to beat our Samael, are they, Selene?" Queen Thema interjected.

Selene smiled weakly, remembering how Queen Thema still didn't know the true purpose of the trials.

The three of them watched as Ghar performed his duties as master of ceremonies, crossing off the names of competitors on a parchment scroll while new arrivals streamed in. The last one to arrive was Drath, looking like the Grim Reaper in a long black cloak, rubbing his six arms together.

When all thirty contenders had gathered, Asmodeus began to climb up one of the scaffolds. It was a windy day, and Selene held her breath as the structure swayed under his weight.

She was surprised by how sluggish the king's movements were. Deliberate, heavy. Was his physical form decaying along with his power? Below, she caught a flicker of concern on Sam's face and knew he had noticed it, too.

Once Asmodeus was in sight of all the spectators, he addressed them with excitement. "Welcome, everyone! The last trial tested the strength and ferocity of our competitors. This trial will determine which among them is cunning, but also favored. The stakes are much higher, for if you fail this test, you'll become one with the river."

A cheer rose from the crowd. Empusa nudged Selene excitedly, which only made Selene's stomach churn harder. Queen Thema clapped delicately.

"Turn your gaze toward the horizon. In the distance, you can see the *Purgatory* preparing to dock," Asmodeus said.

Selene followed the others' demons' gaze, squinting to see through the mist that hung in the air. After a few moments she made out a massive, dark shape moving through the water. A sudden gust tore the mist apart, unveiling a sailing vessel like nothing she had ever imagined.

It was a monstrous fusion of Viking longship and antique steamboat, as long as a river barge and towering ten stories high. A wooden figurehead of a hooded ferryman jutted from the prow, its outstretched hand turned upward as if demanding payment.

"What is that?" Selene whispered.

"The great ship *Purgatory!*" Empusa said. "Any demon who spends time outside the Underworld must purify themselves by sailing home on the *Purgatory*. There, they can spend time in reflection, rid themselves of any mortal attachments, and catch up on the news of the realm."

Selene could see demons hanging off the ship, hooting and waving to the crowd. Misty white shapes darted around the black sails and smokestacks frantically. "Are there souls aboard as well?"

Empusa's laugh wheezed like a lifelong smoker. "Oh, yes. Servitude can be an effective punishment."

Selene was about to ask what she meant, but Asmodeus's voice stopped her.

"I have placed ten coins inside the ferryman's hand. Those who can cross the river to retrieve them will advance to the next round. Those who fail? Well, they will truly understand the river's hatred. May the first contender step forward!"

The moment the trial began, Selene wished she had just stayed in their chambers like Sam had once suggested. Instead of having the competitors try to reach the *Purgatory* all at once, the king had them each compete individually. It was more entertaining for the demons, but gut-wrenching for anyone with human sensibilities to watch.

The first demon, clearly not the brightest, thought he could swim across the river. He strutted forward smugly draped head to toe in spider webbing, seemingly certain it would serve as armor. Or maybe floatation?

With a triumphant battle whoop, he leapt into the River of Hatred. Just as Selene—and probably everyone else—had suspected, the spider webbing offered no protection. His cry dissolved into a gurgling silence the instant he hit the water. A few bubbles rose.

Then nothing.

The second competitor, also brimming with misplaced confidence, believed he could launch himself across the river by having a few friends hurl him like a javelin.

Four demons each grabbed one of his limbs. Then the crowd went quiet as the demon counted down.

"Three! Two! One!"

With a grunting heave, his friends hurled him skyward. He soared about ten feet before plummeting into the river with a spectacular splash. His scream was cut off mid-note, swallowed whole by the water.

And so it continued.

For what felt like hours, Selene watched demon after demon try and fail to cross the river. Some attempted to ride makeshift rafts of bones or barrels, others tried clumsy magick or charms to carry them across. One attempted to part the river like Moses, only for it to swallow him whole when he set foot on the exposed riverbed.

Eventually, a demon of Vanity became the first to succeed. Small and wiry—probably eighty pounds soaking wet—he had bribed a group of imps to fly him across. He snatched the coin from the ferryman's wooden hand with such exaggerated flourish that he immediately fumbled it, drawing a collective gasp from the crowd. But with a swift recovery, he caught it midair, making him one of the winners.

Another demon succeeded by managing to float across on a waterlogged armchair. A third demon, clad in leather armor and a steel helmet etched with a flame, used his wings to fly across the river and back. Though simple, it was an impressive feat, considering most winged demons were too weak to cover such a distance or were immediately thrown off course by the wind.

When it was Drath's turn, Selene cheered alongside the other sadistic demons that he would fail miserably—and fatally. But he successfully crossed the river on enormous iron stilts, sealing his place among the handful of victors. After him, another demon failed to cross, stumbling over a levitation incantation. The next one, however, recited it correctly and made it across.

The longer the trial dragged on, the more Selene's distress grew. The absurdity of it all—the pointless deaths, the howling laughter at each failure—made her hands curl into fists. What was supposed to be a contest of wits and competence had become cruelty parading as destiny.

A few scaffolding rows down, she saw Borias spring from his seat in a burst of anger. He was shaking his head with what looked like disgust. Selene watched him leave, grateful that she might not be the only one struggling with this spectacle.

"I hate this," Selene muttered under her breath.

A nearby demon with double rows of teeth like a shark turned to hiss at her, but when Selene quickly slammed down the pyramid of her mind, he backed off.

Then a thought came to her suddenly:

We should go back to Aurelia early.

She was surprised by the idea, but she didn't immediately dismiss it. If she wanted to, she could walk up to Sam right now, take his hand, and transport them back to Snowmelt. No more trials. No more worrying. Whoever became the Dark Sovereign wouldn't be their problem anymore.

But Sam would never forgive her. That was one of the things she loved about him, his relentless sense of honor. Running away from something hard wasn't in his nature. She might find relief in the moment, but for him, it would be a deep betrayal.

Then if I can't take him home, I have to get him out of the trials.

Determination burned in her chest. Tomorrow, she was going to find something—anything—to give them a clue about who the next Dark Sovereign should be. She would study and read until her eyes crossed. Turn the entire library inside out and upside down if she had to. And if the answer wasn't there? She'd ransack the Hall of Demonic Canon, interrogate every elder demon she could find, and search every ancient building in the Underworld until she did.

Because this was going to be the last trial Sam ever faced.

CHAPTER 36

Sam's plans were going all wrong.

He paced the riverbank, boots crunching against the loose rocks, thinking through everything that had led him to this moment and wondering how he could salvage it.

Was that even possible?

Since the Infernal Combat Trial had been blood-soaked chaos, Sam assumed the next trial would be more nuanced. A challenge that tested cunning, leadership, or arcane aptitude. Instead, the council had decided on a trial where the consequence for failing was essentially death. With every fallen contender, the weight on Sam's shoulders grew heavier. Because the fewer who remained, the more his parents would insist he was meant to rule.

It no longer felt like a trial, but a culling.

Sam could feel Drath's eyes on him as he paced, but he refused to acknowledge the demon's presence. Drath's method for crossing the river had been clever, but not the kind of clever that would impress his parents. While Drath apparently knew how the trials were tied to the crown, he likely didn't know the outcome was ultimately irrelevant. The king and queen would make the final decision themselves.

Thus far, Sam's attempt to recommend a worthy candidate had failed entirely.

He was so deep in thought that he barely noticed a young demon of Mishap approach. "Excuse me, Your Highness."

"Yes?" Sam said absently.

"M-my name is Chort. I was wondering if I could shake your hand." His high-pitched voice ended with an upward inflection.

Sam looked down at the small, bright-eyed demon. "For what reason?"

"For luck." Chort said sheepishly. "You see, it's my turn next. And maybe some of your great power will rub off on me."

Sam stuck out his hand, and Chort shook it vigorously. The demon's skin was covered in small holes, but his palm was dry.

"Dark blessings to you, Chort."

He beamed up at Sam. "Oh, thank you, sir. Thank you!"

A second later, Ghar called Chort's name. The demon skipped away toward the river enthusiastically, leaving Sam to resume his pacing.

Sam would be the last competitor after Chort and he hadn't yet devised a plan to retrieve the coin himself. In truth, he was considering forfeiting his place in the trials altogether so they would no longer continue. His parents would be furious, possibly even humiliated, but maybe stepping aside would create space for the right ruler to emerge.

"And how do you plan to cross the river?" Ghar asked.

"Well, as my aunt Empusa always says: 'The frost remembers what the flame forgets.' So I'm going to try to freeze the river."

"Brilliant boy!" Empusa shouted from the crowd.

Sam glanced up and spotted Empusa seated beside Selene. His mate looked decidedly anxious, which only strengthened his temptation to forfeit.

"Proceed, then," Ghar said.

Sam watched as Chort cautiously approached the river, stopping just short of the water's edge and crouching low. One by one, the small orifices across his skin opened and closed like tiny, gasping mouths. It was an unpleasant sight that was then made worse as water began to drip from each hole, pooling at his feet.

With a look of intense focus, Chort extended a finger and touched the growing puddle. Instantly, a jagged sliver of ice shot from it like a lightning bolt, zig-zagging across the river's surface. It slowed slightly until more liquid seeped from Chort's pores, feeding the puddle and allowing the ice to surge forward again.

"Damnation and ruin!" Empusa shouted. "That's a clever trick."

The crowd cheered. Despite the turmoil Sam was feeling about the trial, a small smile tugged at his lips as Chort took his first step onto the icy path he'd carved.

Slowly and carefully, pausing now and then to steady himself, Chort inched his way toward the *Purgatory.* The ice was slippery and Chort's foot nearly skidded into the water a few times. But each time he righted himself. A hush fell over the crowd the closer he came to the looming ship.

After several tense minutes, he finally reached his destination. He stood beneath the towering wooden ferryman, the prized coin nearly within his grasp. Bending his knees, Chort sprang into the air. One hand seized the ferryman's outstretched arm; the other stretched desperately toward the waiting palm above. The crowd burst into wild cheers.

But the celebration was short-lived.

As Chort hung midair, reaching for the coin, the icy trail he had forged began to melt—dissolving into the dark river below until there was nothing between his small, dangling body and the churning waters beneath.

"No!" Empusa cried. There were gasps from some demons in the crowd, while others hooted with bloodthirsty glee.

Panic overtook Chort's face as he dangled precariously by one arm. The cleverness of his approach, contrasted with the senselessness of his impending death, sent a surge of righteous anger coursing through Sam.

I must stop this.

An image of the hydra he had created flashed through his mind. But this time, he resolved not to be a victim of his own uncontrollable power. This time, he would *command* it.

He summoned the shadows to him. With clear intent, he ordered them to form a long, thick rope. They obeyed instantly, swirling together with a strange eagerness, as if thrilled to finally be given a purpose. The black, mist-like rope coiled around Sam briefly, then shot through the air toward Chort.

The moment the rope reached him, it wound around the little demon's body. Chort wiggled a bit, as though testing the rope's fortitude, then squeezed his eyes shut. Slowly, he peeled his fingers away from the ferryman's arm, one by one. The moment he realized he remained suspended in the air, Chort's eyes flew open with astonishment. He beamed at Sam.

The shadow rope then snaked upward with Chort in tow. It hovered him above the ferryman's hand, just long enough for Chort to reach down and retrieve his coin.

When Chort pumped his fist in the air victoriously, Sam let out the breath he'd been holding. At his mental command, the rope sailed through the air toward the shore. Gently but efficiently, Chort was deposited on dry land, right at Sam's feet.

The crowd erupted into cheers, and without hesitation, Chort threw his arms around Sam's waist in a hug. Sam patted his back awkwardly until Chort stepped away to bask in the crowd's celebration.

Empusa whooped so loudly from her place in the stands, that Sam looked up. But when he glimpsed his parents, disapproval was written across their faces. Perhaps they objected to him aiding another contender?

Ghar's voice rose above the fading cheers. "Another victor— young Chort!"

The crowd erupted again, even those demons who had been hungering for Chort's death mere moments before. Ghar raised his arms to quiet them, and gradually, the noise faded into an expectant hush.

"And now," he announced, "our final contender of the day, Prince Samael."

Sam squared his shoulders. He could do it again—use the shadows to retrieve the coin with ease. But seconds ago, he had made the decision to step away from the trials, hoping his withdrawal might bring the games to an end.

He opened his mouth to speak, to make it final.

But before a word could leave his lips, Chort strode forward and shouted, "No!"

With bold confidence, he seized Sam's hand and pressed a coin—identical to the one he had claimed for himself—into his palm.

"The prince *has* retrieved the coin," Chort declared. "I secured his, as well as mine."

Ghar's mouth hung open in surprise.

Chort gazed up at Sam. "You have my gratitude, sir."

Sam mumbled, "And mine," then looked toward King Asmodeus, who was glowering from his high seat, silent and stone-faced.

"Well... this is highly irregular," Ghar said, his brow furrowing in thought. After a brief pause, he continued, "But the rules state the contender must retrieve the coin—they don't prohibit having a proxy do it for him."

He motioned for the other victorious competitors to gather around him. Once they had assembled in a line, Ghar turned to the crowd and declared, "Demons of the Underworld, behold the victors of the River of Hated Trial!" Several of the contenders waved, including Drath, whose body rippled with pleasure like a caterpillar. "Our next and final trial to find the king's champion will occur in five days."

Sam closed his eyes briefly, grateful that the end of this farce would be soon. He opened them to look at the polluted river, the savage spectators, and the way his father swayed with fatigue in his seat. He had come this far in his quest to save the Underworld—he might as well see it to its completion.

CHAPTER 37

Selene didn't know if there were taverns in the Underworld, but if there were, they'd be packed tonight. She carefully climbed down the scaffolding with the other trial spectators, the air buzzing like downtown Nashville after a Titans football win. Sam had been swept away with the other winners, so she started the walk back to the palace alone.

She was nearly at their chamber door when a gentle tap on her shoulder made her turn.

It was Queen Thema.

"Asmodeus is taking me to Gaia in a few hours so I can go through one of my Aurelian portals," she said. "I wanted to say goodbye."

"Right. I nearly forgot." A pang of grief caught Selene off guard. She hadn't seen much of Thema during her visit, but knowing she was nearby had been reassuring. It was also nice to not be the only non-demon in the realm. Selene reached out to hug her tight.

"I'm going to miss you," Selene said against her shoulder. "Did you enjoy your visit?"

Thema pulled back. "I did, but... " Her words faded into a bitter-sweet smile.

"But what?"

"I miss the person my sister used to be. She is still herself in many ways, but Lamia has been hardened by demonhood. *Lilith* was more compassionate. Charitable."

Selene nodded, secretly grateful that it wasn't just her who found Lamia hard to deal with.

Thema waved a hand as if brushing the thought away. "No matter. It's still a comfort to know she's alive and happy. And with your help, we can keep visiting! When will you and Sam be coming home?"

"I'm not sure. Maybe in another month? Sam has... a few things to sort out here."

"Then I'll see you soon," Thema said. She patted Selene's cheek. "Goodbye."

The next morning, Selene woke up determined to find something to help Sam crown the Dark Sovereign. After Sam walked her to the kennels and left to do whatever he did all day, Selene took off running toward the library with Zetta at her side. If they only had five days before the next trial, she couldn't waste a second.

Once inside the library, Selene surveyed the space, strategizing where to start. Anything about the Dark Sovereign would be buried in the oldest texts, the kind of volumes that hadn't been touched in centuries. That's where she'd begin. She grabbed a precarious stack of crumbling books she'd been putting off dealing with for weeks. Balancing them against her chest, she made her way to a dusty corner table and began her search.

It was slow, tedious work. She took care not to damage the brittle, yellowed pages of each book she skimmed, though a few still crumbled into dust between her fingers. Most were written in Old English, filled with words she didn't recognize or using a dialect now lost to time. She had to guess at meanings, piecing together sentences like a crumbling puzzle.

Her heart jumped when she spotted a minor reference to Baphomet in a battered book about the Knights Templar, but it didn't give her any useful information. A little later, she thought she was onto something when she spotted a few cryptic sentences about the Thronefall Flame, until she realized it was a reference book about astronomy.

As she continued to pore through the old books, the musty scent of aging paper filled the air more than usual. Motes of dust floated through shafts of dim, slanted light filtering through the high, grimy windows.

She had been working for several hours when she leaned back to rub her eyes. She blinked up at the ceiling, then let her gaze fall to the rows of sagging shelves and piles of books on the floor. The hopeful optimism she'd entered the library with had turned into complete overwhelm.

She was starting to second-guess her hunch that something about the Dark Sovereign could be found here. Why hadn't she started with a more traditional place for storing records like the Halls of Demonic Canon or the Chapel of Mourning?

She blew out a breath. The thought of watching Sam compete in another pointless trial made her feel sick. Their plan had once struck her as inspired. Now, it just felt impossibly naïve.

She absently ran her fingers up and down the cord of the traveler's stone, reflecting on how life in this realm was nothing like she had expected. Or like Sam had hoped. She was friendless and lonely; Sam was burdened and overworked. She couldn't wait for the day when they could finally settle into a normal routine. She lingered in daydreams of planting a garden behind their house in Snowmelt and of Brunie patiently teaching her how to bake.

Then she sighed and chastised herself for wasting time.

Get back to work.

She pulled another old book toward her but then realized how dark the library had become. Half the hanging lights in the room didn't work, and the other half flickered terribly. She rummaged through a nearby crate where she'd collected all the half-melted candles that she found. Carefully, she placed them on the desk, nearly thirty in all. For a moment, her heart sank as she realized she had no way to light them. But a grunt from Zetta reminded her otherwise.

Grabbing what was left of a taper candle, Selene crossed the room to where Zetta was happily chewing on a book spine. She had somewhat successfully taught the dog the commands of *sit*, *stay*, and *come*, but they had never tried *speak*.

"Hey, girl," Selene said, ruffling Zetta's head.

Seeing Selene give her such close attention, Zetta shot to her feet, tail wagging eagerly.

Selene studied her for a moment and said, "Now, how am I going to get you to speak?"

"Woof!"

"Good girl!" Selene said, not sure if that was a coincidence or not. She held the candle toward Zetta's snout. "Can you do it again? Speak!"

Zetta tilted her head in confusion, her tongue lolling. Selene repeated the command a few more times, but Zetta only thumped her tail against the floor. Finally, Selene grabbed an old book spine and tossed it like a stick. Zetta bounded after it and dropped it eagerly at Selene's feet, tail wagging. As the hound let out a small, impatient bark, Selene thrust the candle near her mouth, repeating, "*Speak.*"

The wick flared to life, burning with a vivid, hypnotic blue flame.

"Yes!" Selene repeated the command and Zetta obeyed, exhaling another blue flame into the air that quickly evaporated.

"You learned a new trick!"

Smiling, Selene tossed the book spine again, sending it tumbling into a pile of old curtains for Zetta to root through.

Using the taper candle, Selene carefully lit the others. One by one, soft blue flames bloomed, casting an eerie glow across the library. She stepped back to admire the sight. It reminded her of the house three doors down from where she had grown up—the one strung only with blue twinkle lights every holiday season. Back then, the glow had turned her ordinary street into something magical. She let herself savor the memory for a moment longer before lifting her gaze from the desk.

And froze.

Nestled in a bookcase carved with curling lion's feet, a faint blue light shimmered behind a row of dusty volumes.

Selene moved closer, peering between the spines. One by one, she removed the books until only the bare shelf remained. Along the edges of the back panel, a faint outline of blue light pulsed subtly, as if breathing. Grabbing a candle, she brought the flame closer to illuminate the area.

In the bottom left corner, a tiny sigil was carved into the wood. When Selene moved the blue candle near, the sigil glowed softly. But when she blocked the light with her body, it vanished into invisibility.

She ran her hand over the back panel and pressed lightly. Nothing happened.

She pressed harder. Still nothing.

But when she pressed her thumb directly on the sigil, she felt a soft *click* behind the wood. A shiver of movement almost too slight to notice. Pulse racing, Selene pressed harder, and the panel shifted with a faint, grating sound. Holding her breath, she hooked her fingers into the narrow seam that appeared and slowly slid the panel aside.

Behind it, a hidden compartment had been carved deep into the stone wall. Dust poured from the opening, and the air that spilled out was thick with the scent of mildew and age. Nestled among layers of muck and cobwebs rested a thick, ancient book. Its leather cover was cracked and worn, the title barely legible beneath the grime: *The Sovereign's Reckoning.*

Selene gasped.

This wasn't just a clue.

This was the prophecy itself.

CHAPTER 38

Sam's eyes glazed over as he stood in the night-blooming garden, half-listening to a demon of Envy rant about his neighbor's gargoyle statues. From the corner of his eye, Sam spotted Zetta bounding toward him. The urgency in her stride snapped him to attention. Around the hellhound's neck fluttered a note, tied with a strip of green velvet—the same sash Selene had used to belt her dress that morning.

Sam excused himself from the demon's tirade and knelt beside Zetta. He fumbled with the knot, his fingers clumsy with sudden dread, and yanked the note free. It was hastily scrawled across a scrap of torn paper:

Come to the library right now —Selene

A tremor ran through Sam's limbs. Had something happened to her? Was she in danger? Without a second thought, he took off at a sprint toward the library. Zetta raced alongside him, her massive paws clicking against the ground.

When he burst through the library doors, Selene was sitting at a desk, surrounded by dozens of candles burning with eerie blue flames.

"What's wrong?" The words flew out before he could stop them.

"Nothing's wrong. Everything's right!" Her eyes shone with excitement. Then, seeing his expression, she winced. "Sorry, I didn't mean to make you worry. But you're not going to believe what I found. Come here."

He exhaled with relief and crossed the room to drag a chair beside her. As he sat, Selene closed the book she had been reading.

"I used the traveler's stone to scry and see where you were. Then I sent Zetta to find you," she explained, patting the hellhound's head. "I needed you to see this."

"What is it?" Sam asked, still catching his breath.

Selene turned fully to him, her excitement barely contained. "I came looking for information about the Dark Sovereign. Honestly, I didn't expect to find anything more than a footnote." She touched the crumbling book resting before her with careful fingers. "But then... I found this."

Sam looked down at the ancient tome. Letters had been carved into the cracked leather. When he read the faded title, the hairs on the back of his neck rose. "Is that..."

"It is," Selene whispered.

Eyes wide, he said, "I thought it had been destroyed."

"It was hidden," Selene said, quickly explaining how she had found the book. Sam listened intently, his fingers tracing the cracked leather binding, worn smooth by centuries of time. A rusted lock was embedded in the book's binding, fastening covers together.

"Have you looked inside?" he asked.

Selene nodded, her cheeks flushing with excitement. "Look."

When she held a candle near the lock, it popped open with a *click,* allowing access to its contents. She turned the yellowed pages with great care, the brittle parchment crackling softly beneath her fingers. Most were dense with hand-lettered script—looping, archaic characters inked in rust-red, their meanings lost to all but the most ancient scholars. Then she stopped, tapping a page with the tip of her finger.

A rough, black-and-white illustration filled the space. It showed an ancient king with the head of a goat, long curling horns that spiraled toward the sky, wings flaring from broad, human-like shoulders, and cloven hooves.

"The first Dark Sovereign," Selene murmured. "Baphomet. At least, the first recorded."

She flipped forward, more urgently now, but still careful with the fragile pages. She stopped before another portrait, this one rendered in rich paint. The colors were faded but still alive: blood-reds, obsidian blacks, and glints of gold. It showed a young king sitting on a throne, chin raised, authority carved into every sharp feature. A crown of spikes encircled his head.

Recognition made Sam gasp. "It's my father."

The edge of the portrait was uneven, jagged, as though it had once been torn free and then hastily reattached. The pages that followed were loose, crumbling at the edges, their contents written in slanted, archaic script. As Sam read it as best he could, he realized it was the prophecy that predicted Baphomet's fall, and Asmodeus' ascension.

> *Through fire and dusk, where shadows cling,*
> *A demon of Wrath shall rise as king.*
> *By Thronefall Flame, his fate is sworn,*
> *To claim the name of darkness reborn.*

"This is incredible," he said softly. He lingered over the portrait and prophecy, then glanced at the final pages of the book, finding them blank.

"Is that all?"

"Not quite," Selene said.

Carefully, she peeled back the inside edge of the leather binding on the back cover. Tucked within was a folded sheet of paper. Slowly, she pulled it free, holding it chest, shielding it from view.

"Are you ready?" she asked, eyes sparkling with mischief.

"Yes."

Selene laid the hidden page before him. It was another portrait, but it was unlike the others—this one was darker, more vivid. The edges were shadowed, as if scorched, and yet the image in the center was unmistakable.

Vanthee.

Sam blinked. "This... how can this be? She wasn't even born when this book was written."

Selene shrugged. "They don't call them prophecies for nothing."

He leaned in. There was no mistaking her—not with the long blonde hair, the sharp, curved horns, the red eyes. She held her torch in her left hand, its flame frozen mid-flicker. And winding around her right arm was the snake tattoo.

For a long moment, he said nothing.

"And just in case you had any doubt this is Vanthee... " Selene turned the portrait over. "Read this."

Long forgotten, cast away,
Her beacon stirs where lost souls stray.
Deep in the realm where spirits roam,
One lights the path to lead them home.

Between the worlds of land and shade,
Where restless echoes drift and fade,
Awakened now, her power reclaimed—
An enchantress born by Thronefall Flame.

Selene looked at Sam expectantly. "'Her beacon stirs where lost souls stray.' That's her. 'One lights the path to lead them home,'— that's one hundred percent Vanthee."

Sam rubbed his jaw, rereading the passage several times. "But she's not an enchantress."

"No, but who knows how long ago this was written? Maybe they called any woman with special powers an enchantress then."

Sam nodded absently. He watched the strange blue flame of the candles flicker and dance. Vanthee was certainly not who he would have chosen as Dark Sovereign. She had been manipulative, pushy, and disturbingly flirtatious. She had no leadership experience, seemed to have few allies, and lacked the poised grace most that queens carried. But, since the prophecy about his father hadn't been wrong, he had no reason to suspect this one was false.

"What are you thinking?" Selene asked, watching him.

"Vanthee is... an unexpected choice." He glanced at Selene then averted his eyes, weighing the merits of a confession. "I have something to share that may change your opinion of her. Recently, she made advances toward me."

Selene arched a brow. "Oh, I know."

He startled. "You do?"

"She told me."

"I didn't want to upset you, so I never mentioned it."

"It's fine, I wasn't worried. But she also told me her attempts failed miserably," Selene said with a smile that faded into seriousness. "She has an attitude and can be a pain in the neck, but she *does* care about the Underworld. And the dead. More than any other demon I've seen."

Selene paused to look down at the portrait. "She's not the worst Dark Sovereign I could think of. Has the Underworld ever been ruled by a queen?"

"Not to my knowledge," Sam said. "But maybe it's time it was."

The more he thought about it, the more the idea took root. Vanthee, for all her flaws, had something many demons lacked— empathy. He remembered the banquet and her fierce defense of the dead. He remembered how she had argued not for her own gain, but for those too weak to speak for themselves. He thought about how fierce she had been during the Infernal Combat Trial, and how she had eventually had left him alone after their confrontation in the Sanctum.

If they could find a way to put Vanthee on the throne, he and Selene could finally go home. His worries would be settled.

"This is an incredible find, my love," Sam said at last. Knowing he was never meant to be the Dark Sovereign eased a fear he hadn't realized weighed so heavily on him.

"Thank you. How do you think your parents will react?"

"Not well. But if this is true, they don't really have a choice, do they?" Sam crossed his arms, considering how to approach this issue. "Tomorrow, I'll speak with Vanthee."

"It's going to be a lot for her to take in."

"Yes, but since I don't fully trust her, I want to get a feel for whether she's amenable to ruling. I'd like to know if she would fight for the role without knowing she was destined for it."

"I like that plan."

He refolded the portrait and handed it back to Selene. "Even though I'm not the Dark Sovereign, I feel responsible for leaving the realm in good hands."

"Of course you do," Selene said, gazing at him in a way that sent a pleasant shiver through him.

"What does that mean?"

She laid her head on his shoulder. "It means I think I'm mated to the most honorable demon who ever existed."

CHAPTER 39

The next day, Sam sent an imp to summon Vanthee for a private meeting in the pomegranate groves. It was a secluded place where they wouldn't be disturbed. As he waited, he wandered among the trees, their twisted, gnarled branches reaching toward the orange-red sky like grasping hands. Only a few withered fruits still clung stubbornly to the limbs, their red skins shriveled and darkened to near black.

"What do you want?"

Vanthee's voice echoed through the trees, sharp and suspicious. Sam turned to find her standing a few paces away, arms crossed. The seductive look she'd worn the last time they were alone had been replaced by open hostility.

"Hello," he said. "Thank you for coming."

"You're welcome," Vanthee said coolly. "But can we make this quick? I'm quite busy."

"Certainly. Walk with me, will you?"

A gust of wind stirred the grove, rustling the few leaves that remained on the trees. Vanthee hesitated, then fell into step beside him, arms still crossed tight against her chest.

"I want to ask you a few questions. Is that all right?" Sam said.

"Ask away."

"Good. When you competed in the Infernal Combat Trial, what were you hoping to achieve?"

She didn't answer right away. He waited.

"This is just between us," he added. "I have no right to your secrets. I'm only trying to understand."

"I had an enemy among the competitors. I wanted to kill him," she said defiantly. Then, in a quieter tone, she muttered, "I stupidly thought I could impress you, as well."

"I see. But you mainly wanted to harm Drath."

"Harm him? I wanted him to meet his true death. Then my father's debt to him would be absolved, and I would be free." Her voice began to rise with passion. "I have thought of a thousand ways to break our engagement, but a sanctioned way to kill him was too good to pass up. I'm only sorry I didn't succeed."

Sam nodded with understanding. "What debt does your father owe to Drath?"

"It's complicated," Vanthee said flatly.

Her tone made it clear that further questions were unwelcome, and they walked in silence, their footsteps crushing brittle leaves and broken twigs.

"So you weren't trying to become the king's champion?" Sam asked at last.

"Not at that point."

He glanced at her, brows lifting. "And now?"

Vanthee shrugged wearily. "It would be nice. But it's unlikely. Since I already competed in the first trial, I entered the River of Hatred Trial too."

"You did? I didn't see you."

She gave him a sly smile. "Then my disguise worked. I joined on a whim the first time to strike at Drath. But later, I started thinking... if I could win the title of champion, maybe I wouldn't need to marry him. Maybe that would be enough for my father. So I gave it a shot."

Realization hit Sam. "You were the one who flew across the river."

"My wings were sore for days," she said with a half-laugh.

They reached a large ember tree, its blackened bark glinting like coal. Beneath it, a bench had been carved from wood, worn smooth by time.

"Let's sit a moment," Sam said.

Once they were settled on opposite ends, Sam continued, "I want to tell you something, but it's of great importance that you keep it secret. Your father already knows this, but no one else can. Do you understand?"

Vanthee looked suspicious. "Yes."

Sam locked eyes with her. "My father is losing his powers," he said slowly. "It signifies the end of his rule. And that a new Dark Sovereign must rise to take his place."

For a moment, Vanthee didn't react. Then, as if struck, she pressed a hand to her mouth.

"Asmodeus has ruled for centuries!" she whispered. "I can't even imagine anyone else on the throne."

"I know. That's the real reason behind the trials. They're not entertainment. They're a way to find his successor—someone strong enough to rule the Underworld."

Vanthee clutched her stomach. "Oh, I feel sick. Anyone could win those games!" She leaned back on the bench, taking several shaky breaths. When she opened her eyes, her expression had shifted. Disgust gave way to furious understanding.

"That's why my father wants Drath to win so badly," she said, then swore under her breath. "So I would be his queen. Or at least his consort."

She shook her head, a bitter laugh escaping her lips.

"My father wouldn't want the crown himself—he hates anything that demands actual work or duty. But if he could rig it so his daughter has the ear of the king... Oh, Prince Samael, we can't let this happen!"

Relieved that Vanthee grasped the gravity of the situation, Sam turned to face her fully. "My parents want me to be the next Dark Sovereign"—her eyes lit up, excitement flaring in her expression, but he raised a hand to stop her—"but I don't want it," he said firmly. "What I brought you here to ask, or rather, to say, is that I think you would be a good fit for the role."

She drew back. "Me?"

"Yes," he said with conviction. "We don't know each other well, but I've seen your skill as a fighter and Selene has told me of your dedication as a Guide. You have respect for the dead and a deep knowledge of this realm. I've been on the lookout for a suitable candidate for a long time and no other demon comes close."

Vanthee stared at the ground then murmured, "I... I never thought..." She glanced at Sam sideways. "Would I have to take a husband? Or rule with a male consort or advisor?"

"No. Not unless you wanted to. As Dark Sovereign, you would inherit all the powers my father has. You can call yourself queen or empress or anything you want. He reigned alone until he met my mother, didn't he?"

"Yes."

She was quiet for several moments. Sam sat silently, watching a spectrum of emotions play across her face: hesitation, hope, fear, excitement.

"You don't have to decide now. Take some time to think on it," he said.

"I don't need to think on it," Vanthee said quickly. Her gaze drifted for a few moments. Then, with painstaking slowness, her mouth curved into a determined grin. "I don't know if I'm the best choice, but there's a lot I'd like to change here. So I accept your offer."

Sam exhaled. With her acceptance, the pressure to leave the Underworld in a better state than when he arrived lightened even further.

"Excellent. When the next trial is announced, you can compete in disguise as you did before. Did you register with Ghar before the Infernal Combat Trial?"

"Yes, I registered under a false name," she said, lowering her head wistfully. "My mother was called Nahmira, so I chose the name Nyrah."

Sam returned her smile. "Then I will see to it that Nyrah wins the last and final trial."

CHAPTER 40

Sam hadn't appreciated the surprise element of the previous trials, so overhearing a rumor about the next one was an unexpected relief. A day after his conversation with Vanthee, he was leaving the Sanctum when he saw a cluster of imps hovering behind a nearby column. Their hushed voices caught his attention.

"Sire says maze must be cleared," a gray-warted imp croaked.

"Too much green," another said.

"Must destroy green," a third imp replied. "Cut."

"No, pull."

"No! Hack."

Sam listened closely as the imps argued about how to destroy the "green." His parents rarely asked the imps to work together on a task, so he was certain their assignment had something to do with the next trial.

With this new information, Sam asked Vanthee to meet him in the library that evening to strategize. She was sitting on the steps outside when he and Selene approached. Vanthee looked surprised to see Selene was accompanying him and cautiously peered behind her.

"What are you doing here?" Vanthee asked Selene. "Is Zetta with you?"

"No, I left her in the kennels," Selene replied. When Vanthee continued to eye her warily, she added, "I'm not here to interfere with your planning. Sam just asked me to help with some research."

"Oh." Vanthee's expression was unreadable. She began twisting her fingers together as though nervous. "Well, since you're here... I-I wanted to say thank you. For the nice things you said about me to Prince Samael."

Selene's evident surprise made her pause then say, "You're welcome."

"Also... " Vanthee paused to swallow. "I didn't get a chance to say thank you that day in Spirit Veil Valley. For helping Ruth cross over."

"Of course. I'm glad we succeeded."

Sam placed a hand at the nape of Selene's neck, pride warming his chest. "My mate has many skills, too."

Selene beamed up at him then pulled open the library doors. "Shall we go inside?"

Sam had been in a rush when Selene first showed him *The Sovereign's Reckoning,* but now he had time to appreciate the work she had done on the library's restoration. The floor had been swept clean, revealing intricate sigils carved into the black marble below their feet. Though some tables were still buried under books and several pendant lights remained broken, much of the shelving was now neat and orderly. It wasn't finished, but it was easy to imagine how beautiful the space would be at its best. The thought of leaving for Aurelia before Selene completed the project made Sam a little sad, but he was certain his parents would be impressed by her efforts.

Selene pulled out two chairs and dusted them off. "Have a seat. I'll find a cloth to wipe down this table."

Sam sat across from Vanthee. Without preamble, he said, "I have a suspicion that the next trial has something to do with a maze. Do you know of any structure like that in this realm?"

"A maze?" Vanthee drummed her fingers on the table thought-fully. "Only one comes to mind—the Maze of Endless Paths. But no one has been in it for centuries."

"Maybe they're reviving it. What is it?"

"Long ago they didn't have Guides to sort souls as they arrived. They used to send them through a maze to determine where they would end up."

Sam considered this. There was so much of the Underworld's history that remained unknown to him. "Was the path difficult?"

"I'm not sure."

"How large is the maze?"

"Huge, I'd assume, since hundreds of thousands of people die every day." Vanthee turned her head and called, "Hey human—er, Selene. Have you found any books on the Maze of Endless Paths?"

Selene approached with a dust cloth in her hand. "That doesn't sound familiar. Would it be something that's fairly new or very old?"

"Ancient," Vanthee said.

"All the really old and delicate stuff I've found is over there." Selene pointed to a table stacked with the books she'd used while searching for clues on the Dark Sovereign. "Hang on—I think I might have seen a book of maps somewhere."

Selene began sorting through the pile as Sam and Vanthee continued to talk.

"They will probably send us into the maze one at a time," Vanthee said. "Perhaps if we run into each other we can work through it together."

"Aha!" Selene cried, holding up an old atlas. She brought it over, and the three of them leaned in.

She carefully turned each page until Vanthee stopped her, recog-nizing the castle grounds. Though the map was centuries old, the River of Hatred and the cliffs leading to Spirit Veil Valley were still clearly marked. In the corner of the map, was a mess of geometric lines and jagged angles, creating a web of interconnected pathways.

Only a portion of the drawing was visible, hinting that the rest extended beyond the page.

"This looks like a maze, right?" Selene said.

"Yes. What's on the next pages?" Sam asked.

Selene flipped through the rest of the book, but it only contained interior diagrams of the palace. She returned to the map and Sam peered closer. "There's something written here."

Although it was barely visible, scrawled in looping calligraphic script were the words:

To navigate the Endless Path, heed the trail of the ever-turning sun.

"The sun? I've never seen it, but I'm pretty sure it doesn't turn." Vanthee scoffed.

"It must be a riddle." Sam frowned, rolling the words over in his mind. "I hate riddles."

"No, wait—I think I know what it means," Selene said suddenly, excitement lighting her face. "I remember this from science class. The sun *does* turn. Counterclockwise." She lifted her hands, shaping them into a sphere and rotating them in a slow, deliberate motion.

"Really?" Vanthee asked, raising an eyebrow.

"Yes. It rotates just like the planets," Selene said. "I wonder if this means... Have you ever heard of the right-hand rule for solving a maze? My siblings and I used it when we went through corn mazes at Halloween."

Vanthee smirked. "Do humans only eat corn with their right hand or something?"

Selene gave her an exasperated look. "No, it's a strategy. When you enter a maze, you place your right hand on the wall and never lift it. As long as you keep following that rule—always choosing the path that keeps your hand on the wall—you'll eventually find the way out."

She tapped the inscription again. "But this," she murmured, a thoughtful look crossing her face, "this is telling us to follow the path of the sun. And if the sun turns counterclockwise, that means—"

"To the left," Sam finished, realization dawning.

Selene nodded. "Exactly."

"It can't be that easy," Vanthee said. "Solve a maze just by keeping to the left?"

"I don't think it will be easy, but at least it's a starting point," Selene replied.

"True." Vanthee turned to Sam. "So, how are we going to help each other?"

Sam shrugged. "I'll be sure to lose. They usually announce each winner, so I'll stay inside the maze until I hear that you're through."

"But what if another demon comes out before me?" Vanthee asked, then paled. "What if Drath makes it out first?"

Sam stroked his chin thoughtfully. "It won't matter at that point. The king's champion is to be selected from among the trial winners. Just focus on making sure you are one of them, and I'll handle the rest."

"Are you sure?" Vanthee asked.

"What my parents fear most is that the realm will be without a ruler," Sam said. "I'll simply convince them that you are the best choice—and the solution to their problem. They know I don't want the role, and my recommendation carries weight."

Vanthee nodded and bent her head to study the map more closely. Above her, Selene met his eyes with a knowing look. They both understood that even if Sam couldn't convince his parents with words, *The Sovereign's Reckoning* would serve as undeniable proof of Vanthee's destiny.

CHAPTER 41

Sam hissed softly as he sank into the bath Selene had drawn for them, the heat of the water seeping into his sore muscles. It was the first time he had used the bathtub in his chambers, since he usually preferred to bathe quickly under a shower of water. He stretched out his legs and leaned back until his shoulders touched the back of the tub. After years of folding himself into cramped Aurelian furniture, the simple luxury of something that truly fit his frame felt indulgent.

"Too hot?" Selene asked, twisting her hair into a bun and pinning it to the crown of her head.

"No, it'll be fine in a moment." After creating a solid plan with Vanthee yesterday for how to navigate the maze, he was feeling the most relaxed he had since arriving in the Underworld.

"That thing is more like a lap pool than a bathtub. It took forever to fill," Selene said.

"What's a lap pool?"

"A big container of water humans use to swim short distances." Selene motioned to the crisscross of laces at the back of her gown. "Can you give me a hand with this?"

Sam sat up and reached for her. He loosened each tie with his fingers until the fabric relaxed enough for her to pull the dress over her head. She tossed it into a corner and stretched.

"Phew. Now I can breathe again," she said.

Sam watched, captivated, as she slipped out of her remaining undergarments. She had placed lit candles around the tub and on the counter, and he loved watching the way the light played across her skin. The snug fit of her dress had left red impressions on her back that he ached to kiss away. Once she was fully bare, she took the hand he offered and stepped gracefully into the tub. She sank into the water to settle between his legs.

"Alone at last," she murmured, leaning back against his chest. She had poured scented bath oil into the water, and the aroma rose with the steam.

Wrapping his arms around her, he pulled her even closer. Though his shaft was already swelling with the feel of her generous backside pressing against him, he wanted to talk first before losing himself to passion.

"How was your day?" he asked.

"The usual," Selene said. "Zetta has become fond of using broken chair legs as chew toys. I was worried that it might not be good for her, but then I remembered hellhounds are pretty much indestructible. What did you do today?"

"Finished some chores in the Sanctum. Several of the rooms needed repairs, and I wanted to do what I could to take the burden off Borias."

"When do you think we can go home?"

"Soon, I hope. It would be nice to help Vanthee settle into her role before we go back to Snowmelt." Slowly, he began to trail his fingers up and down the sides of Selene's stomach. "What's the first thing you'd like to do back in Aurelia?"

"Eat my weight in Brunie's cooking," Selene said immediately. "I still have nightmares about that 'morning drink' Prickles served me. What about you?"

"It surprises me to say this, but I miss feeling the sun on my face. And I look forward to having leisure time. We can start looking for land to build our home on as well."

"Yes, someplace near the river would be nice. But I still want to be able to walk to Brunie and Eldridge's." She stretched her arms behind her, looping them around Sam's neck. The motion made her breasts jut out of the water provocatively. Sam watched rivulets of water roll down her nipples, now dark pink from the hot water. His cock strained.

He picked up the bar of soap resting on a dish nearby. It didn't smell as good as the ironwood and pine-scented soap she had chosen for him at the Padu market, but it would do.

"Shall I wash your back?"

"Mmm, yes please."

Sam lathered up his hands and began massaging her neck and shoulders with slow strokes.

Selene let out a soft moan.

His hands moved further south, rubbing away those red marks and working into the muscles of her lower back. He bent to kiss the side of her neck then leisurely began tracing his fingers around her sensitive rib cage. Selene's breath quickened.

Lathering up his hands again, he slid them under her arms to cup her full breasts.

"Oh yes, Sam," she whispered. Her head lolled back against his shoulder as his slick palms massaged her breasts.

"What would you like me to build in our house?

"Red shutters" Her breaths were coming faster. "Flowerboxes... bookcases with a ladder... "

Her words faded into a moan as Sam pinched her nipples. Lightly at first, then harder. With one hand, he rolled a tight bud between his soapy fingers; with the other, he kneaded her flesh until she arched her back.

"Why a ladder?" he asked.

"I've always wanted one for floor-to-ceiling"—sinking his hand into the water, he began to stroke her inner thighs until she widened her legs for him—"bookcases."

"I can do that."

Leisurely, he stroked the outside of her core, teasing her with fluttering touches. She shifted her pelvis impatiently, urging him to give her more. He began playing with her clit, rubbing it small, tight circles with his thumb. "And a big bed?"

"Huge." Selene cried out as he pressed a finger against her opening then slipped two inside. Her silken flesh was hotter than the bathwater. He began to thrust in and out while continuing to tease her clit. She started to rock herself into his hand.

"And a walk-in closet."

In her ear, he whispered, "Grind into me. I want you to come on my hand."

Selene did as she was told. Still with her arms over her head, she dug her nails into his scalp. Her breaths came even faster now. Sam felt her body began to tense, causing his own need to surge.

"That's it, my love. That's it."

"Oh, Sam, please… "

"Please what?"

"I want… I need to… "

"You need to come?"

"Yes!"

"Just a little while longer. Don't release until I say so."

Her frustrated groan nearly made *him* come. He pressed his mouth to her neck and shoulders, kissing and nibbling at her scented skin. Between her legs, her folds had grown lush and plump, signaling that she was close to her limit.

Nearly drunk with lust he rasped, "Kiss me." She turned her head and he took her mouth greedily. Then when he had his fill, he said in a low, commanding voice, "Now come for me."

His words had the desired effect. Bracing a strong arm around her waist so she wouldn't sink into the water, he held her as her body stiffened, then bucked against him, crying out her release.

Against his hand, he felt her core pulsate with waves of pleasure, flooding him with as much satisfaction as he had given her.

When her body began to still, lust was pounding through him to the point of pain. Roughly, he whispered into her hair, "Can you take more?"

"I can always take more," she purred.

"Good. Because I'm going to give it to you."

Effortlessly, he lifted her hips to hover over his cock, which now strained desperately for her. Dreamily, she reached between them in the water and guided him into her wet heat. Sam thrust up, driving into her in one brutal motion. She gasped with pleasure, then braced her knees on the bottom of the tub to bounce up and down on him.

Water splashed around them wildly as they moved, extinguishing some of the nearby candles. After making her come so sweetly, he was on fire for her now—desperate, crazed to be as close to her as he could get.

He gripped her hips to drive her down on him harder. "You're taking me so well," he breathed, using one hand to thrum her nipples again.

"It's so good. Don't stop."

"Grab my horns," he said roughly. She reached over her head to wrap her wet palms around both his horns. The surge of pleasure made him buck into her even harder.

"Don't let go," he growled.

"Sam... I'm close."

Normally, he liked to draw their pleasure out as long as possible, but he was about to burst. He could tell she was on the edge again as well. "Come on my cock," he ordered.

The instant the words left his lips, Selene threw back her head, and he felt her climax all around him, squeezing him as if to milk the seed from his body. The sweetness of it made him lose himself, too. He threw back his head, muscles straining, and bellowed his mate's name as he finished.

They stayed in the bath for several moments, both panting hard.

When their breathing slowed, Selene leaned over the edge of the tub to peer at the puddles spreading across the wet floor.

"We've made a terrible mess," she said with a chuckle.

"That's what towels are for," Sam replied, feeling languid and spent. He brushed away a strand of hair that had escaped Selene's bun. "Would you like me to install a bathtub like this in our house?"

Selene looked back at him with a wicked smile. "Definitely."

CHAPTER 42

Though he knew it was coming, Sam was still startled when a pack of shrieking imps announced the next trial was about to begin just as he stepped out of the Sanctum. He watched them soar through the air for a moment, a wave of resignation washing over him—then reminded himself this trial was merely a means to an end.

He began trudging in the direction where the other demons were headed, past the palace gates. He heard the word *maze* in snippets of conversation from those around him, confirming his suspicions about the nature of the trial ahead. Sam scanned the crowds for Selene but didn't see her.

The groups passed a small stream showing signs of infection from the creeping rot that had begun to affect the lakes of fire. To his left, a voice said, "May fate smile upon you, Prince Samael." The tone was unnaturally deepened.

He turned to see Vanthee's red eyes peering out from a helmet. Her horns and hair were hidden beneath the hood of a coat that concealed her figure.

"Same to you, opponent," he replied, and they quickly separated.

As the crowd slowed at the edge of a meadow clearing, Sam threaded his way to the front. He immediately saw his parents, who appeared to hover midair above a dense tangle of vegetation. Then he realized their feet rested on a thick layer of the overgrowth blanketing the top of a stone wall. Behind them, an immense stretch of stonework unfolded, revealing a maze that nature's grasp had long hidden.

King Asmodeus looked down at Sam and gave him a nod. Sam noticed his father leaning heavily on a cane, though he tried to hide it beneath his cape. Dark circles framed his eyes, and his face held a dull pallor.

There were now only six competitors left, including him, "Nyrah," and Drath. They had all gathered at the front. Sam was surprised that Chort was not among them—until he spotted him waving from the crowd, clearly having decided this trial was too difficult.

With a quiet step, Ghar emerged from the maze's entrance between two parallel walls. It had been all but invisible moments before, hidden by a design that tricked the eye.

"Greetings," the demon said loudly. "We are once again here to see who is most worthy of the king's special favor. Welcome to the Maze of Endless Paths. Although, as spectators, we cannot all see the horrors that await our competitors within, I assure you, their screams of terror will reverberate throughout the land."

That elicited cheers and whoops of excitement from the surrounding crowd. Ghar explained that each demon's time would be measured using a candle notched in fifteen-minute increments. Anyone who did not complete the maze in less than one hour would be disqualified.

Ghar motioned for all the competitors to line up outside the entrance. "This will be a solo challenge that each of you will complete one by one, with your entrances staggered. Do you understand?"

Each of the demons nodded, with varying levels of excitement and trepidation. A well-built demon of Depravity named Bradax was chosen as the first to enter. He charged into the maze like he was entering battle. About fifteen minutes later, Ghar waved through the first victor of the River of Hatred Trial, a demon of Vanity called Pekhos. He burst into the maze with equal gusto—only to catch his foot on a tree root and fall face-first. The crowd roared with laughter.

Drath entered third.

"See you soon," he rasped confidently, locking eyes with Sam.

But minutes later, a scream echoed from deep within the maze. Not one of terror, but of raw shock, misery, and grief, fused into a single sound. Sam couldn't tell which demon it belonged to, but the effect was haunting.

Then came another scream—this one definitely Drath's. It was sharper, more anguished. Something in its pitch, its strange resonance, unnerved Sam more than anything he'd faced in the trials so far. What was waiting for him inside those stone walls?

Eventually, Vanthee was the fourth demon to enter. She deliberately ignored Sam as she passed by, marching through the entrance with her head high and shoulders back. All the other competitors had veered to the right when they entered, but Vanthee made an immediate left turn.

Despite the odor of unwashed bodies and demon sweat, Sam detected Selene's pomegranate and vanilla scent drifting toward him. He turned and saw her weaving through the crowd so he roughly pushed the demons blocking her way aside.

"Sorry, I'm late," she said. "I found something in the library and got distracted. Then, when I came out, everyone was gone. An imp told me what was happening. Do you feel ready for this?"

"Ready to be finished," Sam grumbled.

"Me too. Has anyone we *know* come out yet?"

"No," Sam said, understanding her unspoken meaning. "The competitor we *know* has just entered. Also, Drath remains inside."

They stood together, listening for any more sounds coming from the maze and watching the spectators jostle one another.

"What did you find in the library?" Sam asked Selene after a moment.

"A few things about the Thronefall Flame. There's a bunch of blank journals, so I started taking some notes—"

A shout echoed through the maze. Sam's head jerked up—was it Vanthee? But the frantic whimpering that followed was unmistakably male.

"What do you think is going on in there?" Selene asked uneasily.

"Probably just a beast to get past or a trap to escape from," he replied.

Another demon was ordered into the maze. Sam was next.

"Tell me more of what you learned."

"There were some dates listed for when the comet might fall, but they're written in Old English."

Another male scream made Selene wince, but she pressed on. "I tried to do some calculations, but I didn't get very far—"

"Prince Samael! Your time to enter the maze has come," Ghar bellowed, cutting her off.

"We'll speak of this later tonight," Sam said, then bent to kiss her.

"Good luck, I love you."

"I love you, too," Sam said. "See you soon."

He walked toward the maze entrance, trying to avoid his parents' gaze but failing. They had moved from their perch atop the wall; his father now reclined in a chair to maintain the illusion of good health.

"May the darkness be yours, my son," King Asmodeus called. Sam turned and saw pride shining in his father's eyes. Queen Lamia stood beside him, blowing Sam a kiss as he passed.

He stepped between the two looming walls that marked the entrance.

The air was colder inside, smelling of moss, dust, and decomposing vegetation. Immediately, he saw why Vanthee had been the only competitor to turn left.

To his right, a narrow pathway was visible. It was paved with cracked flagstones, but clear of obstacles. On his left, he could take only two steps before colliding into a solid wall.

Sam pressed his hands against the wall, assuming it was an illusion, but it didn't move. He began to pull away the dead roots covering the stone and realized it wasn't a wall—it was a door. Quickly, he searched for a way to open it, using his hands to feel for a secret lever or recessed handle. Nothing.

Minutes passed. The plan had been to go left, but the door refused to yield.

Sam exhaled in frustration. How was he supposed to help Vanthee if he could barely make it past the entrance? Then, it hit him —Vanthee must have used her powers as Guide to get through.

The thought steadied him. He was wasting time abiding by a plan they had only guessed would work. He needed to make progress to help Vanthee win—or risk her disqualification when her time ran out.

Taking the right-hand path meant enduring the humiliation of passing the entrance again, exposing his mistake to the crowd. He did so swiftly, ignoring the hoots and jeers that echoed behind him as he ran.

Once he came to his first obstruction, he paused. He needed to know when Vanthee emerged, so he focused on his hearing. The sounds of the crowd had faded, but he couldn't hear any other movement. Even the wind had vanished. He strained to detect the rustle of another contestant, a whisper of movement—anything. But there was only the sound of his own heartbeat.

Reasoning that the announcement might be more audible near the end of the maze, he pressed on.

After hitting two dead ends and a corridor that looped back to a path he'd already taken, he was starting to get annoyed. He could see the footprints his boots had left in the lichen and dirt, which was helpful, along with the faint traces of other contenders.

But it wasn't until he turned the next corner that he began to feel it: the presence of someone behind him.

He stopped and looked over his shoulder. Nothing.

Still, the sensation lingered—and then he heard footsteps. Multiple sets. Some heavy, others light. Again, when he turned, the sounds stopped.

He was becoming unnerved.

How long had he been in the maze without encountering another competitor? Had they all made it out already?

He veered right and crashed straight into a wall. Staggering back, he turned, only to find himself face-to-face with a spirit.

Sam inhaled sharply, more startled than afraid. Yet something about the apparition tugged at his memory.

It was an Aurelian. A wolf-like Lycah with a strong build and scornful gaze. The side of his ghostly head was caved in, and one arm dangled uselessly from his shoulder.

"Hello?" Sam said cautiously. "What do you want?"

The Lycah's lips curled back, exposing translucent canines. His scorn twisted into rage. With his good arm, he gestured first to his shattered skull, then to his mangled limb.

Sam took an uneasy step back. "Do you need help?"

The question made the spirit's form seethe, mist swirling violently. He bared his fangs in a silent snarl, fury shining through his hollow eyes. And suddenly, something in Sam's mind sparked.

Recognition.

"Who are you?"

The Lycah lunged. Sam barely had time to stumble before hitting the ground, the spirit hovering inches above him. Then, out of the shadows, more spirits surged forward—silent, desperate, their empty eyes drilling into him.

Hatred. Accusation. Fury.

Sam's skin began to tingle as an unlocked memory crashed through his mind.

Crowds cheering as the moon rose in the sky. A pale figure yanking me out of Brunie's arms. Rough hands pushing me into the ring. Eldridge's voice begging for them to stop. Someone coming toward me. A fist driving into my stomach. A blow snapping my head back. More cheering. More pain. My fear slowly fading, replaced by the burning rise of demonic rage. It soon consumed me, and then—

Sam blinked up at the Lycah. He had come face-to-face with the first person he had ever killed.

He opened his mouth to say something—to apologize, repent. But one by one, the other spirits came closer. Some were covered in burns or badly bruised; others held their heads in their hands. He searched their faces, realizing they weren't just random spirits sent to slow his progress.

Sam tried to push them away, to stand, to run. But their ghostly hands pressed against his skin with desperate insistence.

And all at once, Sam began to relive every death he had ever caused.

CHAPTER 43

Selene chewed her fingernail worriedly. *What is taking him so long?*

The candle measuring Sam's trial had long since burned out, yet there was still no sign of him. Hours ago, Vanthee had breezed through the maze so fast that Selene worried it might draw attention and jeopardize her identity. But then the first competitor stumbled out behind her, sweating profusely and babbling about nightmares so wildly that he captured everyone's attention. Others made it out with only a small pool of wax in their candle—shaken but relieved.

Most demons watching the trial had grown bored and left. King Asmodeus and Queen Lamia remained, though they both looked disappointed and weary. When the Eventide bell tolled in the distance, Lamia motioned to Ghar and whispered in his ear.

Ghar cleared his throat and announced to the remaining spectators, "The Maze of Endless Paths Trial has ended. However, due to its complexity and grueling nature, any competitor who failed to finish within the time limit remains eligible to be the king's champion."

When a few nearby competitors began to grumble, Ghar's gaze snapped to them. "Protestations on this decree are forbidden by order of the queen. All demons are to depart this area at once."

Selene watched King Asmodeus stumble to his feet, while Queen Lamia spoke quietly to Ghar. Cautiously, Selene approached the king.

"Your Majesty, should we be worried that Sam hasn't come back yet?"

The king looked at her, then to the maze, then back at her. "I'm sure he's fine. All that time in Aurelia likely dulled his sense of direction."

"What's actually in the maze? Why were so many demons screaming?"

Asmodeus looked thoughtful. "You know... I can't remember."

The sinking feeling in Selene's stomach grew worse. Was Asmodeus losing his mental faculties as well as his physical ones?

"Come, darling," Lamia said to Asmodeus, ignoring Selene. "Ghar is bringing you a horse to ride back to the palace."

"But... " Selene watched helplessly as the remaining demons swarmed away from the maze. In the distance, two great black horses were being led in their direction. A tug at her sleeve made her turn. It was Vanthee, eyes gleaming conspiratorially through her mask.

"Hide with me until they all leave," she whispered.

Selene nodded, deeply relieved that someone else shared her concern. She hung back with Vanthee behind a thicket of brush while Asmodeus carefully climbed on the horse. Once Lamia made sure he was settled, she mounted the other. And without even a backward glance or word to their daughter-in-law, Sam's parents set off for the palace.

When everyone was completely out of sight, Vanthee beckoned Selene to approach the maze's entrance with her.

"What's really in there?" Selene asked.

Vanthee shrugged. "For me? Nothing, really. I kept to the left as we discussed and made my way out. I hit a few dead ends and crossed paths with some spiders, but nothing to make me scream like the others."

Selene placed a hand over her racing heart, hoping to calm it. "Maybe Sam tripped and hit his head or something. Or one of the walls collapsed and he's pinned under it. Or what if—"

"Stop that," Vanthee said sharply. "Making up stories isn't going to help anything. I'm going in."

"So am I," Selene said, following Vanthee through the entrance.

The demoness immediately turned left, but Selene reached for her hand to pull her back. "No, he didn't go that way. He tried, but after a few minutes, we all saw him go the other way."

The confidence in Vanthee's face faltered. "Well, there's one reason why he hasn't come out. All right, human. Let's go."

Figuring they could reverse the left-hand rule, Selene kept her right hand on the wall while Vanthee walked ahead through the maze. The air was damp and reeked of rotting leaves, but so far, no monsters or boogeymen leapt out at them.

"Sam?" Selene called out now and then, but silence was her only reply. They took several wrong turns, and as the sky darkened, it became even harder to see where they stepped.

When Vanthee slipped on a puddle, she huffed in frustration. "Forget this." Reaching under her dark coat, she pulled out a torch that must have been strapped to her belt. With a quick tap of her fingers, it flared to life.

The burst of light and warmth eased the tightness in Selene's chest, but it also revealed new hazards—cracked flagstones, foot-snaring vines, and scattered heaps of broken stone. When Vanthee stumbled on a loose rock, she said, "If I get to be Dark Sovereign, one of the first things I'm going to do is tear this ruin down."

Selene was about to agree when a faint sound froze her in place. "Uhhh... "

Vanthee's head whipped around. "Did you hear that?"

"Yes!"

They sprinted toward the sound, which wavered in volume with each turn. Vanthee was much faster, rushing ahead while Selene's lungs burned with every stride.

Eventually, Vanthee disappeared around a corner. Selene heard her gasp sharply, followed by, "He's here!"

Even though she could barely breathe, Selene forced herself to move faster. But before she reached them, Vanthee's voice rose again, this time in alarm. "What are you doing? Go away!"

Selene rounded the corner and skidded to a stop.

In a corridor that funneled into a dead-end Sam lay curled on the ground in a fetal position, his body still. Above him, a swirling mass of spirits pulsed, each one diving down in turn to torment him. Their relentless assault contrasted with the faint, aimless shadows drifting listlessly through the air.

Selene took in the scene with horror, her heart pounding so hard she feared it might stop altogether. Vanthee was trying to reach Sam, shouting and swiping at the shadows, but they ignored her. The worry and fear Selene had dealt with all day morphed into anger.

She rushed toward them, shouting, "Get away from him!"

Instantly, the spirits halted. Then, as one, they abandoned Sam and hurtled toward Selene. She barely had time to react before they were upon her, a blur of movement so fast it sent her stumbling backward. When the back of her head touched the wall, the spirits descended.

Speak again!

Can you hear me?

What are you?

Help me!

Whispers and wails crashed over her like a hailstorm, their voices sharp and relentless. Selene held her hands up defensively.

"Get back! You all need to step back!" When the spirits failed to comply, she shouted, "I said back off!"

Something in her tone changed the air around them. A large spirit Selene recognized as an Aurelian Lycah made a motion with his ghostly hand. The other spirits drew back, giving her some space.

When a few moved toward Sam again, Selene said, "I will speak to you all in a moment, but stay away from my mate. I mean it. Wait over there."

The spirits reluctantly drifted over to the corner she pointed to. Selene fell to her knees beside Sam, whom Vanthee had covered with her coat. She touched his face, which was wet with tears and sweat. "I'm here, Sam. It's okay."

His eyelids fluttered slightly, but he didn't respond.

Selene began to stroke his hair, noticing his skin was burning hot to the touch. She exchanged a panicked look with Vanthee.

"What do you think they did to him?" Vanthee asked.

"I don't know," Selene whispered. She glanced at the swarm of spirits—some watching her with pleading eyes, others glaring with contempt. When she caught the eye of the Lycah, he charged forward.

"Stop. Don't go any further," Selene said firmly. "What do you want?"

We want our vengeance!

"What do you mean?"

The Lycah pointed at Sam with a clawed finger.

He took our lives—all of us. And was never punished!

Realization crashed over Selene like a tsunami.

Vanthee shot her a frantic look. "What are they saying?"

Emotion overwhelmed Selene so completely she didn't answer at first. Then, she whispered, "These spirits... they are all the lives he took in Aurelia."

Vanthee's eyes widened, and she covered her mouth with her hand. "Oh. That's why the other competitors were screaming. They were faced with their regrets."

Sam's head lolled to the side. "What do you want from him?" Selene asked the Lycah.

To make him suffer as we did!

"Haven't you already done that? I'd say he's pretty traumatized."

It's not enough. He is the reason we're trapped here!

"That's not true. You can leave any time."

"Translate, translate!" Vanthee insisted. When Selene relayed what the spirit said, Vanthee's face knotted with indignation. "Tell them they should have followed me like they were supposed to! I can't be responsible for every angry spirit who wants revenge—"

"I know. It's not your fault," Selene said, cutting her off. She looked up at the Lycah. "Are you ready to go to the Afterworld?"

Yes!

Yes, I am.

Take me!

No, take me first!

The spirits who had hung back swarmed again, talking over each other and pushing their way closer to Selene.

"Easy, easy! Vanthee and I will take you, but not now."

When?

Why not now?

Do not betray us!

"Rest assured, we will get you where you need to go. I know you're all angry with him for taking your lives, and you have every right to be. But you've done enough."

She looked at the desperate, pleading faces of the spirits. "What do you need to move on?"

None of them spoke for a moment. Then the Lycah floated forward.

Hear my story. I was born in the territory of the great Queen Keebee under a waxing moon. When I had seen nineteen winters, I left to go in search of adventure. Along the way, I met a vampire...

As the Lycah spoke, the others began to push in front of him, each wanting Selene to hear their story too. Sam was growing paler, and his breathing more irregular.

"We've got to get him out of here," Vanthee whispered as two spirits visibly began arguing with each other. "It's like he's been poisoned by their anguish."

"I'm scared the spirits won't let him go."

Vanthee glanced at Sam, then at the sky, and finally at the approaching turn in the maze before saying, "Keep listening to them —I'll get him out."

"He's too weak to stand."

"I know," Vanthee said. Then she bent down and effortlessly lifted Sam onto her shoulders in a fireman's carry. She adjusted her grip, securing one hand on Sam's dangling thigh over her left shoulder while firmly grasping his bicep with the other.

Selene stared at her, wondering if there was anything Vanthee couldn't do. "You've got him? It may take some time before you make your way out."

"I'm fine. I don't like leaving you here alone, though." Vanthee replied.

"I'll be okay," Selene said. The spirits were growing restless around them, clearly agitated that Vanthee was about to remove their punching bag. Selene waved her arm at Vanthee. "Go!"

"All right!" Vanthee said as she hurriedly backed out of the corridor, careful to keep Sam's horns from brushing the ground. "Dark blessings, human!"

"Same to you, demon."

As Vanthee disappeared around the corner, Selene squared her shoulders. Turning back to the spirits, she shouted, "Listen up!"

The spirits stared at her with hungry eyes.

"I'm sorry that you're no longer among the living. But if anyone wants to share their story or send a message to Aurelia, I'd be honored to carry it back." She pulled the writing pad out of her pocket and flipped to a fresh page.

Eager cries rippled through the throng of spirits, their voices rising in a collective, desperate strain. One by one, they surged toward her, but their urgency was so intense that they soon merged into a chaotic blur of misty white forms. The very air seemed to pulse with their sorrow as the raw weight of their heartbreak enveloped her in a tide of grief and regret.

CHAPTER 44

Selene held up her arms as the spirits pressed in around her, pushing and shoving to get in front of her, each one trying to be heard, eager to relay their message into her ears. Although she could make out individual faces before, now the spirits blurred together.

"Step back," Selene said weakly. The shadows that carried her words to the spirits were faint. "Give me a moment... "

She dropped her head, trying to breathe, but the spirits only pushed in closer. Cold fingers brushed against her body and tangled in her hair, pleading for attention. From the way her knees wobbled she knew she was close to curling up on the ground, just as Sam had done.

"Help," she whispered.

She thought she could handle it, but she was wrong. There were too many of them, and they were too desperate. Eventually, she would have to be carried out by Vanthee as well, assuming she didn't lose her mind first. Or perhaps she might suffocate, drowning above water since her air supply was choked off by spirits.

But then, she heard something that made her freeze. She lifted her head, trying to focus on the faint sound.

It was barking.

It was distant at first, but it gradually grew louder. She dismissed it as her imagination. A result of all the spirits trying to get their messages to her.

She caught the sound of another bark, followed by a high-pitched yip. Then a third, unmistakably like Zetta's howl.

Suddenly, she felt a blast of heat, like a furnace flaring to life, and the horde of spirits surrounding her broke apart.

Selene's legs gave way, her knees slamming painfully into the ground. She squeezed her eyes shut, bracing for what might come next. Then something warm, wet, and gasoline-scented swiped across her cheek. Gasping for breath, Selene opened her eyes to find Zetta sitting in front of her, tail thumping.

But she hadn't come alone.

The hellhounds had arrived—all thirteen of them—and they were herding the spirits away from her like a pack of determined sheepdogs. Some of the hounds were blasting burning red fire from their throats. Most souls zoomed away down the maze's corridors to escape; others pressed themselves into corners, watching the hounds fearfully.

Selene looped her arms around Zetta's neck, hugging her with relief. "How did you know?" she asked into Zetta's fur. The hellhound leaned into her, resting her great head on Selene's shoulder.

Ahem, said a Drago floating above her. ***You said you would listen to our stories!***

Selene leaned back and replied, "And so I will. But one at a time." This time, the shadows easily zipped from her mouth to the spirit.

Meanwhile, a hellhound with streaks of gray in his coat was barking furiously at a trio of Nereid spirits huddled together. Another dog, with eerie yellow eyes, stood on his hind legs, paws pressed against a wall to snap at a trembling Goblyn. Seeing her pack so worked up seemed to excite Zetta, and she started zooming around the other dogs.

Selene watched her for a moment, then called, "Zetta, come!"

Instantly, all of Zetta's counterparts froze. One by one, they turned toward Selene, then bounded toward her expectantly. She stared that them, dumbfounded for a moment. Until a slow smile spread across her face.

"Sit," she said hesitantly.

Without hesitation, the hellhounds obeyed, settling onto their haunches in front of her. Now that they were still, she studied each dog more closely. Some had blood on their muzzles, and a few were favoring one paw. It made her wonder how they had all escaped from the kennels. Surely, they couldn't have run all the way here... could they? She had only spent time alone with Zetta, but now every single one of them was gazing at her with unwavering devotion.

Looking past the dogs, Selene saw the spirits of Sam's victims still hovering, impatiently waiting for her to fulfill her promise. She looked back at Zetta and said, "I don't know how to train you for this, but I need to see one spirit at a time."

She held up a finger and repeated, "One at a time." She pointed to the spirit, then to the dog. "Do you understand? One at a time."

Zetta tilted her head with confusion, and Selene made a frustrated noise.

This is never going to work.

But before she could think about a plan B, the gray-streaked dog stood and trotted to the nearest spirit, a Sasquatch-shaped Vowa. With a gentle nudge of his nose, he guided the spirit forward, causing Selene to clap excitedly. "Yes! Good job!"

The gray dog seemed delighted by the praise. Selene continued, "Can you keep doing that? Bring me one spirit at a time."

When the Vowa spirit floated hesitantly toward her, several others tried to follow. But the gray dog blocked them with a low growl. A few other tried to sneak around the Vowa, but the other dogs herded them back.

Without waiting for an invitation, the Vowa began to share his story. He told Selene how he had gotten into debt from a bad business deal. When a traveling wagon show came to town, he thought he could win some of his losses back by fighting a demon...

The other dogs, less interested in herding, closed in around her as the Vowa continued his story. One hellhound rested its heavy chin on her thigh. Another flopped down at her feet. Zetta curled up against Selene's hip, as if supervising the gray hound's efforts to usher the spirits to her, one by one.

And so, Selene remained there for many hours, surrounded by hellhounds, listening to the stories and carefully recording the names of each spirit Sam had killed.

When the last spirit told his story, the sky was growing orange with the light of morning. Most of the hellhounds had fallen asleep, but Zetta and the gray-streaked one—whom Selene had nicknamed Smoky—remained as alert as ever, carefully watching the spirits and barking warnings whenever one ventured too close.

None of the stories were easy to hear. Most of the Aurelians Sam had killed were either those who had entangled themselves in vampire affairs and paid the price, or brash hooligans seeking notoriety by challenging a demon.

Each had died with regrets. Fractured families, wasted potential, and poor choices were a common thread among the stories. Many demanded that Selene help them cross over the moment they finished their tale, while others simply vanished before her eyes. Most only wanted messages of love conveyed to their families.

She had expected to see more vampires from the rampage Sam had unleashed to kill his captors, but since it was technically their second death, they must have transitioned immediately.

Slowly, she rose to her feet. Her back ached from sitting on the ground for so long, and her knees had grown stiff. The hellhounds began to stir too, yawning and extending their front paws to stretch their backs.

In her fragile mental state, she reflected that the divide between human and demon had never felt more stark. Now that she had truly seen this part of Sam, she understood why he had always tried to hide it from her. Although she was well acquainted with his tender side, his full demonic nature was formidable. It hadn't bothered her when she had seen him brutally slay vampires, but hearing how he killed those far less lethal was harder to reconcile.

When all the dogs were awake, Selene said wearily, "All right, pups. Let's get out of here." She looked down a corridor that split into a fork, contemplating the best way to navigate out of the maze. The thought of stumbling her way through, hitting multiple dead ends, and possibly retracing her steps made her already aching body throb.

As she considered which path to take, Smoky lifted his head to sniff the air. Then he did a little twirl and began trotting with determination down a corridor. The other hounds watched him for a moment before following—some barking with excitement, others jogging along dutifully. Selene glanced down at Zetta, who met her gaze with a soft chuff, and together they took off behind the trail of hellhounds.

Either Smoky had the makings of a brilliant search-and-rescue dog, or he was exceptionally lucky, because the pack took only a few wrong turns before Selene could hear the caw of the death-ravens that lived in the surrounding forest. The scent of roasted meat filled the air, spurring the dogs to quicken their pace.

Selene watched them all burst through the maze's exit just ahead. Then she heard someone screech. Rushing out of the maze with Zetta, Selene spotted Vanthee scrambling up a nearby tree. Below her, a small fire flickered weakly, practically stamped out by the hellhounds in their frantic attempts to get to the steaks she had been roasting.

"Vanthee, what are you doing here?" Selene asked hoarsely.

Vanthee gestured to the now extinguished fire. "Helping you get out. I saw that all the hounds were gone and I figured they were with you. I thought roasting meat would give Zetta a scent trail to follow."

Selene slumped down on a fallen log. "That was a brilliant idea."

"Are you all right?"

"Exhausted and slightly traumatized, but otherwise fine." She gestured to the notebook. "I've got a lot of letters to write when we get back to Aurelia."

"Did you really need this much backup?" Vanthee asked, watching the dogs scrabble over a hunk of fat.

Selene began to roll her stiff neck. "I don't know, they just... came."

"Did you call all of them?"

"No, not consciously. But they were a big help in there. What's going on with Sam?"

"He's all right. Blight met us at the gates on a horse and took him in. To his chamber, I assume."

Vanthee passed her a full waterskin, and Selene drank it down gratefully.

"What happened in there?" Vanthee asked.

Selene described how the spirits had crowded her, then how the hounds came, and how she had listened to the stories each spirit had to tell. She shared snippets of a few memorable ones, and Vanthee listened attentively. But some of the questions, and the confusion behind them, reminded Selene that Vanthee had never left the Underworld. She couldn't fully grasp the joys and sorrows of mortal life the way Selene could.

They both sat in silence for a few moments, watching the dogs. Then Vanthee asked, "Now that the trials are over, what do you think will happen next?"

"Sam has to convince his parents that you should be the Dark Sovereign." Selene poured some water into her hand to splash her face.

"But what if they don't believe him?" There was a hint of vulnerability in her tone.

"They don't have a choice," Selene said, stifling a yawn.

Vanthee blinked. "Of course they do. Why would you say that?"

Selene gave her a long look. "It's your destiny. Come to the library tomorrow, and I'll show you why."

CHAPTER 45

S am wanted nothing more than to rest his pounding head on the table of his father's state room and sleep, but the arguing voices surrounding him wouldn't allow it. He closed his eyes, fighting against the pull of exhaustion.

Queen Lamia's voice sounded on his left. "Let's do it tonight. Why delay such a joyful occasion?"

"The coronation should be held on a date of significance," countered Blight, general of the Legion of Punishment. Sam could hear the buttons on the sleeve of his military uniform clang against the table. "The anniversary of Asmodeus's coronation would be poetic. What day would that be, great king?"

"You know I can't remember details like that," King Asmodeus growled. "Why do you taunt me? I am still king of this realm and—"

"Apologies, apologies. I only wanted to honor you," Blight said.

Sam opened his eyes and rubbed his temples, trying to recall the events of the past eight hours. After the souls of his victims had nearly driven him to madness, he had blacked out. He vaguely remembered Vanthee carrying him up to the palace gates, his body jostling over her shoulders. Then Blight had run up to them, yanking him from Vanthee's grip and forcing him to stand.

Vanthee had hurriedly told him that Selene had stayed behind in the maze to communicate with the spirits so he could escape. Panic surged through him, and he'd tried to turn back for her. But his legs couldn't hold him, and he collapsed. Blight hauled him up, but Vanthee was already sprinting back toward the maze, shouting over her shoulder that she would take care of Selene.

"Who won the Maze of Endless Paths Trial?" Sam rasped.

"Why, you did," Queen Lamia said. She gently rubbed his shoulder. "Just rest now. We will see to all the details."

"Listen here! Events like this take planning," Empusa said, smacking the top of her cane. "We need time to spread the word across the realm. And invite demons working in Gaia back home for the coronation, if they wish to come."

Queen Lamia looked thoughtful. "Yes. We must summon all the demons back, not merely *invite* them. Sam must start his rule with all subjects pleading absolute fealty."

"What? No," Sam said, panic rising.

Asmodeus stamped his hoof three times. A few seconds later, a trio of imps swooped into the state room. When they appeared, he commanded, "Send word that all demons must return home for their new king's coronation at once."

The imps nodded and buzzed out of the room.

Sam placed his palms on the table, trying to steady himself. "What's going on?"

Lamia gazed at him fondly. "The trials are over, and we have found the Dark Sovereign. It's you."

Sam gasped. "No, I didn't win." He tried to shake his head, but the motion made him dizzy.

"That doesn't matter," Lamia replied. "We went along with your games to placate you, but now they're over. Ultimately your father and I have final say, and we've decided that you will rule."

Sam tried to stand, but the after-effects of so much trauma left his legs leaden. "It's not my destiny. It must be Vanthee. She is the one who deserves to rule. She completed all the trials—"

"Pit-spawned foolishness," Mammon interrupted with a snort. "My daughter doesn't have the intelligence to possess a toad."

"No, she competed as Nyrah. The prophecies—"

"I have an astonishing idea!" Mammon's slippery voice cut through Sam's words. "Every king needs a queen. Why not combine Samael's coronation with a primitive yet sentimental tradition... a royal wedding?"

"You want him to marry a *human* at his own coronation?" Blight asked incredulously.

"Not Selene," Mammon purred, his tone sickeningly smooth. "If Vanthee was truly one of the competitors, as he claims, he could marry her."

When Sam moved to grab Mammon by the throat, the demon quickly added, "Selene can serve as your mistress if you're that attached. Vanthee won't mind. I'll see to it. And Drath can be your Royal Chancellor. Oh, this is coming together so well!"

"I said no!" Sam said desperately. "If I marry anyone, it will be Selene. And there won't be a coronation because I'm not the Dark Sovereign." He clumsily leaned toward his mother and gripped her hand. "Please, you have to listen to me. In the library, Selene found the bo—"

"Shhh," Queen Lamia interrupted. She straightened the collar of Sam's tunic. "I know you're nervous about your new role, so let's not complicate it with a wedding so soon."

"Perhaps we can have a wedding once Selene becomes a demon," Asmodeus said.

A ripple of delighted murmurs spread through the room from everyone but Mammon. Sam dropped his head into his hands as a cacophony of coronation plans began to take shape, voices overlapping with excitement.

The weight of his situation crashed down on him like a warhorse at full charge. Arguing with them was pointless. His parents would never listen. Even if he showed them *The Sovereign's Reckoning*, they might choose to ignore it. His wishes would never be respected.

There was only one solution.

They had to flee the Underworld and return to Aurelia.

Tonight.

Sam lifted his head, pulling himself together as best he could. Slowly, with false excitement, he said, "Can we have cinnamon sweet buns served at the coronation?"

Queen Lamia beamed. "Of course!"

"Good. But Empusa is right—we need more time," Sam said, each syllable an effort to form. "I'm in no shape to be coronated tonight. Everyone should be there, so you must give the demons in Gaia time to travel."

Asmodeus inclined his head thoughtfully. "True. It takes at least two weeks for those who journey on the *Purgatory*."

"So perhaps everything should occur in one moon cycle?" Queen Lamia asked, looking around the room. Blight and Empusa nodded enthusiastically though Mammon glowered like a child denied a toy.

"Then it's settled," Lamia said. "I'll start making plans. Rest now, my son, and we will talk more tomorrow."

Although Sam was bone-tired when he returned to his rooms, all the worries racing through his mind kept him awake.

He had asked Prickles for a report on what was happening in the maze, but the imp flatly refused to leave the palace grounds. That left Sam alone with his thoughts, haunted by what might be happening to Selene and how she might be changed by the experience. How would the spirits twist her, consume her, break her? When he saw her again, would she still look at him the same way? Or would he see fear in her eyes?

Now she would know the full extent of his violence. The unfiltered truth of who he was. The blood on his hands, the rage that had burned so hot inside him—she would witness it all.

He must have eventually succumbed to sleep, because he awoke face-down on the bed when he heard Selene open their chamber door. He sat up, focusing on her silhouette as she moved through the darkened parlor into their bedroom.

When the light fell across the strain in her face, he immediately knew his fears were justified.

"Hi," he said tentatively. "H-how are you?"

Instead of sitting next to him on the bed, she lowered herself into an armchair.

"Tired."

"What happened in there?"

Selene leaned her head on the back of the chair wearily. "The spirits swarmed me all at once. There were so many of them."

The rawness of her voice was excruciating for Sam to hear. He didn't say anything until she continued, "But then the hellhounds came. All of them. I don't know how they knew, but they drove the spirits back so I could hear each of their stories. One by one."

She patted a flat, rectangular shape in her pocket. "I wrote down all of their names and if they had a message for their families."

"That was very clever. And generous," Sam said slowly. He searched for the right words. "Do you want something to eat or drink?" The question sounded inadequate when what he really wanted to ask was, *Do you still love me?*

"No, thank you."

For a moment, the only sound was the dripping tap in the bathroom. Then Sam, unable to stop himself, blurted out, "Do you want to leave me? I don't blame you if you do."

Selene sat up straighter to look at him. "No! Sam, I love you. Hearing those stories was hard, but it doesn't change how I feel about you." She bent to pull off her shoes and tossed them in a corner. Running a hand through her hair, she exhaled and said, "I'm just struggling. With this place. With everything. "

"Struggling in what way?" he asked carefully.

"Sometimes I wonder if I'm really the right person for you. Maybe you'd be happier living in the Underworld instead of Aurelia. If you were born to punish people and use your strength the way you did with those Aurelians, you shouldn't have to bottle that all up just to be with me."

Sam rose from the bed, even though he was still shaky on his feet. He dropped to his knees in front of her and placed his hands on her thighs. The scent of the maze still lingered on her clothes.

Before he could speak, she asked, "What if I'm just too... human for you?"

"No. Absolutely not. You are the right one for me. I hated doing all those things. And being here, delivering vengeance, it's not all that I imagined it would be. I have loved seeing my parents, but I don't like it here much more than you do."

She placed her palm on his cheek, and he leaned into her touch. When their eyes met, he said, "Selene, I think we need to flee."

"You mean... " She touched her fingers to the traveler's stone.

"Yes. My parents and the council have decided that they are crowning me as the Dark Sovereign. They're making plans for my coronation."

She sucked in a breath. "What? When?"

"In a month. They want all the demons in Gaia to come home to attend."

"Okay, so we have a little time."

"Yes, but why does it matter? Let's leave tonight. Right now, even."

"Honey, I don't have the strength to use the stone tonight," she said quietly.

A prickle of shame coursed down Sam's spine. "No. Of course not."

"But also, there's something I need to do before we leave. In the maze, I promised the spirits I would help them cross over."

"Did you tell them when? I can help you." He swallowed. "Seeing them home should be my burden to bear."

"No. You can't communicate with them and it would raise too many suspicions. I'll ask Vanthee if I can take them tomorrow."

"If you're certain that's best."

"I want to show her the prophecy, too. She needs to know about it."

"I agree," Sam said. "Once we're gone, she may have to fight for her rightful place."

They were both silent for a moment until Sam tapped the notebook in her pocket. "And when we get home, I'll deliver these messages to the families myself."

"That would be nice. Oh, I just realized something... " He watched Selene's eyes suddenly fill with tears. She looked upward, trying to blink them away, but failed. "I'll need to say goodbye to Zetta." Her voice hitched.

Sam wiped her tears away with his thumb. "Of course," he said gently. It pained him to see her hurting, but the promise of returning to Aurelia filled some of the emptiness he had been carrying. "Take care of everything tomorrow. Then we'll go as soon as you're ready."

CHAPTER 46

The next day, Selene asked Prickles to deliver a message to Vanthee, asking her to meet later in the library. Sam was going to tie up any loose ends he had at the Sanctum, but he still walked her to the kennels so she could spend one last day with Zetta.

Selene had ditched the gowns in favor of the pants and T-shirt she had worn when they left Aurelia. Ogrin was working in the kennels and raised an eyebrow at her unconventional appearance but didn't comment.

She had to hold back tears when she opened Zetta's kennel, but she managed to keep it together until they made it to the library. After a good cry, which thoroughly perplexed Zetta, she was taking one last, bittersweet look at all the progress she had made on the library when Vanthee burst through the doors.

"I don't have much time, but something's happening," she said breathlessly. "My father just cornered me ranting about how I need to beguile Prince Samael!"

"They're planning Sam's coronation," Selene said quietly. "His parents decided last night that he's the Dark Sovereign."

Vanthee made a choked sound. Her surprised expression shifted to heartache, and her shoulders slumped. "I guess him nominating me didn't go so well. I knew it was too much to hope for."

"It's not going to happen because Sam and I are leaving tonight," Selene said. Speaking the words gave her a tingle of excitement. But when Zetta nudged her head under Selene's hand, her throat swelled with grief.

"You are?" Vanthee asked.

"Yes, so I need to show you this right now." Selene grabbed Vanthee's arm and pulled her behind a bookcase.

Vanthee looked around. "Show me what?"

"Do you know what *The Sovereign's Reckoning* is?" she whispered, suddenly conscious of being overheard, even though they were alone.

"Of course, but it's only a legend."

"No, it's not. I found it."

Vanthee inhaled sharply. "Are you serious?"

"Yes, but it's tricky to get to." Selene called Zetta over. Grabbing a candle from a nearby table, she held it in front of Zetta's nose. She explained to Vanthee, "You need blue fire to get to the book."

When Selene commanded Zetta to speak, the wick lit instantly. Selene held the candle in front of the hidden panel in the bookshelf. Vanthee gasped with understanding when she saw the sigil in the wood glow. Selene slid the panel aside and retrieved the book nestled within.

Balancing the ancient book in one hand, Selene explained, "The legend is that Baphomet destroyed the prophecy that put King Asmodeus on the throne. But it's not true—someone hid it. Look."

Carefully, she hovered the candle near the book's lock until it popped open. Inside, she showed Vanthee the prophecies of Baphomet and Asmodeus. By the light of the blue flame, Vanthee's red eyes glowed purple as she studied the portraits.

"How did you find these?"

"Pure luck. It took me a while to figure out the lock, though."

Selene ran a finger over the jagged edge where the book's remaining pages had been torn out. "I thought this would show us who the next Dark Sovereign is, but someone ripped out the pages." She set the book down on a nearby table. "Then I found this."

She pried back the book binding to reveal the hidden portrait. Carefully, she held it out. First, Vanthee squinted at it, leaning in for a closer look. Making a startled noise, she reached out to touch it, then quickly pulled her hand back. "Is this real?"

"It's real. And it's definitely you."

"How is this possible?" she asked breathlessly.

Selene shrugged. "I've learned to stop asking that question."

Vanthee swallowed as she gaped at the portrait. "But what does it mean? How am I supposed to take the throne?"

"I don't know. Read the prophecy." Selene flipped to the portrait over and held it close to the candle to illuminate the words.

"Oh my." Vanthee touched her horns nervously then rubbed her tattoo. "It was one thing when Prince Samael suggested I compete in the next trial, but this is a lot."

"I know. But Sam and I believe you'll make a wonderful queen."

"Will I?"

Outside the library, a distant voice screeching "Vanthee!" made them both jump.

"It's my father. We can't let him see this," Vanthee said, stuffing the book back into the hole with shaking hands.

"But you saw how I opened it, right?" Selene closed the panel and stuffed several books in front of it. "You'll have to get over your fear of Zetta."

"Yes," Vanthee replied. "I have to go. I don't want Father to know I'm here and it's nearly time for the Hailing of Souls."

"Can I come with?" Selene asked. "I promised I'd help all the souls Sam killed pass over before we leave."

"All right, but we have to hurry."

CHAPTER 47

Selene thought it would be a challenge to round up all of Sam's victims, but on their way to Spirit Veil Valley, she spotted one floating near the Chapel of Mourning.

"Hey, excuse me!" Selene called. The spirit turned, his pale face lighting with recognition. "If you're ready to pass into the Afterworld, we're going right now. Tell the others. And anyone else who wants to come."

The spirit stared at her, then nodded before floating off. From the corner of her eye, she saw Mammon skulking in a dark corner near the chapel, so she hurried after Vanthee.

Word must have traveled fast because as they made their way into the valley, a small procession of spirits gathered behind them. Unlike yesterday in the maze, the spirits weren't looking at her with accusatory eyes or bitter glares. Selene could tell they were excited—euphoric, even.

Soon there were nearly twenty-five lost souls ready to transition, drifting behind her like a shimmering patch of fog. A few tried to engage with Zetta playfully, brushing her fur with their translucent hands or attempting to scratch her ears. To Selene's surprise, Zetta responded to their simple commands like "sit" and "shake," confirming that, like her, Zetta could hear the voices of the dead, too.

As Selene descended the rocky stairs in the heart of the valley, the strange lights of the three domes looked different, now that she understood their purpose. The red one still seemed ominous, but the white and blue domes felt hallowed, more sacred to her now. She was grateful to be able to give Sam's victims peace before they returned home.

"I'm late!" Vanthee said, rushing past her when they reached the bottom. From the entrance of the white dome that connected the living world to the Underworld, she called, "I'll take your spirits after I cross over the others. Be right back!"

Selene waved her off and stood with Zetta to wait. The lost souls drifted through the valley—circling each dome and hovering outside the entrances. As time stretched on, their anticipation grew increasingly restless.

When is it our turn? one spirit asked. His question caused others to chime in impatiently.

We've waited long enough.

Lead us through!

"Vanthee will be back soon," Selene replied in a raised voice. "Don't go too far."

The spirits continued to grumble until, moments later, Vanthee returned with the usual horde of the recently dead. She began sorting them as normal, but the action made the once-joyous energy of the lost souls that Selene brought to turn frantic. They began to swarm Selene, just as they had in the maze.

It's our turn! We were here first!

Unlock the gates!

I want peace!

"No, wait! Vanthee will help you through in just a moment," Selene cried. Zetta began herding some of the insistent souls away from her, but not all obeyed the hellhound.

Vanthee's face twisted with panic. "No! I'm going to lose them all! Get yours to wait by the Afterworld!"

Selene waved her arms and pleaded, "If you came with me, wait over here!"

Zetta backed her up, steering some of the drifting souls in the same direction, but it wasn't enough. Her fierce barking startled some of the newly dead, making them scatter like birds, colliding and mixing with the lost souls into a great swirling mist.

Selene found herself in the middle, shouting directions and gesturing wildly to the two groups, but no one was listening. Then they began to flock to Vanthee.

"I can't take you all at once," Vanthee cried, even though they couldn't hear her. "I have to unlock the gates one by one!"

The horde that had surrounded her was beginning to break apart and Selene watched helplessly as some of the newly dead drifted toward the palace, about to join the multitudes of spirits who hadn't crossed over. She continued to shout and gesticulate to any spirit who would listen, but it was all turning to chaos.

Then, without warning, Zetta darted protectively in front of her, a blur of black fur and canine muscle. Her lips peeled back to reveal glistening fangs, snarling more viciously than Selene had ever heard. The growl rumbling from her throat made the hairs on the back of Selene's neck stand on end.

Startled by the hellhound's reaction, Selene leaned down to whisper, "Hey. Zetta, it's okay. We'll bring them back—"

Her words were cut off as something slammed into her chest like a battering ram. Hard and brutal. The impact stole the breath from her lungs and sent her reeling backward. Instinctively, her fingers latched onto Zetta's thick coat, grasping for balance. Her eyes scanned the valley, but it was difficult to see anything through the murk of spirits.

Then she saw him.

Mammon.

His face loomed in front of her, bathed in the blue glow of the Afterworld gate. His features were contorted with triumph and spite.

She heard Vanthee scream, "NO!" just as her body was jerked back, and the world around her began to dissolve.

Sound dropped away.

The ground vanished beneath her feet.

Light bent and folded inward.

And before she could stop it, the blue haze of the Afterworld enveloped her—swallowing her and Zetta whole.

And everything went still.

TO BE CONTINUED...

The *Shadows of Aurelia* series continues in *Awakened by Shadows*, coming in 2026.

Cass, Selene's sister, never believed in otherworldly realms—until she meets Hal, a mysterious demon living in Nashville, Tennessee. When Hal reveals that Selene now lives in the Underworld, Cass fears her sister has been taken there against her will. So when Hal is summoned home for the coronation of a new king, Cass convinces him to take her with him, posing as his wife. But upon arrival, Cass discovers that Selene's fate is far more dire than she ever imagined. At the request of her sister's grieving mate, Cass and Hal embark on a journey across three dimensions to find Selene—unraveling not only the truth about their worlds, but the secrets they've kept from each other.

Acknowledgments

I broke a lot of "rules" when writing *To Dwell in Shadows*, and I'm grateful to everyone who enabled me to do so. Some say romances shouldn't end on a cliffhanger. That continuing with the same couple is boring. That you must release a new book every six months to build a loyal readership. In some cases, they're right—but one of the joys of being an indie author is the freedom to follow your creative instincts wherever they lead. I'm incredibly thankful to the readers who stuck with me while this book slowly came to life.

Originally, *To Dwell in Shadows* was meant to be a short novella focused on Sam's reunion with his parents. But as I began writing, it became clear that the next part of Sam and Selene's journey wasn't so simple. I wanted to see how the old saying, "You can't go home again," would apply to a demon seeking redemption. And because so many readers resonated with Selene's struggle with eldest-daughter syndrome, I knew I had to show how breaking toxic patterns doesn't happen overnight—it's a complicated and ongoing process.

Yet when the "novella" started to grow into a book, I began to lose my way. One of the first people to get me back on track with a new direction (and a juicier plot) was Susan Barnes. Thank you, Susan, for pulling me out of my creative rut and offering suggestions I never would have come up with on my own. It was after our sessions that I felt like this story finally started to come together.

To my most trusted beta readers and merry band of Pals—Brad Buchanan, Peako Jenkins, Jason Maynard, Krissie Mulvoy Williams, and Megan Roggendorff—thank you for your honest feedback and for propping me up when I needed it most. Thank you to Aileen Bishop for your beautiful narration of the *Unbound by Shadows* audiobook, which attracted so many new readers and helped me achieve a major author milestone. I'm also grateful to Audra Davis for keeping me gainfully employed as I juggled fiction writing with grant proposal writing.

Bethany Seabolt, thank you for your editorial insights and for knowing Sam and Selene almost as well as I do. Samantha Peirce of Radiant Editorial—your little reader reaction notes were an absolute delight, and I'm grateful for your permission to fully embrace the em-dash.

Thank you to The Porch for your inspiring classes and for giving me the chance to share everything I know as an instructor. I'm also appreciative to everyone who's ever joined a Nashville Romance Writers meet-up at The Porch, and for our off-campus coffee shop chats and Discord adventures.

Finally, I want to thank the two most important people in my life—my mom and my husband, Grant. Grant, you have furthered my author career both as a supportive spouse and as the audiobook producer of my dreams. Even though hearing the spicy scenes I wrote echo through the house while you worked made me cringe, I'm so grateful for the care and precision you brought to every part of the process.

Mom, thank you for giving me a childhood where the library was our second home—it has clearly left a mark on my writing! You have always been my biggest fan, and I'm so lucky to have you as a mom. Also, thank you for that time you took my Instagram post asking for chocolate and coffee literally and mailed me a box of both. You truly understand the fuel writers need to thrive!

About the Author

Avalon Griffin is an indie author who writes paranormal fantasy romance with unique characters, far-away settings, and a healthy dose of heat. She is the author of the novel *Unbound by Shadows,* its sequel, *To Dwell in Shadows,* and the short story, *The Vampire's Library,* which was published in Once Upon a Book Club's 2024 Book-Club-Mas anthology. When not writing, she can be found traveling the globe in search of kitschy roadside attractions, off-beat museums, and cryptozoology legends. She lives in Nashville, Tennessee, with her husband and a crew of formerly feral cats. To keep up with her or subscribe to her newsletter, visit www.avalongriffin.com.

instagram.com/avalon_griffin

facebook.com/authoravalongriffin

tiktok.com/@avalon_griffin